T0274046

How People See

A Novel

Terry Ades

TUMBLEWEED PRESS, INC.

ISBN: 978-1-998270-04-0

Printed in Canada

Tumbleweed Press - Toronto, Canada

Table of Contents

Part 1
How It Came To Be

Chapter 1

For the greater part of the day, Oscar Horvath dozed. A shaft of sunlight drew a yellow bar across his hairless chest. On his left nostril, a web of blood vessels bloomed against his white flesh. A thin stream of saliva trickled from the corner of his mouth to the pillowcase. He swallowed and awoke.

He did not recognize the pine dresser on his left, did not know where the door was. A partly opened tube of hand cream on the bedside table lifted his disorientation. He was in the upstairs bedroom that should have been his but was not. It belonged to a mortgage company that was on his tail for a debt that rose— rose for god's sake, as deliberately as the murky water in a blocked sink. The company owned his son's room and his wife's kitchen and all the white walls and brown floors down to the naked concrete of the unfinished basement. The rest of it, the number 117 door and its front steps, and the scrap of a cement patio on which they were allowed to place their three vinyl chairs belonged to the condo association. For those red bricks shared by a hundred other families and for the weedy lawn and the one parking space neatly marked by the number 117, he also had to pay.

He looked toward the last light of the sun. A spider scuttled up the curtain and disappeared inside the folds. Louise would have an absolute fit if she saw the insect. She'd go after it with a slipper and a broom slapping at every speck in the room.

"Louise," he shouted.

She scuttled in like the spider, on heels for some reason and all duded up in her thin black dress.

"Going dancing?" He pulled her into the bed.

"Os-car," she trilled. "*We danse quand tu* come back." She hugged him and pulled away. "We have dinner now. *Viens.*"

He didn't have time for a full dinner but there, on the dining table was a roasted chicken surrounded by potatoes and sweet onions pungent in the air. Steve clattered down the stairs, his shoelaces trailing behind him and the three of them sat together long enough for the boy to gulp down his meal and lean back with his ever-present phantom guitar clutched to his chest. Grinning, Oscar plucked at his fork.

Much of December had seen his cab perched on the hoist of the Tony Garage. The Malibu often acted like a hormonal teenager, refusing to budge whenever the urge hit. The week before Christmas the transmission had seized. Second time with that vehicle. All week, Oscar faced the television unaware of the images on the screen, thinking only that the cost of repairs was increasing with each passing commercial. His ear flea hissing, he'd dip a quarter teaspoon of instant coffee into a mug of boiling water, glance inside the sugar bowl, and push it to the back of the cupboard. According to his

4

calculation, a jar of coffee could last six months, maybe more. Back at the television, he'd jab at his calculator figuring out the coffee and bread and home heating ratio till his credit card balances could be tolerated. That's if the bank stopped sending him waste-of-paper letters that demanded interest on interest on a mortgage that might have been paid two lousy days late or maybe just five minutes late. They knew how to add but not subtract.

Twenty-nine coffees later the car was resurrected. Tony handed him the bill, took it right back, and discounted ten percent off a figure best forgotten.

"You don't have to pay it all at once." A cigarette hung on the side of his mouth. "If you have a couple a hundred now. The rest– no rush."

"Cigarette money."

"Yeah– I don't want to smoke them all at once."

Earlier in the day Louise's mother had pressed them to celebrate the eve of the new year with the family and on her third call, blamed Oscar for never taking time for them. She said, "The least you could do is drop our daughter and grandson off. They should be with the family on the *reveillon*."

You'd think the South Shore was two stop signs down the road, the way the old hag said, Bring them over. Bring them. Sure. In what? The Malibu? As if he was perfectly free to do every little thing she wanted. Paid, that drive was worth over fifty dollars plus lost time. And if

Louise's brother were to pick them up, Oscar would have to fetch them himself using up gas and mileage on the tiresome commute over the bridge. And besides, he was the family. No, he said. No. So when they finished eating he said, "Louise, that was delicious," even though it had been rich enough to put him to sleep and the coffee would make him want to pee every twenty minutes.

Louise took her men by the hand. "*Bonne Année mes chéris. Tout ce que vous souhaitez.* And good health more than anything."

Steve looked away. "You too."

And Oscar, full of food, and inarticulate love, wrapped them in his arms and bumped them in a dance between the dining chairs. "Here's to 1995, the jackpot year."

Whoa. A brilliant start. Oscar hadn't paid his stand fees for months and had long ago given up the radio with which to receive calls. He was a cab driver unassociated with a company, an independent. But when he rolled up to his old stand, only one driver zoomed in ahead of him. A second later the guy jumped out of his cab and handed Oscar the address that had just been radioed in. "Come back when you're done, man. We can't keep up with the work."

The calls came in ten at a time. After the evening rush, Oscar taxied his reserved clients from one party to the next in the latest trend to arrive late and leave early. At around 11 PM, he dropped his last passengers off at the gleaming bronze doors of a downtown hotel.

"Want me to pick you up? I'll be on the road till breakfast. And you might not find a cab later on."

"No thank you." There was an oily adolescent sheen on the face of the boy who held out his pay. "We've got a room." This skinny, tie-clad child was able to pay and tip and spend the night at a five-star hotel.

Oscar parked at the deserted hotel stand and took a breath. The wads of money in his pockets were too thick for comfort and too thick to unfold safely. But in the quiet glow of the hotel lights, secure in his corner, he slid the money out of his pockets. Below the dashboard, he began to sort it by denomination. There were enough fifty-dollar bills to pay January's mortgage, the condo fees, a couple of weeks' groceries. He sorted a good quarter inch of twenties and another of fives and tens into orderly piles– not yet enough cash for the little gifts he wanted to offer Steve and Louise but later in the evening, in this new year of promise, yes, tons more would float straight into his pockets. He gazed at the money on his lap till he heard a motor.

The spanking bumper of a Crown Victoria hovered beside his car. Narrowing his eyes, the driver moved on just past the cab stand. A moment later he sauntered up to Oscar's window. Oscar locked his doors and sat on his money. The cabbie tapped at the glass.

"Ruby only." His stubble of yellow hair brushed against the window.

Yeah, yeah, the Ruby cab stand. Oscar thought he knew the man, a name that likely started with a K– whatever it was, a hard letter. He cracked his window. "You look familiar. I used to be with Ruby. I don't know, maybe twenty years ago?"

"Well you're not with Ruby now. You can't stay here."

"Hey– it's New Year's Eve. You'll run out of cabs in about five minutes."

"Go park on the curb."

Oscar rolled up his window. "Too bad, Ruby. I was here first."

The guy backed away muttering. That he was indecipherable didn't matter. Oscar understood him perfectly, pretty much could have written the script– Yeah, I've seen you before asshole. You can't even pay your stand fees. And your car looks like shit–. The taxi driver pulled at the massive hotel door and slipped in. It was twelve minutes to midnight. The street lights appeared to dim in preparation for the big pop. A couple more Rubys pulled up to the stand and a moment later the doorman tapped at Oscar's window.

"Sir, this is private parking." He looked like an army cadet in his red jacket.

Oscar unrolled an inch of his window. "What'll you do when you're short of cabs?"

"I'm sorry, sir. Ruby taxis have the license for the hotel."

Five, six cabs were lined up behind him.

"Hey– give me a break, man. You know perfectly well you need the cars."

"Sir– I'm warning you. Get your vehicle off hotel property."

"Yeah? What are you planning to do? Pick up the car and carry it out?" He rolled up his window and revved his motor.

The doorman leaned against Oscar's car, his weight dark over the front window. Keeping his car in park, Oscar pressed his foot on the gas. The vehicle pulsed and shivered till Red Jacket backed away, his arms up in surrender. Oscar grinned as the guy pulled at the hotel door.

Oscar lifted each side of his rump and gathered the warm bills from under his rear. From the corner of his eye, he saw the driver of the Crown Victoria slink out of the hotel, his jacket hood pulled over his eyes. He approached Oscar's car and then strode right by it, heading to the Ford that stood behind the Malibu. He climbed into the Ford and a moment later, his friend craned his face out the open window.

"Horvath– get the fuck out of my way."

Yeah– so they knew him too. Ha-ha. Raising his middle finger, Oscar grinned with only his teeth. The Ford's window rolled up and the motor started. Oscar's provocative tongue twitched at the cabbies. The Ford began to edge around the Malibu. Oscar put his car in gear, hit the gas, yanked the wheel, and slammed on the brakes. Eraser face brandished a fist. It froze midair as a collective cheer erupted from the building. A cacophony of noisemakers reverberated from restaurant to restaurant. One of the cabbies thrust open his door and blew a whistle into the darkness. They applauded, called out Happy New Year wishes. Docile in the freshness of the new year, the Ford backed away.

In packs, the after-midnight fares left the hotel. The first was a thirty-something couple, tired already and rushing home to relieve the babysitter. Oscar dropped them off in the suburbs and returned to the hotel where sure enough, there was a lineup of clients and no cabs. He was set for a princely night of easy driving. Even drunk clients would be sweet.

By five a.m. there was not a soul heading out of the hotel and not a cab left to push him out of his place. For a while he idled at the hotel entrance for nothing, then set to cruising Sherbrooke Street past the wrought iron university gates and onto the side roads, pausing at lit-up clubs and at an all-night breakfast bar, its neon DEJEUNER glinting in his windshield. He passed it by, thought to grab a coffee, and circled the block. And right in front of the joint as if granted by his fairy godmother, was a finger pointed in his direction. Oscar pulled the car up to a tassel-hatted boy and a couple– a boy and girl studded with matching nose diamonds. The three jumped and hollered, wagging their wrists at him in unison. Tipsy and frowzy, they climbed into the back seat and slammed the door.

"Where to?"

They burst into hiccuping giggles.

"Come on, now. Where are you going?"

"Breakfast," the girl heaved.

"That's right here. Now get out."

There was a collective whoop while they rolled on his upholstery. One of them finally paused long enough to say, "Take us to a bank machine."

Oscar watched them wriggle through the rearview mirror. If he wasn't so tired, he'd have kicked them out. Instead, he turned and eyed them till they stopped tittering. They were children, their mouths pursed and ready to laugh. When they were utterly silent, he turned the wheel away from the curb and drove.

"You'll have to tell me where to go."

They began again to giggle. One of the boys burped. Oscar stopped the car. He'd give them one more chance. "Which way?"

Tassel Hat pointed a thumb at the left window. Oscar turned the corner and following the boy's thumb, turned again. The boy grunted left or right at almost every corner leading them across the Pine interchange into the residential Plateau at the base of Mount Royal. Left, right, left, right, they circled to the boy's thumb till Oscar stopped the car and the meter. These people had no place to go and no money.

"Hey man, we're not there yet," Tassel said.

"Yeah? You owe me ten-thirty-five. Pay up now."

"We'll pay when we get there."

"We're not where we want to be," the other boy piped.

"Shut up, Alex."

"Look. I don't know where you're going. I don't care. I want you to pay me ten dollars and thirty-five cents and get out of my car."

"You're just leaving us here in the middle of nowhere?" It was the girl, high-pitched.

"Right now." A motley row of darkened houses stood on either side of them. They couldn't have been more than a block from the bus stop.

Tassel rustled in his pockets.

"I can't believe it. This guy's just dumping us," the girl squealed.

"Catherine, get out of the car. Me and Alex will take care of it."

Oscar gazed into the rearview mirror. The couple with the nose rings were wearing jean jackets without coats. Spoiled kids with no brains. It was below zero and getting colder. A slick of ice coated by a fine layer of snow lay on the asphalt. The snow was coming down wet, almost sharp on the windshield. Catherine opened the door.

"Go on," Tassel said. "Get across the street. Keep walking. We'll join you."

She left, crossing the street on spiked sandals, her pale toes bare in the snow. Not even a nylon covered them.

"Stop ogling her." Tassel opened the door and threw a handful of change at the dashboard. Oscar ducked. A second later a fist struck the back of his neck. There was a crack, the dashboard on his forehead.

The chill breeze from the opened door brought him out of his stupor. His forehead throbbed. He saw where they'd gone. Their tracks were like arrows on the snow. He checked and found the wad of bills safe in his back pocket then felt around for the coins on the floor. Weird– eleven dollars in change. They owed him nothing but good health. For that, there was a price. They could have killed him with that blow. His shoulders ached, the back of his neck was raw. What kind of steel-ended fist was that?

He put the car in gear and followed their tracks on two narrow streets up to the rim of Mount Royal Park. Beside a wood bench and beneath a ridge of Christmas trees the girl's stiletto heels branded their passage. They'd gone past the slope of the mount. Oscar parked the car and went into a small wood. They couldn't have gone far, her bare toes in the snow. On a hiker's path made close by the taut growth of spindly trees and brush, Oscar tramped behind their footprints. He felt his throbbing neck and felt a smear of blood. His shirt was ruined. He didn't have a million of them. Rigid branches scraped his hands and face. He'd have gone home if it hadn't been for the warm trickle on his neck, the red signal that urged him further into the winter-barbed landscape. Each step was dimly lit by the haze of distant lights. He cracked a switch off a bush and lumbered on. Further ahead, flickering shadows warned him to stop. He was about to give up, he just about did, when he heard the girl, sharp in the silence, whining and swearing– You assholes, I'm frozen. Where the hell are we going?

Oscar edged in, one ponderous step at a time till he could hear the rasp of the girl's breath. They had cleared the snow off a log and were huddled like chickens in the rain.

Tassel pulled out a cigarette. "I'm not the asshole. He is."

"He's a garbage man," Alex agreed.

"I'm talking about you. You hit him for nothing."

"What are you talking about? Were we supposed to tolerate his bullshit?"

"He didn't do anything. He wanted to get paid," the girl said.

"Shut up," Tassel said.

If they weren't drunk and cold and young, they'd have heard Oscar grunt. They'd have seen him raise his stick, seen him aim at Alex's head.

Tassel turned to light his cigarette. He saw the shadow of the monster, its short legs, and its huge arms, heard its breath. As the branch came down crashing, he jumped as high as an acrobat, shoved his friend off the bench, and drove his knee into the monster till it lay clutching its side in the snow, crying like a lonely dog. Alex gave it a kick. A few bucks fell out of its pocket. Tons. There was a bank in there. They emptied the bank and ran.

Chapter 2

Oscar became aware of the sun flickering over the wood. He lay on his side, one eye in the snow. With his other eye, he saw that the sun was high in the white-blue sky. He turned his head to get a glimpse of his watch but fell back when a pain shot through his chest. Okay, pain. So what? For a moment he couldn't fathom why the snow was in his face. He began gradually to lift his leg" No— the drill in his pelvis too sharp, he took hold of his surging breath, pushed his tongue against the snow, and with that bare lick of moisture, cried out for help. His croak was swallowed by his ice pillow. He lifted his neck high enough for clearance and this time opened his mouth as wide as it would go. The scream that emerged was barely audible. He howled at the distant houses at the base of the hill and again, snow the silencer, muffled him. The hoarseness of his breath was the only sound left in the world.

He forced himself to lengthen his breath, and in that moment, heard motors at a distance and closer by, birds on the wind. Such full sunlight on his back. Noon, he conjectured. He called out again but somehow, his voice remained as soft as a bird's, it too, carried away. His cab was parked in a tow zone. They'd hook it to a truck and take it away and get him good with a big fine if he ever found it. Flexing his arm muscles, he tried with his elbows to pull himself above his melting sinkhole. His head lifted briefly before he slid back onto the plate of ice. His face was stiff, already numb. And the time between numb and frozen could be short. On a New Year's morning, nobody would be tramping in the snow.

He wanted to rest his head on a fallen branch but could not reach it. For a time he called for help, for Louise, for Steve, for his sister Paula, and maybe for his dead mother. Only the weather-hardy birds responded and only to complain about his existence. Let them. He was beginning to feel his drowsiness pleasantly. Maybe a long sleep would come out of it. He had not slept in weeks, no time for it except for that one day before the new year but that one was pitted by street noise and his impatient anxiety. And now, sleep was finally dimming the lights. There was the boy with the tassel and the long legs to thank for it. Oscar smiled and dropped his cheek in the snow. This moment was a gift. So simple. A long sleep– imagine. He stopped a rumble of laughter from descending to his throbbing pelvis. To sleep time away, be rid of his hours of work, the cab, and the bills. What a brilliant idea. He couldn't understand why he hadn't thought of it earlier.

The knot in his pelvis loosened, the pain familiar, now cozy. A squirrel scampered over the fallen branch and over Oscar's back. It felt like the slip of Louise's hand on his body. He smiled at the squirrel though it too had dashed away.

He would have to leave everything to Louise. Nothing to Paula. Except for an old shirt maybe. Louise could let the cab rust on the shores of the St. Lawrence River if she wanted. The bills could burn to cinder in her mother's fireplace. Her girlhood room on the South

Shore had in any case been kept intact for her return. Her parents would only have to turn down the bed. Thrilled they'd be to have her back.

The squirrel twittered at him. Oscar saw his glimmering eye and one side of his erect ear. It disappeared and came on him again. It would not let him sleep. These animals were not so quiet and not so small. To say hello, Oscar tried to purse his lips into a whistle. He blew soundless air at the rodent, took another breath, and hissed between his teeth. In a second, the squirrel jumped up a tree and was gone.

You thought I was dead. Oscar grinned. Not yet. What will you do when I'm stiff? Eat me? You'll have to wait till I defrost. He closed his eyes. He felt himself rise, that last moment before sleep, too light to touch the ground. Too light to feel pain. Too light to hear the hysterical skiers, to feel a mouth over his, the blanket of bodies wrapped around him.

You'd think you were in a disco. So many people crowded under the trees were screaming louder than the belligerent squirrel. He tried but wasn't strong enough to shove them off. He hissed at them like a devil, like a snake, but they snared him good, tied him to a gurney, and lifted him high off the snow. They said: what's your name, what's your name, what's your name?

Chapter 3

Louise's brother unfolded an army cot in the back corner of the dining room. An entire toolbox he lugged in just to adjust the rusted springs. He finished peering at his handiwork and pretended to squirt Oscar with lubricant.

"Don't worry. You, me, and your feet have risen up those stairs into this house. And next, you will get into bed too. Now– put your hand on my shoulder." And with that, Marc pushed him into the bed.

Oscar had spent almost a week in the hospital and faced weeks more on this backbreaker of a mattress. From where he lay, he could see the reverse end of the couch and on the yellowing living room wall above it, the top half of a cardboard poster– snow in all its facets– winter in Quebec– as if they didn't get enough of it. Louise had a gift with glue and old calendars.

Time was interminable. Still, he preferred to lie supine on his board than totter to Louise's bidding. But did she allow it? Not her. She shook at him relentlessly till he rolled off the bed for his so-called morning walk. Her elbow hitched through his, she forced him to limp around the circumference of the dining table, through the corridor, and into the kitchen where she sat him on a pillow-topped armchair for the better part of the day. If Louise wasn't pressing at his buttons, Oscar wouldn't budge even to pee. But she egged him on through the drilling pain, obliging him to lift and lower his legs on every hourly dong. A windup toy he'd become, as intractable, as mechanical.

There was a constant buzz of visitors. Everybody, every single neighbour, every lousy acquaintance heard Louse's truncated version of the story. People Oscar had never spoken to marched into their vestibule, their kitchen, and right up to his drooping silhouette to present their blaring regrets. The house became a hotel where the morning coffee was gratis. Only the police refused to come for their doughnuts. They had complete descriptions of the crooks down to the pink polish on the girl's toes, but they didn't care. Thank you and goodbye. We'll let you know.

And the Dumonts– one after the other they trooped in on their lumbering feet, sometimes a whole gang of them, ten, fifteen at a time. They crowded into the living room and as at a funeral home, took turns to nod at the body. His final resting place. If only it was. If only Mariette Dumont did not come with a roster of treatments for the broken pelvis.

She spoke to him in deliberately loud French, intoning every syllable. *"Os-car– je t'ai apporté de la soupe. Et une tisane pour ta digestion."* And a porridge that would magically reduce the inflammation in his pelvis and bowels all at the same time.

"It tastes like paste," he spat at Louise.

She poured a little boiling water into his bowl and sloshed it around. *"Manges, ça va t'aider."*

He swallowed. Worse, pasted more tightly in his throat than the never-ending porridge came advice from the in-laws on how to conserve money. As if they ever had to do it themselves, or could really know. What Oscar owned was dwindling. Even the armchair on which he reclined smack in the middle of the kitchen floor, might already belong to the bank.

The present difficulty, Marc dutifully made clear. His little glasses damp with condensation, he placed a notebook and calculator on the table and pulled up a chair.

"We will figure out if your insurance benefits cover all your expenses. I can put the figures on a spreadsheet for you. I'm sure they do, but just in that case, there are ways to make the money go farther."

Oscar clenched his fists over his blanket. The clan knew altogether too much about Horvath business.

"Good thing I have a strong arm." Marc grinned like he had a key to the coffers. "Not for nothing I'm top salesman. All that silly accident insurance I forced you to buy. Perfect for you now."

Except that there no longer was accident insurance or mortgage insurance or life insurance. There was no pension fund, nor a university tuition fund. Marc had not been there to explain, from the magnified view of his steel-rimmed glasses, how money made money when the premiums had to be paid. Smiling dimly, Oscar let his brother-in-law prattle. The minute the topic of insurance opened and it always did, Marc could fly you to another planet with all his talking. Good place to land in.

Somehow, they managed through the first month. Louise's mother brought cardboard boxes filled with frozen beef and chicken and whole macaroni dinners. The father passed Louise a few bucks each time he came, always waiting for Oscar to look away, or pretend to. Things they didn't need appeared in the house. Louise bought a standup lamp for the living room, a large cooking pot, oven mitts. She bought striped runners for Steve. The boy clomped around in his funny shoes looking awkwardly big-footed. The grandparents took him out when Oscar was asleep and he returned with bags of oversized shirts and pants. Big enough to last a few years. That's how the Dumonts got rich. When it was all accounted for, they didn't spend that much.

Oscar might have rented out the cab if it weren't so temperamental. Some people reaped substantial benefits by renting their cabs to poor schmucks who didn't know better. The owners worked half-time, bought more cabs. Money on money for them. Oscar wasn't about to shoot anybody in the foot. Besides, except for the mechanic, Oscar was about the only one who could start the car in the winter. Anybody else was liable to flood the motor. Or slam the doors till they refused to open. As long as Oscar dozed on the cot, thoughts came and went without making a difference.

He heard the squish of the sofa. More visitors– women– her chatty friends. Louise rushed into the kitchen and reappeared with coffee that smelled of old shoes. He tried to slumber past the ricocheting voices till Louise announced that all she had to do, was sign up for a little test that would get her a cab license. "And then I will be the *chauffeur de taxi* in the family."

Oscar opened his eyes. Their heads rose like little peaks above the back of the couch. A stiff tuft of red hair wagged back and forth. Louise sat facing them, cross-legged on the floor. They jabbered on about cab licenses and cabbage salad and Louise's leaky boots.

"And the taxi won't be wasted in a parking lot," one of them cooed. "Oh– but then I won't have anybody to talk to. So I'll come and keep you company in the front seat."

"Flora–" Louise squealed. "I need to take de customer."

So it was Flora disguised in red hair. Blowing hot air, what a surprise. Always feeding Louise stupid ideas.

With Flora's guidance Louise had been reading the highway code from a pamphlet that she displayed like a doily on the coffee table. Flora quizzed her and maybe by now, Louise knew the highway code perfectly. And maybe if she could actually pull the car out of the driveway, she might pass the test. But Louise couldn't even get to the corner without hitting a curb. It took her twenty minutes to climb into the car and adjust the mirrors. And forget about getting anywhere.

Roads and their directions were a mystery to her. And what would she do when she had no time for her daily friend fix?

He craned his neck in their direction. "Hi Flora. Know anybody who wants to rent a cab?"

"Oscar– I thought you were asleep. How's that pelvis doing?"

He grunted and closed his eyes. If she kept her mouth shut, he could get some peace.

Except for the mechanic, the visitors were hers and not his. Tony showed up a good week after Oscar came home. From his armchair in the kitchen, Oscar could see Louise's head bob, probably to air-kiss him on each cheek before rushing him and his cigarette odour into the kitchen.

With dirt-ingrained fingernails, Tony held out a box of almond bark. "I didn't want to bother you. So– I didn't come right away."

"To-nee. You don bodder hus," Louise simpered.

Oscar grinned. Tony left his scum of dirt wherever he sat, but he was quiet. The guy would keep Louise hovering with her broom and her rags. She served reheated coffee barely lightened by skim milk.

"I've got another couple of weeks in this coffin," Oscar said.

"And then?"

"Back to work."

Tony let his hands drop between his knees. He turned over his wrists and looked at them while his coffee cooled. "You can hardly move."

Louise was washing up, using too much hot water. In a moment she'd be dragging her rag over the counters.

"Look. I've got this Mazda on my lot. It's got six years on it but it's in great shape." Tony took a sip of his coffee.

"Yeah?"

"It's got some mileage, but you know, those Japanese cars last."

Louise wiped the counter. She'd be at the kettle next and the stovetop and the tile work behind the stove after that. She'd be up there cleaning all day if there was something to listen to.

"The owner was an old man with Parkinson's. A real quiet guy. Kept miles from the potholes."

Oscar snorted.

"I swear to God. It's the truth." Tony swigged back some of the coffee and shifted his chair as Louise passed the broom between the men. "If you're planning to drive your passengers farther than around the block, you might want to think about it."

"I can't do it. Not now."

"I can give you a really good deal."

"You should be charging me to keep the Malibu in your lot."

"Nah–"

Oscar gazed at the floor.

"Hey– I don't want money for the Mazda. I'll lend it to you. As long as you keep the repairs at the shop."

"Lend? What does that mean?"

"That means you can use the car and when you have to fix it, I'll charge you for the repairs."

"You want me to trade one disease for another."

"Os-car–" Louise raised her hands to her ears. This was the signal. She was about to start explaining. And when she did that, she never ended. "Dis is too kind for Tony, *dis opportunité*, is some-ting we must talk about."

"There's nothing to talk about."

"Maybe, we can bo-rrow *l'auto* and af-ter, to pay."

"Pay with what?"

"We will 'ave in-come, Os-car."

"Sure. Income."

Oscar didn't owe a flat cent to the mechanic. Not yet. So far, he had paid off everything, sometimes in fives and ones, sometimes in chunks every couple of days. The guy was scheming up another way to make a buck, like he needed it, like he was about to buy a bunch of used crap cars just so he could sell them and keep a running tally on the repairs.

"Look. This car's in better shape than your Malibu. Whatever you have to fix will last."

"My eye it will."

"You think you're the only one with trouble?" Tony gulped down the rest of his coffee. He wouldn't insult them by wasting it. He placed his mug in the sink. The woman was wiping her wet fingers with the dripping dishcloth. Her hair drooped over her shoulders, little bits of girlie blond speckled through it. Any sign of a morning hairbrush was gone. He reached a hand out to her, stopped short, and turned to go. The veins on one side of Oscar's nose were almost purple.

Steve opened the fridge and poured himself a glass of milk. From the window Oscar watched Tony get into his truck and speed away just ahead of the snow crews. An entire cavalry dealt with the snow. And he'd never noticed it before. Not in so many words, not to be able to turn around and describe it to his son.

"Do you know how they take away all that snow? Did you ever really look?"

Steve rolled his eyes.

"It's an assembly line. You've got this plow that shoves the snow into two piles, left and right. Come to the window. Come quick."

Outside, the rotating blades of a blower scissored through the icy mounds formed by the plow, sucked in the snow, and a moment later, blew a grey geyser of it into a truck riding alongside. Full up, the truck rumbled away and another took its place.

"See that?" Oscar leaned back in his chair.

Staring out the window, Steve scratched his ear.

"I guess you've seen it a million times."

"Ya."

"Did you get all your homework done?"

"Almost."

"You go to university, you won't have to drive a taxi."

"I'm not."

"You're not what?"

"Being a cab driver. Not because– I mean, I still might want to drive something."

"Don't. Do something else."

"I mean– like a plane. Maybe a plane."

Oscar nodded. Maybe a plane. Why not fly away?

Up from his cot, Oscar staggered to the toilet, peed, flushed, and washed his hands. Before Louise had a chance to race over with his crutches, he got to the kitchen and eased himself into a chair. Throughout the entire month of January, he had kept an eye on the weather via the windows, practiced sitting and standing, and counted the minutes till he could walk to Tony's garage. Well. The countdown was over. He slapped his hand on the table. "I'm ready to go."

But would she let Oscar go alone? No way. Not Louise. She set a bowl of oatmeal in front of him, her mouth pursed, a spoon raised to her ears as if to thrust it into his mouth at the first opportunity. He polished up the porridge just to keep her away, pushed aside the bowl and shuffled to his cot. Grasping the mattress, he eased one leg into his trousers before he had to stop and wait for Louise to angle the other foot into his pant leg. She pulled the pants over his navel and when he was done buttoning his shirt, handed him a cardigan.

"I don't need that."

"Il fait froid."

It was always cold according to her. He put on the sweater and a puffy, too-short parka that must have been donated by her brother. Tied up in scarves to keep out the chill, they descended the front steps into minus forty-degree temperatures, the February wind sharp on their faces. Louise clung to the sleeve of his nylon parka as they limped on sidewalks that were almost dry, the cement paths narrowed by a crusted snow wall that peaked as stiffly as beaten egg whites along the curbs. She weighed him down but he didn't say it. Here and there, a slick of ice shone along the four residential blocks to the garage. With the scarf that barely allowed him to see and Louise stepping on his heels, any minute he could roll into the traffic. But getting to the garage, the very effort, made him grin. As long as he could walk this gauntlet, he could easily drive.

The Malibu was parked snugly beside the brick wall of an apartment building. It was Steve's job to start it up every day, let the engine warm, then turn off the ignition. Tony kept an eye on him. He called Oscar to say that Steve was doing a good job even though, "The boy always looks as if he's about to turn the steering wheel and let go of the brakes. The last thing we need is to have the thing bang through somebody's bedroom." That was a joke for Tony. He called every time he took it out for a spin. As long as it wasn't burned by a foot heavy on the gas, the Malibu turned the corners obediently. And if it whined like an old dog on a leash about to stop and relieve itself you never knew when - Tony would know what to do.

Louise opened the car door. Oscar peered into the interior, took off his gloves, and passed a hand over the seats. The sagging upholstery was frozen rigid. He tried to lower his knees and get in, his bunchy coat a cushion to his pelvis and a barrier to his entrance. He might have been able to sit on the passenger side but could not fold himself behind the steering wheel. He walked around the car and back to the open door and for nothing, bent his knees again, not knowing how to make himself thin. He smashed his fist on the roof, then on the windshield.

Louise lifted her curled fingers to her ears. "Os-car," she called. Her voice was as thin as a whistle.

Oscar slammed the door, his pelvis aching from the effort and stumbled away from Tony's entreating face.

Louise answered an ad and got a job stuffing envelopes. At the rate she worked, she made about fifteen cents an hour and when her mother came to help, about five cents more minus the price of coffee. In front of the television, they set out a lethargic assembly line of envelopes. Some kind of soap opera flickered out images while the mother slurped down gallons of coffee. Louise jabbered on and on about politics, of all things, putting big halts to the assembly line.

"And the minute we become our own sovereign country, nobody will ever again need to be *bilingue* to get a good job."

Yeah right. The talk made Oscar seize up. He'd been in and out of the toilet all morning, all month really, waiting for a movement. He made his way up the stairs to the bathroom and sat, leaving the door ajar. Louise went on singsonging at the top of her lungs about how, when the province became a nation, life would be more efficient smarter and cheaper. A Francophone country– at last– could handle its affairs entirely in French and nobody would have to struggle with that other language. And all the money that ran to taxes for the Canadian roads and bridges they would never see would be put back into their pockets. And then, the ladies reasoned, they'd have themselves a little vacation, a week at an all-inclusive in the Dominican Republic, why not?

He made out every last word they said. Louise had spouted it out a thousand times. When once he had asked her why in the world she was so against his culture, she rushed up to hug him.

"Os-car– dis 'as noting to do wit' you. *C'est juste de la politique.*"

"Just politics," had infiltrated the house. Didn't need a radio or television. Louise spouted out her own broadcasts. It was a relief to get away even if it was just to sit on the toilet. On the days that had seen him stiff on the cot in the dining room, the Dumonts flitted around him like fruit flies, impossible to bat away. Whether he slept or not, they talked about him– if he was better educated– if he was not so stubborn– if Louise had become a nurse–. She was married too young. They went on and on as if he was too stupid to understand their French.

He should never have married a woman like Louise but when you're young, you're too young to know what's good for you. She served tables at a greasy spoon, always giggling, shouting at the kitchen help. She passed you the ketchup before you asked for it and was always pouring extra coffees. It was the way she closed her eyes when she laughed that got him. That he could not speak to her was entirely irrelevant.

He put her in his cab, a Crown Victoria as plush as they come and took her to a movie that he did not understand and that she did not listen to. Afterwards, he asked her to join him for a drink. But she pouted about the bar he'd chosen or was it the drink itself, he didn't know, and they ended up having ice cream at a plastic, outdoor table. She was more relaxed with the cone in her hand than she had been in the close theatre and spoke to him with her little giggles, a few shrugs, her hand on his wrist. She knew how to say thank you in English. And, *fun*, and he learned to say, *un petit bizou*, which meant, a little kiss in any language. She threw her head back and closed her eyes and breathed out words that filled him with a sense of community. Together they were as one with the pimply boy who served the ice cream and the two-child family at the next table and the old lady who sat alone with her handbag clutched to her breast. Louise described the flavour of her ice cream to them and parts of the movie and maybe how her calves hurt or didn't hurt now that she was sitting. The children's ice creams dripped as she talked.

Every day he sat where she could serve him. She'd list the special of the day, "*Un bon pain de viande, un bon spaghetti, une belle omelette*– and he said yes, no matter what it was, just to see her toss back her head. Amidst her French vocabulary she began to scatter English words, never connecting them properly. And he used a kind of French that made her burst into laughter. What mattered is that she began to address him with a warm, birdlike, Os-car. His name, twittering from her throat made his ears burn. Though she chattered too rapidly, he began to understand almost everything she said, understood that she was not quite eighteen, that she would be a nurse if school wasn't so tiresome. The French part of his responses got tangled in his mouth and soon, he spoke to her mostly in English. It didn't matter. She was the girl his mother hoped for. On Sundays, she helped the old lady up the stairs of the Catholic church while Oscar searched for parking. She sang all the hymns and at his mother's bidding, went into the confessional. After church, she kept her arm folded across her breast, a couple of hours separation that was too much for him. What sins she had admitted to the priest, she kept to herself. He only knew that he needed to marry her.

*

Oscar could fairly bounce up the stairs and into bed but could not sit long enough on the toilet to squeeze out a turd. He concentrated a minute longer without any luck, wiped and flushed. He stood at the mirror and washed his hands. The red trails of a blood vessel flared unhealed on his nostril. It had been lurking there all his life but when his smile folded his nose into his cheeks, it was barely visible. The toilet whined and the voices downstairs rose back at him. Because of her, the little bit of hair that still clung to his skull was already grey. The blood vessel throbbed into his temples. Her unwavering ambitions were tearing at his guts– a vacation in the sun, new boots, an entire new country, for god's sake. He wanted to please her. But what could a small man with a bald pate do for a woman, but bleed?

Chapter 4

Louise's solution to the problem was leg lifts. Oscar lay on the floor in the afternoon dusk and picked up his legs at five-minute intervals. Sixteen years they'd been married. With every request, she ate him up with her desolate gaze. He had no choice but to say Yes. Christmas was the last time he had thrust a roll of dollars into her limp hand. She needed hair gel and hand cream and tons of sanitary pads and it was he who provided it all plus stuff she didn't even need. Stuff. Stuff to have just for the fun of it. He squeezed his fist and aimed it at the glowering walls of their ridiculous condominium. If he'd only insisted on staying in their rental, they wouldn't be in this mess.

But no. He lifted his legs, lifted and grunted. As far as Louise was concerned, the apartment was uninhabitable because the refrigerator smelled, because you couldn't even fit a pear in it, never mind a four-litre bag of milk, because, because. So in came a gigantic refrigerator. And out went a gigantic cheque. And with that fridge came the voracious guests who sucked hundreds of dollars' worth of groceries right out of that fridge. If it was only about food, they could have managed. But then she needed a dishwasher. On and on she went– if only they had a dishwasher like everybody else– if only there was someplace in their teeny-weeny kitchen to put it, her hands wouldn't get so very dry. So what do you know? Her chapped hands needed a bigger house to go with the dishwasher. And to go with her new soft hands, they had to have a fancy dining table with two extensions and to go with that, a set of matching floral dishes. And with the gleaming condominium came a gobbler of a mortgage and tax bills that were dropped like ten-pound weights through the mail slot. He grunted one last time and lay still. The walls seemed to throb while the last streak of daylight dimmed in the window pane.

"Louise," he shouted. "What do you want me to do next?"

Oscar bunched up his coat. Under it, Louise's flannel nightgown formed a flaccid girdle around his midriff— Louise's form of cushioning. He folded himself over, slid into the driver's seat and clamped his foot to the gas pedal. He turned on the engine. In the rearview mirror, Tony's cigarette flickered against the yellow brick wall of the gas station.

The car coasted backwards into the boulevard and there he was, Oscar back on the road, back on the job. His eye out for prospective passengers, he felt the velour seat on which he perched. Except for the bouncing chassis against his aching pelvis, the car felt prosperous and friendly. He drove along the boulevard past apartment buildings. A handbag beckoned him. His first fare, caught in less than ten minutes, hauled herself into the back seat. Oscar patted the dashboard. He couldn't help it. He felt like kissing the car. Three fares in a row for Oscar— men, women, with or without shopping bags flapping in the wind, it didn't matter who they were. They waved him down, gave an address, and while the Malibu sniffed at the ground, Oscar got paid.

He drove into a strip mall pausing long enough near the grocery store to get a few irked honks. There was not a soul in the lunchtime hours who was not walking to their car. Everybody and his dog owned a car in the suburbs. Not the best place to drive a cab, but never mind. He pulled up to a parking slot at the far end of the lot and turned off his motor. In this dead winter of impatient weather and barren branches, birds were singing. He turned down his visor to shield himself from the glassy stare of the snow. To blunt the noisy birdsong, he turned on the radio and let the voices of a call-in show rage with the same old discussion– the choice of the people.

We should be free to choose, a man kept saying.

Which should it be, the host shrieked– A united Canada or a free Quebec?

This, the caller said more than once, Will be decided by the people of Quebec. We–

Thank you, sir, and now for our next caller, here's the question for you: Should the Parti Quebecois government hold a second referendum that will let the people decide for once and for all if Quebec should remain in Canada, or– should we respect and make final, the outcome of the 1980 referendum where the majority of the people of Quebec chose to remain within Canada. Should the taxpayers be paying thousands of dollars for our government to ask the same question? Let us know what you think. Call us at—

Shut up— Oscar clicked off the radio. His legs were stiff. The cold rode up his back but as long as he had no fare, he would not waste gas. He stretched his torso over the steering wheel. He was on the waiting list for a physiotherapist not that he needed one. Perfect waste if all they did was time his leg lifts. If you had insurance, Marc Dumont had shouted at him, you could go private for a physiotherapist and then take all the time in the world to recover. They'd be paying you to lie in your bed and rest. You wouldn't have to worry about anything. It will be months before you can sit in your car, never mind drive around the city. A couple of dollars a month, the insurance would have cost you. One less pizza.

When Marc Dumont shouted, he didn't raise his voice.

Oscar turned on the radio and adjusted the dial until classical music soft enough to sleep to drifted through the speakers. He looked at his watch, snuggled against Louise's nightie, and let his eyes drop. Why not take a little rest, Louise would advise. Good idea. He began to count downward from one hundred. At zero, at the first and last digit of all time, he'd look for another trip. He allowed his eyes to close and reached for the light switch.

The stores across the asphalt stood in a fluorescent row. Oscar yawned and straightened. He turned the key in the ignition. Nothing. He pulsed the motor. Twice, three times the starter clicked. The smell of gas in the air was too indistinct to be a sign of life. He leaned against the dashboard and rubbed the little horseshoe that dangled from the key. Come on. Gradually, he turned the key. Got nothing, not even a croak of disdain. He slammed his fist on the dashboard and flung open the door. Bent over his throbbing pelvis he slid out and edged toward the hood. He plucked at the tin fastener. A hollow click should have released the hood. But the rusted hinges refused to separate. He tugged at the hood to no avail. Tears fell out of his eyes. Because of the cold pricking at his tear ducts. Luck– just a sip would do. He rubbed the useless horseshoe and felt himself gasp. He leaned against the chassis and listened to his breath.

The uneven row of buildings faced him. At the end of the row, a red phone booth stood like a beacon. Call someone. Oscar limped across the parking lot. He pushed the little numbers on the keypad. Louise's shrill erupted from the receiver. He wanted to tell her to shut up and listen but his breath skittered. To get to the mall from Tony's garage you need to pass three lights and two stop signs. But don't call Tony. He didn't know the name of the shopping centre though he'd often passed it.

He heard the coin drop, must have told Louise something. His car was somewhere on the lot or on a curb or maybe around the corner. Cars everywhere but his was the broken one. He. eased out of the booth and there was Tony springing toward him, his grey tuque flattening his forehead.

"What did you do? Leave the lights on?"

"What kind of battery did you put in there? The thing's not even a year old."

"Nothing wrong with it this morning. Get in the car. We'll jump it."

Oscar got in. Tony unclasped the hood.

"I told you. I keep telling you. The Malibu's finished. Take the Japanese one. What's the big deal? You'll do me a favour, get it off my lot. All you have to do is change the permit. So it'll cost you a few bucks in taxes. Then you'll be free. No more broken anything for a while. Now turn over the engine. Go."

Oscar lay on his living room floor. The first thing he needed was rest. Then he'd think up a plan if he could think at all. Steve was at it again with his music. It was enough to make a man scream. But it was Louise, Louise with her stupid ideas who got to him most. She'd given up stuffing envelopes in favour of Tupperware. The catalogue splayed on her lap, she prattled on for hours– It is so easy. First, you sell to your friends and then to their friends. And if you buy for yourself, well, you get a discount. And if you want to be serious about your business, you have to show the merchandise. And look at the bee-u-ti-ful things they have. And the *qualité*. Smiling like a baby girl in front of a Barbie doll, she turned the pages of her magazine. It had seemed harmless. As long as she talked about selling things, she didn't wear the yellow house dress that made her look like her mother. And she didn't rub at the counters with her rags. As long as she only talked, everything was fine.

As he lay on the floor trying to repair himself, Louise showed him her plastics, taking brand new bowls and tumblers from boxes, turning them over in her hands. On top of that, there was the smell of cake in the air. Cake, for God's sake.

"Yes but where did you get those plastic doodads? Who gave them to you? And when? Was I asleep? You didn't pay for them, did you? Did you? My God. Don't tell me they made you buy that crap."

"Os-car. You give me dat look. 'Ow can I to sell if I 'ave noting to show de cus-to-mer?"

"They made you buy it?"

"It is a kit. For making sale."

"And you paid with what, may I ask? Since you couldn't have had more than fifty cents in that little drawer of yours."

"Os-car— *la carte de crédit*. You say it is for emer-gen-cy." She was making faces, a soft trembling in her chin.

Another debt another debt another debt, all of them emergencies. Oscar rolled onto his hands and knees. It was a surprise to him that his body, as petrified as it had become, could get up at all. But up he went, he always had. It was up to him to clean up the mess.

"You'll have to give them back."

"*Mais non.* I cannot. I am in business now." Louise raised her hands tautly to her shoulders. "*J'ai une surprise pour toi.* Tonight I 'ave a Tupperware party. All de neighbour is coming."

So that's what it was. A party. People coming to eat and drink. Coffee, eggs wasted in the cake. Where was she getting the funds? None of it was free. To depend on Mariette with her pinched mouth and her packages. Now that was a crime. Weeks, he'd been on his back, always taking, giving nothing in return. Later the Dumonts would expect plenty. Reciprocity was in their code. They'd want him to take Mariette to her appointments in the city– the arthritis doctor, the podiatrist for God's sake, all the way from the South Shore. Hours on the road and miles of gas. He had married a woman who couldn't add and subtract. And with her, came her family. He held his noisy breath in his contracted chest till it slowed all the way to nothing. Almost nothing.

"Even cake costs money." His voice was like the sugar in the cake.

"My mudder 'elp me."

"I know."

"You must say, tank you to 'er."

"Of course, of course. I'll take her wherever she needs to go." Oscar lay back on the floor and closed his eyes.

More than anything he needed to sleep. But no. Louise was arranging and rearranging her plasticware on the coffee table, matching shapes, colours, who knows what else. You'd think it was a flower show. Later she'd bring out a supper of hot dogs and potatoes and the boiled cabbage that was now stinking up the house. *Des bonnes saucisses*, she'd shrill, as if she won the lottery.

He tried counting backwards. His shoulder twitched. He felt Steve looking in. He let the slit of his eyes confirm what he already knew. The boy was leaning against the wall plucking at his fake guitar. He had an instinct for his child. When his infant barely stirred, he was the one who awoke. He'd have to bequeath something to his son. He once had a watch with a gold band but that time was gone and if you have nothing, what do you give? He squeezed his eyes tight. Well. Maybe advice. Better his than Louise's. Or if the advice was no longer relevant, maybe some part of his wisdom– some sort of life statement. No. Never mind that. He had nothing brilliant to offer. And, what would some philosophical line do for Steve? Better to teach by example, give him some part of his experience. The boy swayed to his head music. Probably he wasn't even aware that Oscar was lying on the floor, two feet away from him. Oscar opened his mouth, about to release a list. Before he could say one word, Steve lifted the invisible guitar above his head and bowed.

Chapter 5

Louise bought herself a white blouse that made her look stiff-necked and all week, went gallivanting around with some Tupperware lady. Big shot nonstop talker she'd become. If you got anywhere near the plastic containers laid out like museum pieces on the coffee table, she'd be at you. For dinner, she fried eggs and kept on talking. Du profit pur, she said as she laid the table and again as she dipped toast in the soft yolk of her eggs. Never mind that she couldn't calculate. While Louise sloshed the dirty dishes in the sink, the puffy sleeves of her fancy blouse rolled up to her shoulders, she told Oscar that in one night all her expenses would be paid off and the rest would be—

"Yeah, I know. Pure profit."

How stacking the fridge with a chocolate layer cake and some kind of gelatinous mold thing would be profitable, was the big question. Oscar clutched his pelvis and climbed up to bed. He refused to see them arrive. Guests he didn't need. He tucked the corners of his coverlet into his ears to dull the squeals of the women but couldn't avoid the peck peck peck of his mother-in-law's call up the stairs.

"Yeah," he yelled back. And finally went into the darkened hall just to put a stop to her voice. "I'm fine. Trying sleep."

As if she even cared.

Too much noise for sleep. He edged down the stairs toward the din, smelled them before he saw the seven fully perfumed women decked out in high heels to buy plastics. Duded up in his grey school pants, Steve dashed into the kitchen with the coats. Double red kisses were pasted on his cheeks. Louise fluttered around and eventually gathered them into a single huddle facing the pyramid of plastics. She passed around the Tupperware explaining how each one could be best used, showing off their secrets– a cheese grater on a bowl, a water bottle with a compartment for hiding keys. The big surprise was how the women fondled the containers. And how Louise dismantled her pyramid and built it up with the skill of an engineer.

Steve approached and began to finger the water bottle. Receptacles. Who'd have thought they'd be interesting to the boy? They were almost scientific. *Il y a des trucs dans l'Tupperware*, his mother had told Steve. And if you get to see the tricks in that Tupperware, well– you'd be converted in no time.

"*Regardez*," Louise told the ladies. She held up her hands as if to start the show and nodded at Steve. He nodded back and went into the kitchen.

"The best jello mold in the world," Louise announced as Steve returned bearing a green Tupperware. She took off the lid, turned the thing onto a platter and pulled off the middle piece. She was smiling. Oscar could almost hear a drum roll. Louise jiggled the plastic container and lifted it off in one swoop. Everybody applauded. But for what? A sculpture made of jelly that would disappear as quickly as everything around it.

Just as he'd been instructed, Steve placed milk and sugar on the dining table and returned with the cake. The applause got louder. As the coffee brewed, Louise displayed the Tupperware mould that had produced such perfect ridges on the gelatine. Steve handed her the official order pad but she pushed it away.

"*Sois pas impoli*, Steve." Two red spots appeared on her cheeks.

"*Oui mais, faut prendre les commandes.*"

Ah. But Louise would never be rude. And to ask for payment– in her own home– Never.

Oscar could have done the asking. She expected him to be rude. He reached out to beckon the ladies and instead teetered on the stairway as if attached to a spring– a little man in a capsule, begging.

Louise cut up the cake while her mother tittered over the prices in the catalogue. The women munched and giggled, Louise the loudest. Take the orders, Oscar growled through his glued teeth. She would, he knew, make some kind of eventual sale. They'd all come knowing that they were expected to buy something. Politeness showed itself in many forms. Oscar slumped against the bannister. Patience was the key. After an endless wait, Mariette called out that she had decided to buy three of the largest storage bins available– a matter of faith in the brand and in Louise and to thank her for the beautiful get-together and such lovely colours and–. Oscar turned his quivering legs and went up the stairs. If all went according to the plan, Louise would remind them that they too, could host a Tupperware party and that if they did, they would earn Host dollars and receive a Membership Card. Right. He heard nothing in the soft voices below that sounded like anything more than thank you and goodbye. Forever goodbye

Louise dwelt on the plentiful weather. She dispensed advice on healing the natural way, whatever that was. Her new money-making scheme was to buy a batch of lottery tickets and blow on them for good luck. While she waited for the cash to roll in all by itself, she sat in the kitchen beside her radio and played solitaire. Seemed like she never stopped talking.

Oscar shuffled toward the tinkle of music. He opened his mouth to tell Louise to get her puffy white blouse out of its bath of soapy water and sell something. But no. Louise laid the big orbs of her eyes on him as if to say, what the heck are you doing here? He shone a smirk on her and dropped back into thoughts that could not be shared.

"You look good *quand tu* smile," she said. "You must to sleep. You 'ave black *cercles* under you' eye."

Yeah, and an ugly blue pulse on his nostril.

The Tupperware order pad lay blank by the phone. Not a surprise. Louise couldn't even play a good game of cards. If she ever had to support herself, she'd have some other kind of party and starve. Never mind. Soon he'd jump off his taciturn bed and into the awakened cab.

Except that his car was dead. There was the other car, the one Tony told him to drive. The one he didn't own was waiting for him in Tony's parking lot, its obedient nose face to face with his truculent Malibu. If he took it on the road, it would own his job and it would own him. He wasn't about to do something so stupid, not right away. For now, he would let himself be free. if only to sleep.

Days on end he woke up in the late afternoon, companion to the receding sun. With dinner, he liked a glass of sweet tea the way his mother used to make it. Louise ate watching the soporific TV while he gazed into his tinted glass. In the depths of the silent weather, the sweep of Steve's clothing as he shuffled around the house was the only sound that likened itself to some kind of conversation. Soon after swallowing a few mouthfuls, it was already dark and time for bed again. Oscar was finally living without the need to speak. It had taken him fifty-one years to get there.

The bills came in. His sister would have piled them beside her toaster. Sheldon took care of her. Even divorced, he took care of her. Oscar took care of Oscar and his wife and his son. It was his job. He settled himself in his chair, the blanket spread over his torso and opened the envelopes. The telephone bill showed four months arrears. His sister's telephone number had probably not changed in two years but there was no sense remembering it. He could still dial the telephone number of his childhood without consulting a phone book. Regent 14406, the number that never rang. The mortgage company threatened to foreclose on the house. And on the Visa bill was a row of numbers that started with the price of Louise's blouse and ended with the plastic boxes still displayed on the coffee table like offerings to the saints. When he had announced his engagement to Louise, his mother told him, Once you marry her, she's yours forever. Till the very end, you take care of her. The numbers on the bill blinked without a pause. He had something of a headache. And there was Steve trolling through the living room, his fingers on the chords of his imaginary guitar. Thanks to his grandparents' latest gift of technology, his indifferent ears were plugged to Nirvana. Thanks to the grandparents, the Horvaths ate.

"I can't bear it." Oscar covered his face with the blanket. Heat was wet on his face. He threw off the blanket, rolled to his feet. Oscar ran. In and out of all the rooms, into the kitchen. *I can't bear it I can't bear it.* Just ahead of him, Steve bounded up the stairs.

Louise laid down her cards. How that man could run with his pelvis not healed? And what was he screaming about anyway? Sometimes he lost his temper for some little nothing and then he'd calm down. A good meal helped. She had the onions and the potatoes on the counter. He owned one very distinguished suit, dark grey. They used to dance. When he wore it and when his pelvis was straight, he looked wonderful.

CHAPTER 5

*

He took her into his arms. *I can't bear it*, he whimpered. There were onions on the blade but that didn't matter. He always took care of her. He held her close, kissed her throat. I can't bear it, he whispered into her open mouth. He had things to tell her but first, she'd have to close her mouth. Please stop talking. He pointed the knife to a moist spot on her lips and easy like, drew it down, cutting a seam through her Adam's apple. She clung to him like she never had. Yeah, easy. Such a long cut. Sticky too. Never mind. She'll sew it up later.

Part 2
Math Days

Chapter 6

The disembodied branch of a tree wavers just beyond her living room window. Could be that, or a willful drawing created by her eye-brain. Could be something else too– a long-handled spade stuck in the ground, a crooked metal hanger suspended from a ledge. Either way, it's a warning. The people who are supposed to bring him home might not show. Three p.m. they should have been knocking and now, nine minutes to four– no, eight minutes–there's definitely no car at the curb. Her eyes on the tree's forbidding finger, she rotates her face till the brown scum of March snow appears below her with perfect clarity. She grips the window's wooden frame and wills them to drive up to her door. Wills so hard, her jaw clenches. Time ekes on to half past four. Her arms cramp before she acknowledges that she's been tricked. She's about to flop onto the couch but as if willpower alone turned on the correct switch, hears the slam of a car door.

A slender, quarter moon image appears on the side of her eye and billowing like the loose wrapping on a package, a red jacket shimmers. Steve. She knows him by his height, by his stick-like body. Behind him, his grandfather– it must be him– climbs out of the car, hugs him briefly and goes back in. Steve bends into the wind and hoists something out of the trunk. Ahead of him, his mother's brother and wife carry boxes. And she's there too, at the tail of Steve's jacket, her chin angled to the sky.

Paula knows them by their shapes. They huddled beside Steve at his mother's funeral, the grandmother sobbing for her Louise, her chin The grandfather grimly taciturn. Hunched over the judge's desk, Marc and his wife demanded that Steve be given to his mother's family. For the sake of the boy's safety. The defeated now mount the concrete steps to her apartment for the single purpose of delivering Steve to his lawful guardian.

Throwing open the door, she hustles past the aunt and uncle and draws Steve into her padded embrace. There's a duffel bag between them and around them, the close buffer of his relatives. Afraid to let him slide backwards toward his clingy grandmother, she only lets go when he ducks out of her grasp.

Marc and his wife remove their boots and step in. To decipher one featureless face from the other, Paula fixes her attention on Celine, a half a head taller than her husband.

"We are late," Celine says in her pronouncedly French accent, "because Steve want to drive near 'is new school." She glances back at her mother-in-law.

Still in the alcove, Mariette Dumont is diminutive in her tent of a camel coat. She eyes the coffee table and tucks her nose into the collar of her coat. As if the place stinks, as if the white stain on the wood table is an infectious blemish. Too bad for her if she thinks the frayed newsprint drawings on the wall are trash. Too effing bad if she thinks the sunken couch belongs in a dump. Stones, jars, a noise maker, piles of greeting cards and photographs– Paula sees it the way they would– clutter the tables on either side of the couch.

Paula retreats to the kitchen and plugs in the kettle. Too bad for them. The law is the law. She raises the volume of the nattering radio to make herself feel as if she too is surrounded by a crowd. While Steve lugs his belongings down the narrow corridor into the bedroom, Paula strides back into the living room and flicks a hand at the couch, determined to give some appearance of welcome. "Sit down," she shouts into the din of the Dumont's silence. "I'll make tea."

"*Non merci, non.*" Celine wrings her hands. "We are late. If you let Steve stay wit' us like he want, we will not rush to de city *comme ça.* Tomorrow is school. The Jacques Cartier bridge is close' again. We have to drive almos' one hour."

From the alcove, Mariette's eyes bulge like blue marbles above two splotches of rouge. She cranes her neck into the recesses of the apartment. "*Steve, où es-tu?*" she calls through a pursed mouth red with lipstick. When at last he returns, she squeezes him in a breathless hug. "*À bien-tôt, mon beau Steve. On viens te chercher Samedi.*" They turn and leave. Frightened birds. That's what they are.

As their steps recede down the concrete stairs, Steve leans back against the closed door. At fifteen he's taller than his aunt, a spike to her broadness. Paula taps him on the shoulder, takes his hand, and leads him to the kitchen.

"What did they say?"

He shrugs.

"What's this about Saturday?"

"They're picking me up."

She looks at him like what he's saying is in another language. Or he's just plain stupid.

"It's not a hotel here. You can't just stop off for a visit whenever you feel like it. You live here now." Paula stares ahead of her as she speaks, looking past him. "I don't suppose you drink tea. Too old lady-like? You want a glass of milk? No? You're too old for that? I guess you don't want to grow taller than you already are. What are you now? Six feet?" She sidles up to Steve and lifts up a hand to measure.

He averts his head.

"I have orange juice."

"Look. I'm not a two-year-old. And I'm not stupid."

"You eat, don't you? Sit down. I have cookies."

Paula pours Steve a glass of juice and another of milk, butters two slices of whole wheat bread and piles them on a plate beside a handful of chocolate wafers. Nursing her tea, she sits across from him, her eyes like spy holes. "You'll need to pick up your strength before you unpack," she says.

Steve's belongings are parked in the back room only because there's nowhere else to put them. He has no intention of eating in Paula's house, does not intend to sleep here. He certainly will not fill the dresser nor hook his shoes on the metal rods of the shoetree.

His aunt's droopy eyes stare at the wall on his left. "Go on, take something." She pushes a glass toward him.

The juice dribbles down the side of the glass. Only to keep it from spilling further, he leans over, touches his tongue to the rim of the glass and allows a few drops to slide down his throat.

"Go on, eat now."

He hasn't changed his mind about staying, is not hungry. He bites into the polite edge of a cookie. That's okay. Cookies aren't real food. He gulps down the juice even though he's not thirsty. Juice might be real but waste is not polite. He tucks the cookie into his palm and takes a step away from everything else at the table. He'll save the cookie for the trip.

"You can hang anything you want in that room. Sharon put thumbtacks in the top drawer for you." She talks about his cousin constantly– Sharon this Sharon that.

"You brought any pictures?"

Ya. Frozen smiles in a cardboard box. Should have been dumped in his father's grave. To keep him company forever.

"Posters?"

He stares at the seam between the ceiling and the wall. "Wrestlers, movie stars? Zebras? Whatever it is, you can hang it."

"I need it."

"What?"

He shrugs. From that angle, he appears as concave as a plate. Everyone on his mother's side is just as narrow. From his mother, he inherited sculptured bones almost visible through the skin. From Oscar, he got his colour. His cheeks are so pale, they're white, close to translucent. But the pinkness of anger, he doesn't possess. Not yet, as far as Paula could see.

He slides his hand over his back pocket.

A bulge. She nudges him. "Go on, let's see what you have."

He turns and walks away.

The two-by-four you can't even call a room, reeks of used sheets. The door opens barely halfway before it knocks into a pink dresser. Pink. The frilly bed skirt is pink. Even the walls are pink.

Steve jams his boxes into the closet and lies on the bed. Nothing but junk in those boxes. His uncle dumped most of his parents' crap into a few garbage bags and practically had to beg some charity to take them away. The upholstery and the beds, the rusted fridge, the washer that needed a kick start, he left for the bank to enjoy. The rest of the condominium he must have cleared with a broom and a dustpan. And a barrel of disinfectant. Because according to him, decent people hand over their empty homes clean. He told Steve– Take something. Maybe you want your globe? Your father's watch? Nah. Steve wanted no part of it but was still obliged to take his mother's fake pearls probably got from a garage sale, and the waste of time photographs. In the end, the only thing he got of any value was a car he wasn't even allowed to drive. And the privilege of staring at his aunt's open-closed eyes. They're so dim, he can stand right in front of her and be invisible.

He pulls off his running shoe. There's a watery blue line around the heel. Expensive shoes. Fast movers. He pulls back his arm and hurls it at the dresser. Amazingly, the crash does not alert his aunt. He plugs his ears with his fingers comforted by the hollow sound of a cave. When the shoe stops rocking against the floor, he pulls out the wad from his back pocket and smells the damp paper.

Chapter 7

Hunger wakes Paula. Too early for daylight, the luminescent street lamps glinting into her window urge her to roll off the bed, search for slippers, and feel her way to the bathroom then the kitchen. It's a few minutes past four A.M. but time, since Steve's arrival, has no logic. After waiting for Steve all day, she continued to mark time during a weird, supperless stretch– waiting for Steve to sit at the table with her, to pick up his fork, to join in any kind of conversation. Dinner finished with his concise, Thank you as he got up and left the room. Time then for Paula to pack up the leftovers and spend much of the night peeking in on his exhausted sleep.

She makes coffee and toast and eventually sunlight glints on the silver kettle. Another round of toast, more coffee. Good God, it's eleven already. Will that kid never wake up? She flicks on the radio and keeps raising the volume till a rustle emerges from the back room. The door creaks, the toilet flushes. Paula sips her cold coffee. A rock sits on her intestines. An eternity later, Steve pads into the kitchen, his wet hair caked across his forehead.

"Good afternoon."

He grunts.

"Sit down. I'll make you some eggs."

"No thanks."

The rock becomes a boulder. "There's no no's around here."

"I never eat breakfast."

"What breakfast?" She hears her voice rise. "You missed breakfast. It's lunchtime."

Staring down at the linoleum, he shuffles out of the kitchen.

The year Steve was born, Paula and Shelly spent hours with Oscar and his Louise. They sat on the diminutive floor of the Horvath living room laughing at every other word. Eight-year-old Sharon picked through Steve's baby toys. While they ate pizza, Steve slumbered on the quilt at their feet. In Louise's exotic French mouth, the word olive sounded like curtains opening. O- leeve, o-leeve. Oscar kept running his hand through the blond freckles that ran through her hair. She smelled of warm talcum powder and of the red lipstick on her smile. She kept touching the back of his neck, his shoulder.

So– why?

Paula called them a couple of times. "What's with you? You forgot you had a sister?"

"You're the one who forgot. How's Sheldon?"

"Okay." She spoke as if she was still with him. "You see him once in a while?"

"Him yes, but you, I haven't seen in months."

"Yeah– I'm working seven days. Trying to pay off the cab. I just renewed the mortgage at fourteen percent. I don't know– this home ownership deal isn't such a great deal."

"It's a cute place."

"Yeah."

The next time she saw him– a year later, a couple of years? He sat in her kitchen, his eye sockets looking like rubber gaskets. Seated together between the chrome legs of the table, they were as close as children but sallow and wrung out. She passed him a plastic bag filled with clothes for Steve. Oscar glanced at her gift then thrust his clamped fists into his pockets.

"What?" Paula didn't see the taut angle of his jaw. She felt it.

"Nothing."

The fathomless grey of his eyes widened the chasm between them. What he wanted and what he didn't, his joys and his angers, he kept masked in that expressionless pit of grey. But Paula knew. He already had two thousand dollars that were her part of their used-up inheritance.

"You think I have more money for you?" She snapped the elastic of her panties against her waist. "You want my underwear too?"

Oscar pushed away a full cup of coffee and grabbed the bag of clothes.

He took away Steve's clothes and took away Steve. Took away all contact. He didn't answer her phone calls or Shelley's knock at his door. And when Louise eventually cracked it open, Shelly had to reach in to grab her hand.

"She was like a little kid," he told Paula, "like she was playing some stupid game of hide-and-seek and couldn't speak."

It was chance that eventually brought the rumpled Steve, too tall for his clothes, to Paula. Camouflaged by the green dappling of leaves, he romped right in front of her face. "Aunt Paula," he called out.

They were in a park, in the shadows of sixty-foot trees. She grabbed his outstretched fingers and pulled him closer. He smelled of a rusted faucet, of outdoor sweat. By her calculation, he was already twelve miles away from his parents and how that was possible, she couldn't understand. He shook her fingers and laughed but didn't stand still long enough to remain in her sight. She looked around and he was gone. The path that led to the duck pond was vacant and so was the clearing. Not a soul on the park benches. Two years vacant till he appeared again. This time she bumped into him at the mall a couple of short blocks from her house. She saw a lanky boy, his face level with hers, a smear of dark hair across his forehead. She wouldn't have known him if he hadn't cocked his grin to the side of her left eye. She hugged him. His outdoor smell had been replaced by an abundance of sweet hair gel, his new voice husky. For a moment, she stood close to his face asking for news of his parents. Whatever she said made him laugh, always laughing that boy. Or he was too busy jousting with a few buddies nearby to even hear what she said. One of them called his name and with a half-second movement, maybe a shrug, Steve jumped out of her clutch and disappeared into the crowd of shopping bags.

Two months later Paula's ever dwindling visual memory had already erased Steve's features. So when a teenager with a crumpled red face and a neck as wobbly as a baby's was brought to her in a police car, she said, Who? The police had to tell her his name.

Wait and watch. Nothing else for her to do. Somewhere in the middle of the week, she manages to grab a hug. His bones feel thinner than the cartilage of a chicken, as breakable. Cut up by the blind spots in her eyes, he's not much more than a ghoulish imprint of a real person. She sees his pallor. Hard to miss, even for her. He might have scoliosis, anemia maybe. Or something that hasn't yet been discovered. Better food, any food, won't hurt. But he keeps his mouth locked. No words no food. Her only option is to scuff along behind him offering almonds, carrot sticks, and whole wheat cookies made edible with chocolate chips. Inevitably he flits away, even from the pure junk any other kid would gulp down in a minute.

"As if I smell," she tells Shelly. "I don't know what to do anymore."

They look like the three Musketeers except that Shelly's a dwarf not even as tall as Sharon and his aunt is wider than both of them combined. They're forcing him to go to a restaurant. If Shelly lets go that is. The minute his uncle got into the apartment, he grabbed Steve in a hug that circled the room. Kept saying, Stevie, Stevie. Just wouldn't stop. His mother used to call Shelly, Steve's little uncle, until he and Paula divorced and then she called him, le petit juif, because she didn't think she was supposed to be friendly with Paula's ex even if she still liked him.

Sharon gives Steve a sliding high-five and they all cram into Shelly's car.

Hockey games light up every wall of the barn-like restaurant.

"So Steve, how's it going? Getting used to the neighbourhood?" That's Sharon talking nonstop. Talking to herself. She rolls her eyes at her father. For a while, they all stare at him. Like he's some kind of thing. He stares at the hockey. He could be just as fast as any one of those hockey players. On skates, everybody's fast.

Shelly jiggles Steve's dish. "Go on. Hamburgers are the best food. Eat up. If you don't eat, your Aunt Paula will make you a big dinner of liver and spinach."

"On the same plate, disguised with a layer of apple sauce."

Steve glares at the screen. Ha ha. So funny I forgot to laugh. A Blues hockey player swings at the goal. It's not even a Canadiens game. If somebody scored right this minute, they'd all yawn. And there's Sharon dabbing at her mouth with a napkin. Like, what is she? Queen Victoria?

"There's a great arcade at the mall," she tells him. Nothing makes her shut up.

"The last thing he needs is an arcade," Paula says. "No. Absolutely not. Young men can play basketball, read a little, study. They can watch some TV if they don't overdo it." Like he's a giant doll, she pats his hand. He pulls it away but she keeps patting. Pushes her away, pushes hard.

"Sweetheart–"

"Damn it. I don't play basketball."

Now they really stare. Like who knew he could talk.

"Take a bite," his uncle says.

"If she's making you sleep in my old bedroom, paint the furniture. I don't care. I'm done with pink," Sharon takes off her wire glasses and leans over her plate. Her thin hair brushes the tomatoes on her salad. "Hey, guess what I've been doing? I'm the interpreter for an admitted gang member. Do you know how weird that is? The guy hardly speaks a word of French and his whole gang is French. He's not even scary except when he's he's creepy. And that's all the time."

"Which gang?"

"Dad. You know perfectly well I'm not supposed to say."

"The Hell's I'll bet."

"I don't like that job of yours."

"It's her career, Paula. Just say yes or no. Is he with the Hell's?"

Steve turns back to the hockey. His cousin's a translator for some kind of court thing. All day she talks in front of judges– not a hard job. He could get that kind of job without even studying. His French is much better than hers and probably his English too. If the job pays half decently, he might do that for a living. If it doesn't pay, forget it. Some people can't even afford the clothes they wear.

"Steve," His aunt as usual. "You don't like the burger?"

Shelly pokes him on the shoulder. "Go on. Your food's getting cold."

His aunt is blinking very fast. Even the droopy eyelid flutters. Her eyes are colourless where the colour's supposed to be and red where the white's supposed to be. Both parts are watery and bulgy. Not his fault if she up and cries like a two-year-old. If she thinks he's about to eat just to make her happy, she's got it wrong. But to shut her up– don't bawl old lady– he touches the bread with his finger. Somehow, he's got a dot of ketchup on the side of his hand and on his mouth. He only wants to get rid of it. Licks off the ketchup and pulls back. His mouth opens. The smell of the meat forces it wider. All by themselves his lips close on the burger. He bites and swallows and bites again. Shelly and Paula look at each other. Like he's too stupid to understand the secret. He rolls his tongue in his mouth but the automatic door won't obey. He bites and chews and swallows.

Chapter 8

Paula pulls him in by the cuff and while the principal stands behind his desk holding out his hand, she blathers on about him– how he's an orphan, how his dead parents left him a car he's too young to drive and how, now that he's in the apartment with her, he gets nutritious meals three times a day. Like the head man even cares. For about twenty seconds she shuts up, swings her massive purse over the guy's desk, stares at his outstretched hand, and wiggles it. They sit and on and on she goes– his behaviour citation, his English award, how she washes his favourite pants every other day. The principal stands and sits, wipes his hand on his sleeve and rolls his eyes at the ceiling.

"The car is six years old and looks brand new. Their mechanic was so heartbroken, he fixed it for free. Looks like pure silver except it's not silver. And he drove it all the way to my place and then stood at the door with his cap in his hand and gave his condolences. Come to think of it, I have no idea how he got home. "

"Usually it's the children who kill themselves with their parent's vehicles. The police hauled two of my students out of such a wreckage. One of the girls cannonballed through the windshield and landed right here," The principal jerks a thumb at the window, "her face flat against the blue spruce." He slaps the top of his desk. "There was broken glass all the way up to the Moss Rose. Yards past the tree. She was in the back seat– not buckled in. So. Do you think children should be allowed to drive?" He thumps twice on the table. The judge forcing everybody to listen. "Well I don't. Children whose parents are foolish enough to hand them the keys to the car when they can barely read are forbidden to park anywhere near the school. Take the bus. Walk. Jog, ski if it makes you happy. Just don't show up with your hands on the wheel."

Paula ducks her head in her bag, rummages around for his papers. "My daughter went to school here too," she peeps.

"Thank you, Miss Horvath." The principal hustles around the desk and opens the door. "Would you like somebody to show you out?"

She wraps her feet behind the chair legs. Like she's in for life. "I'll wait."

The pregnant guy trots back to the desk. "Steve Horvath," he says.

The clouds are actually very weird– white and fuzzy like it's not about to rain but is.

"Look at me."

Steve glances from the window behind the desk to the principal. Any minute the guy'll give birth to a thirty-pound baby gorilla.

"Steve–"

Whatever.

"Mr. Horvath–"

"That's not my name."

The principal's brown-yellow eyes get smaller. They look like overlapping fans. His name is Rickie. Chickie Rickie. The guy turns to

Paula. "I've been the principal of this school for nine years. Nine. Time enough to know what I will tolerate and what I will not." He flashes his teeth at Steve and goes back to Paula. "The barest show of temper, the barest insubordination, is not permitted in this school." He pushes a sheet of paper toward Steve. "Now— write in your name, date of birth, and address."

The three of them are completely silent. Outside the room, the telephone rings as if to wake them.

Paula edges her chair closer to him. "Please, sweetheart," she mutters.

"How're you doing there?" Rickie says. "Need help with the address?"

Steve cups his arm around the paper. In the stifling room, he can smell himself.

"Five solid minutes to write nothing on a document that asks only for your name and address?" Rickie smiles. "Is he able to write?"

"Yes of course." But really, she doesn't even know.

Rickie taps his finger on the paper. "Get going on that."

He's got the pen pointed to the line where his name goes. His knuckles are rigid. They can wait for all he cares.

"Survival in this school, Ms. Horvath, is not complicated. All a student needs to do is use the right vocabulary— yes sir, no ms, thank you, good morning, I'll be happy to, excuse me, I'm sorry— Are you familiar with those words, Steve?"

"Steve is always polite," Paula says.

"I was speaking to your nephew. He doesn't appear to know his own name."

Steve begins to print letters on the first line but even as he writes, he crosses off the part that starts with H, scribbles in something else and stops midway. He knows his own name. He leaves the address blank.

"Steve. Dumont." The principal reads the page backwards. "Is that his name? I thought it was Horvath."

Paula squints at the floor.

"What's on the birth certificate?"

She looks at the Steve, her eyes almost closed. "Horvath."

"And Dumont?"

"His mother's name."

"Fine. If that's what you want, it'll be Dumont-Horvath. We'll use your aunt's address, since it's your address. Let me know if you move." Rickie heaves himself out of the chair, shakes Paula's hand again, and takes her to the door.

Then it's him alone with the pregnant guy and the smell of his sweaty shirt.

There's a rectangular rug between the two armchairs and on the wall, a picture of a lollypop tree. No window. No way out except by the closed door and she has the key. Ms. Boneti. The toes of her shoes are so pointed, they look like arrows.

"Grab a chair," she says and when he doesn't, she says, *"Veut-tu qu'on se parle en français?"*

Steve takes a step backward toward the door. The lollypop hangs its head. Oh. Made by some kid in therapy.

"I'd like you to sit down." She's back to English. Ping-pong. She sits in one of the chairs and points to the other.

He slouches into it.

"Thank you."

"Whatever."

Her arrows aim straight at him, her ankle bones lock like triggers. Then nothing. Only the floor and the rug, a green rectangle between them without words. Green for the environment, for grass, for reuse, recycle. He wants to jump up and scream.

"Your parents–"

What the fuck. The whole world knows.

"Tell me about them."

He breathes because he has no choice. The sign on the door says Guidance Counsellor and Rickie's long finger pointed to it. Inside the room, there's the flying carpet under his feet that can't take him anywhere. Guidance nothing. He wants to hurl the chair at the window. Except there's none. Nothing here but the sound of shoes falling down the stairs, not even the sound of a sharp shooter's arrow whizzing straight into her forehead. He erases the thumping shoes and hears the whisper of the heater. I can bear it, he tells himself.

She just about waits a year before saying, "They died in a car accident?"

"Ya." Ya. Smashed right into the blue spruce.

"Would you like to talk about them?"

"Sure. My father was a kook. And if you must know, she was also a kook." He smiles.

"Alright. Time for you to go to class. And whenever you're ready, we can talk again."

"Ya. That would be great.:"

"Okay. Good enough. Now let's go." She stands. "Just remember one thing. You're welcome here anytime. Anything you say in room 123 is private. I won't repeat it to anybody else unless you want me to."

Call it the guided tour led by the guidance counsellor. The building is one giant circle on two floors with hallways lined by lockers. He gets one of the metal clinkers and on they go, practically running. Boneti points to numbers on the doors as if he can't read. The bell rings. She races ahead and dumps him with the homeroom teacher.

Fat or thin, tall or short, what the teacher looks like, is irrelevant. She, or maybe he, calls attendance and when he hears his name, he raises his hand. Big stupid Horvath mistake. But it makes no difference. Nobody knows he even exists. At the sound of the bell, he's released into the hordes circling the merry-go-round. He pastes himself to the wall till a second bell rings and the last of the students scurry into their classrooms.

Steve trudges along the path. Lectures– Geography, Math, History, Moral and Religious Instruction& drone from the open doorways. No matter how many times he circles he ends up in the vicinity of the same boring voice, male or female, the same. He passes room 114 twice and shrugs it off. He could walk out the front door right now. If he was completely ready, he would. On the third round, he stands in front of the half-opened door watching the History teacher open and close her huge mouth. There's no advantage to school but he could tolerate it till he gets his act together. Eventually, she stops squawking. Steve neither moves nor breathes. But she must have heard his breathless breath, the white noise of his sweat. She pulls open the door— *"Oui?"*

He thrusts the yellow, admittance paper into her hand and immediately regrets it.

"Ah -un nouvel étudiant. Je suis Mme Dufour." She makes him stand in front of the class. *"Je vous présente* Steve Dumont-'Orvat'.*"*

There's a low chorus of unenthused *bonjour*'s from the students. The teacher seats him beside the window at the only available desk. He opens his notebook on the wood surface of the desk. Keeping his eyes rigidly facing the board, he writes:

Mar. 17. At crummy school. Will leave first Monday in May or earlier. Need $$$ for travel expenses.

Sunlight arcs into the window. A crust of grey ice coats the ground. Somewhere past the window, there's a blue spruce smeared with somebody's brain. Chalk scratches on the board. The teacher seems excited by some date in history. He drops his ear to his shoulder and hears only the shuffling of the boy on his right. He looks over. The boy is stretching an elastic band at the teacher's butt. Twang. He shoots another and another, never quite reaching. After a while, he snaps them at Steve's feet. Steve steps on the elastics as they drop. He writes:

Fat kid in for it. Will set up explosives under his fat ass. Will blow him to kingdom come. Bye-bye Charlie.

Steve shoots an elastic at the kid's knees. The kid grins and kicks it away.

Steve writes:

Must get out of this dumb school. Might rent houseboat on Pacific Ocean. Plenty of houseboats near Vancouver Island.

"Neeck–"

The bag of elastics drops. Steve covers it with his foot.

"*Lève-toi.*"

The kid stands to the whoops and giggles of the class.

"Empty your pockets."

Out pops an eraser, a few coins, scraps of paper.

"Elastics please."

"It was an accident. I only had one."

"Is it possible that only one can make such a ruckus?"

"Sorry?"

The teacher glares. "Since you're so keenly interested in the elastic, you'll love writing an essay about it. I want three pages on the uses and manufacturing process of the elastic on my desk by Wednesday. Is that clear?"

As the teacher turns to the blackboard, Steve retrieves the elastics and shoves them under his notebook. Nick raises his eyebrows and grins.

The bell sounds. Among the surge of students in the hall, Nick punches Steve on the shoulder. "Thanks man. That teacher doesn't let anybody have any fun. Man, if you don't have fun in there, you fall asleep. I prefer to save my afternoon nap for Math. What do you have next?" He glances at Steve's schedule. "You lucky guy. It's Algebra 312 with Brosseau. I love that teacher. He puts me to sleep in five minutes."

They stop in front of their classroom. Steve turns toward the circular hallway. Round and round and round you go.

"What's wrong? You don't speak English? *Veux-tu que j'te parle en français?*"

"I speak English."

Nick scans the open door and lowers his voice. "Only the geeks don't speak English around here."

Steve never heard his mother say an unbroken word in English, even if it was only about the weather, even to say, Please– her accent so heavy, it was easily misunderstood. And yellow tulips only speak French.

Nick rams papers into a binder, his knee pulled up under the stack. "This guy loves you if you're neat. See?" He closes the binder and tucks the loose papers between the covers. "If you have a three-ring binder you're in with him. He'll tell you to put in a divider for Algebra and a divider for geometry because math is math is math." He laughs. "You'll see."

A few passing students stop to poke Nick. Somebody tosses him an apple. He throws it back. "I only do bananas, man." The bell rings. "Come on. I already have to write one essay. I don't need another one."

Steve doesn't move.

"Don't worry man. Three pages are nothing. I write big."

"You think I care?"

"What the hell. I didn't say anything."

"I'm not a geek."

"Who said you were?"

"I speak French, my mother, my grandmother, my–"

"So what? My mother speaks Greek. They can speak whatever the fuck they want." On the second bell, the boys rush into the classroom.

Chapter 9

Paula leans on her cart, takes a can off the shelf and shakes it. If sound alone informed her, she'd be independent and wise. Last week she ended up buying bony salmon instead of tuna. Neither she nor Steve would eat it. Twelve years of free-delivery-Tuesdays at this grocery store and still, she never finds what she!' looking for without imposing her super-sonic glare at the stuff on the racks. She follows her cart through each aisle, feeling the packages, sniffing the labels. She jiggles a bag of something that sounds like chips or some other combination of chemically enhanced starch, eyes the minuscule list of ingredients with her magnifier and plops it in the basket. Whatever. Doesn't have to be nutritious. As long as he likes it. He'll eat salami from the deli counter. She tells to clerk to cut off enough salami for seven sandwiches. Okay, make it ten in case dinner makes him squeeze his nose. The guy knows her. With a, see you next week, he places the cold cuts directly in her carriage.

Paula pays, limps out of the supermarket and through the long mall corridor till the food court presents itself in a surge of dizzying colour. There's a place that sells coffee in there. Beyond the steam tables at the butt end of the mall is a bowling alley and attached to that, an arcade. Even during school, the arcade is full of kids, boys primarily.

According to Shelly, a lot of the teens get high. "And do you know what they do?" She knows. He only told her a million times. "One of them buys a little trinket and while he's paying, his buddy grabs something a whole lot more expensive and stuffs it in his waistband. And when the merchants complain, all the police does is stroll through the mall acting tough. Not."

Not. Not that she believes what Shelly says, or even cares.

Paula's table faces the over-priced fortune teller's booth. Some kind of cloudy lavender thing drapes the box. Looks like glued-on tissue paper. Across the top, a banner bills the fortune teller as Arrnie the– must be Annie the Fortuneteller: Palm-something, Astro-something, the Healing H something. Maybe it's Head or Harmony or if not that, it's a number 4.

Marnie solves two crossword puzzles in less than an hour but can't gather up her next twenty bucks. She forces her thoughts away from miscellaneous words and onto the business of making a living. She needs at least two customers a day to pay the rent. For the most part, she gets them. It's just a matter of visualizing that special person, a person of clarity and vision and a whole lot of confusion. A needy soul who will trust Marnie's every last word. Ah– there's one– a child in an upside-down umbrella dress that floats her straight to Marnie's booth. She presses her gooey mouth to the table. Bright little thing. The mother holds her back, snuffing her curiosity. Come back in fifteen years, if I'm still here. Marnie folds her hands over the crosswords and scans the food court. Somebody who needs her is there. Ah. Yes. It's the woman with the thrust-forward head and the hulking back. She's drinking from white styrofoam oblivious to ecology, desperate for help. Marnie nods at her. Hi, there. She waves.

Unresponsive, the woman sips her drink. All the time in the world she has, completely unaware of her own desperation. Fine. No rush. She'll come. And sure enough, she crushes the styrofoam and looks right into Marnie's eyes. Then nothing. She's glassy. Three minutes pass. Four, four-and-a-half. For some reason, she's glued to her chair.

Marnie crosses the food court. Keeping an eye on the hulking back, she buys a large Orange Crush, strides to the woman's table and sits. "Good to meet you."

The woman angles her face away from Marnie, her eyeballs turning like globes on an axis. Marnie flicks her fingers at her face. She blinks.

"You're awake. Good. You've been in my presence all morning. All I could think about was you and how I could help you."

"Are you talking to me?"

"Yes indeed. I have the sixth sense. So what's your sign?"

"I don't know what you're talking about."

"Never mind. I already know. You're an Aries.

"I don't believe in astrology."

"What's belief got to do with it? It's obvious who you are. You've got the head of a bull. Don't worry. I'm not talking about how attractive you are. It's the way you sit, your head past your shoulders."

Paula straightens her back. "You're that person over there." She snaps her wrist at the fortune teller's booth. "I do-not- believe in mumbo-jumbo, whatever you call it."

"That's because you read the newspaper horoscopes. There's no science in that."

"You're not invited here. Go sit somewhere else."

"I thought we were sharing the earth. Share the earth, share your table. What's your name?"

"None of your business."

"Your business, my business, no difference. Think of me as your guide and we'll get along perfectly. Now what's your birthdate?"

Paula opens her mouth and closes it.

"Okay never mind. How old are you? Twenty?"

Paula snorts.

"Okay, no more jokes." Marnie wants to take her hand but both are gripped on the purse. "I'm being serious. You were meant to be here at this time and I was meant to read your birth chart. That much I'm sure. You need help and here I am." She gulps down her orange drink.

"My back's killing me." Paula's face is red. She's still attached to the chair.

"It's Lola, right?"

"Wrong."

"Something like that."

"Paula, if you must know."

"You were born around the time of the war. I'd say between 1942 and 1945. Right?"

"What's it to do with you?"

"If you don't like astrology, I can read your palm. Or your tarot. On Tuesdays I offer discounts for the tarot. Ten dollars. Half price for you today."

Paula wraps her arms around her purse. She normally devotes ten dollars to her monthly lotteries. "No thank you."

"Wouldn't you like to know your fortune?"

"I have no fortune."

"Of course you do. And with accurate information, you'll be able to plan for the future.

No mistakes no problems."

"Look–."

"If I tell you what to expect you can make the changes that will bring you luck."

"Some people aren't lucky."

"It doesn't work that way."

"Last month I lost my brother and sister-in-law."

"What do you mean, lost?"

Paula hugs her purse. "If the future's as bad as the past, I don't need to know."

"Since you're suffering," Marnie tugs at Paula's hand. "I'll make you a deal. If you come back next week as a paying client, I'll read your palm for free today. Two sessions for the price of one. And for free today, I'll tell you one very important thing." The woman's plump fingers lie damply in hers. "You just ran out of all your bad luck. No more loss as long as you make the right decisions. Which I'll help you make."

Paula pulls away. "Forget it."

"Well, Lola. You don't want to lose the opportunity of your life."

"Paula."

"Paula, when somebody offers you a hand, take it." Marnie dips her nose into the remnants of the ice, gives up on the drink, and straightens her turban. She tugs Paula up by the hand and leads her to the booth.

Marnie turns on a light bulb shrouded in a fluffy mound of satin. To please her clients, she sometimes flutters her fingers at the globe and mutters an incantation. If customers feel confident with pronouncements from an apparent crystal ball, fine. She covers Paula's hands with hers and turns up her palms.

"Looks like you're right-handed." Marnie traces her fingertips over the creases of each palm. Three breakups before Paula's fiftieth birthday. "I see here, that you're divorced. Twice?"

"No."

"You've had one man or two?"

"One."

"Then you separated."

"So would you if your husband was glued to his cellphone."

"How many siblings do you have?"

"I had my brother."

"So. Here's what it is. You had a breakup with your parents at a young age. Another with your husband. And the third is with your brother."

Paula clenches her fists. There was an argument with her parents on account of Shelly– that she was planning to move in with him though Paula didn't tell them any such thing. What Paula actually said was, Sheldon and I– and before she could continue, her mother interrupted her thoughts with a long stare of disapproval and disappointment. And her father explained that Shelly came from a different world than hers and– Come down to earth for a change, her mother shouted, You live in la-la land. Paula refused to shout back. But she had to be heard. Maybe she bit her tongue on the insults that were threatening to erupt. Maybe she whispered the words. Maybe she screamed her heart out, saying that she'd live with the man she loved and be happy for once. And before she could change her mind, her mother threw the entire contents of Paula's oak armoire into a steel-sided suitcase and two paper bags and pushed them out the door. Paula towed her luggage down the hall of the apartment building, heard her mother– Paula, Paula, silly girl, come back– took the elevator down and caught a cab straight to Shelly's hesitant embrace.

"I never broke up with my parents. We had an argument and later they died but–"

"Dead, yes but that's not what I'm talking about."

How, under that turban, the fortune teller's mind works, Paula has no idea. Her father died without memory, his vacant eyes weirdly framed by soft blond curls, his back as straight as the chair he sat in. Till the end of her days her mother held it against Paula that she married that Sheldon Shapiro without standing in front of a priest– that without taking vows to become a Jew, Paula ate like a Jew, had a daughter who was a Jew, talked and acted so much like one, that her nose grew.

In the last of her days, Paula's mother stopped walking. From her chair beside the kitchen window, she watched Paula fill her fridge or empty it, heat up a plate of food or throw it out. Paula prayed that her mother would lose her recollections but not her mind. But the slack line of her mother's mouth never eased into anything that resembled a smile, never said a word that held praise. Her pencil point eyes bore in on Paula as every day, she passed a washcloth over her mother's hump neck, slid a dress over her head, combed her few grey strands.

"Twenty years dead," she tells Marnie.

Paula did not know who to invite to the funeral– if in fact the people who pay their respects to a wooden casket, are guests. Or by some magic, would they know that her mother had died and show up to the funeral home wearing black? Her mother must have had friends but Paula had no idea who they were. She could not remember a telephone that rang in that house except for the occasional solicitation for money. Nobody came for tea, nobody borrowed sugar. Only the four of them sat around the table. Never in the parcelling of their meals was there an accommodation for a visitor. The cabbage rolls were counted and divided into four portions well before they sat down to eat. Conversations were as sparse and dry as the salt that was passed around.

She and Oscar passed by the church as if to pause at a traffic light. Shelly had stayed home with Sharon. Oscar's bride, no longer a schoolgirl, was with the baby, safe in her parent's diocese. None of their friends knew of their mother's existence. At the church their mother had regularly attended, Paula and Oscar sat at a pew holding hands while a priest recited a prayer that was unrelated to their mother. They left a donation with the priest and went on to the funeral home for the next portion of the kind of burial their mother had not wanted. Except for the white vase and the powder that filled it, the place was vacant. Thankfully, the old lady wouldn't notice.

After fetching the vase, they ate at the drugstore counter close to their mother's apartment. Paula should probably have held some kind of reception for the family, but her listless preoccupation with the funeral took up all her concentration.

Oscar chewed systematically, as if lining up his tax documents. "This is not how I want to end my life."

"You mean the funeral?"

"I mean all of it. How did she get to be such an odd duck? She was, you know."

"No odder than anybody else."

"No odder than you. You look like her."

"I don't and it's not about looks anyway. It's about how you act. And how you live your life." Paula tossed her head at him, tossing away all thoughts of her misfit self.

"I'm trying to tell you something. Listen up now." The fortune teller waves a hand at Paula's face. "All parents die. Everybody dies. I'm not talking about separation through death. She unfolds Paula's fingers and taps the fleshy nodules on her thumb line. "There was bitterness between you and a parent. Or both of them. Right?"

Maybe it was regret. Maybe it was just that they had nothing to say to each other.

Again Marnie applies her fingers to the tracks on Paula's open palm. "There's illness here, in the upper part of your body." She pats the top of Paula's head. "What is it? Migraines?"

"If I have to answer all your questions, you're not much of a fortune teller."

"Who said I was a fortune teller? Only amateurs tell fortunes. For twenty dollars I teach essential life skills."

"You said it was free."

"Are you kidding? It's a two-for-one deal. That's what we agreed on."

"We didn't agree on anything." Paula gathers up her coat.

"Hey–" Marnie stretches out her narrow fingers. "Sit with me and you'll see something new. The power in my hands comes from my heart. A shaman empowered me." She turns each of Paula's hands to the side, half closing them. The traces of a child borne early in Paula's life and another decades later cling to the woman as tenuously as thinly secured ribbons. One big wind could tear them away. On the right hand, the children are barely formed, not really hers. But on the left, the hand closest to Paula's heart, the children are interwoven into her life. "It says here that you're a caring mother. And that you're not a giver-upper and that your life will change."

It's already started to. The second destiny line is clear on the woman's left hand. Another is forming on her right. Changes then– imposed on her and created by her. For some, it means a second career. For others a move. For Paula, the changes came in the shape of that last child. This kid is rearing its head, kicking and demanding. A break with the past. But all this, Paula doesn't understand. Nor is she listening.

Paula withdraws her hand.

"For twenty dollars I read the palm. But for fifty, I'll translate my heart's feelings for you. Do you want me to do that?"

"Forget it." Paula thrusts her purse under her armpit. "I don't have fifty dollars. I don't even have twenty."

"I'll take ten."

"No."

"I'll take whatever you have. And I'll give you a few deep thoughts for free. Didn't I say I would? I always do the most I can because the power came to me at no charge when I was six. A bird lady put her talons on my wrist. My fingers kept growing just to absorb all the power she was transferring. Look. Look how long they are." She shows off the length of her tapered fingers, wriggling them for emphasis.

"Forget it. There's no scientific proof for all that stuff." Paula slings her coat over her shoulders.

"Sit down. I have nothing against science. My wrists and fingers were tiny then but all the necessary power to look into your heart was transferred to me. Sit." She grips Paula by the wrists and forces her down. "Now. Tell me about your head."

"Goodbye. I'm leaving."

"One thing I can predict for sure, is you won't have to leave the province. The big winner in this stupid referendum will be the No side."

"Goodbye."

"I guess you're voting No. You're not a separatist I'll bet."

"Good. Bye."

Marnie lets go. "I'll see you next week. You owe me twenty."

"I did not sign a contract. I owe you nothing."

Marnie closes her eyes. She needs to see a paying client. If she was a magician, she'd conjure one up. This cheap client is lumbering away on her crepe soles, her lopsided pant hem sweeping up dirt. She'll be back. The minute she finds a good excuse to sit and listen.

The girl's barely fourteen. There's a glint of silver in her nose and another in her eye. Looks like a star in the distance to Paula but definitely, she sees it. Take that ring away from your eyes, child– Paula tells her. The girl brushes by. She probably can't even read.

Well, guess what kid– Paula mutters. One of these days you'll be walking with a white cane. See how much fun that is.

Paula's cane is in the back of a closet, another useless dust collector. Those who need canes see the world as pinpricks on beige paper towels. Everything– buildings, light posts, people– looks like ghosts floating by. Except for a few indecipherable street signs or clocks too dark to tell her the time, her sight is absolutely splendid.

And if she can't recognize the matted face of some acquaintance on the street, it's no big deal. She waves at them all.

She's used to seeing the wavering dots that glitter unceasingly in front of her eyes, used even to the careening boulders that appear without notice, about to smash her face off. How and when her concrete and concise vision softened, she can't recall. At one time shopping, like brushing on two coats of mascara, like reading and recognizing what she saw, was automatic, not a thought around it. Now, just to get to the mall, she needs to feel the border of the curb before stepping off. She used to do secretarial work for a living. At lunch, she browsed the shops. She flicked through clothing noticing collars, pockets, buttons, the colours of the fabric. More or less. Less and less. In her teens, she was taken to a series of doctors who promised worse to come. Nothing could straighten the slide– no medicine, no surgery, not even a vitamin to make her feel better. She had a one-hundred-per-cent-full-scale eye disease. Whatever they called it didn't matter. That one word, disease, meant decrepitude, meant to be eaten away from the inside out. Oscar used to stick out his tongue at her. "Ha ha, you saw it. Nothing wrong with you." He meant to make her feel better, she knew. But as they grew older, he also said that she was their mother's twin, her clothes as stained and dishevelled, her hair in disarray, her face as faded as her eyes. Yeah, but Paula's mouth surely didn't hang open when she concentrated. Nor did her saliva drip to the front of her blouse. Paula's disintegration came from a yellow spot in the back of each eye. Spots, for God's sake. By the time she had Sharon, she no longer knew if her child was dressed in pink or yellow. Paula's vague and shrunken perimeters became her sole landscape.

Paula squints at the outskirts of the parking lot. Oscar's Malibu is out there in the shade of a clump of trees, the polished chrome nose of the car pointed to the asphalt. She meanders between the cars looking for the right trees.

Vegetation– not a car in sight. No vegetation either. She trips over a bump. Looks like there's a street ahead but she doesn't know where it would take her. She's gone too far. She scans the lot. Forget this. Go back to the mall. Where the heck's the mall?

"Steve–" He's hidden under the trees with the hidden car. "Nick–"

"*Moi?*"

She swivels. They're right in front of her nose, slouched over the hood of the damned car. Steve is underdressed in his red windbreaker. Too bad she doesn't have a salami sandwich to give him.

She says, "I have to go home and wait for the groceries. Is that you, Nick?"

A cropped head bobs beside the car.

"We have a chocolate chip cookie delivery. You coming?"

"We're going to the arcade." From Steve, it would have been a belligerent statement but from Nick, it's information.

"Isn't there a cheaper form of entertainment for you? I can stop at the bakery– Steve, wouldn't you like Nick to come for a visit?"

"We're going for a drive," Nick says.

"You drive?"

"The minute I'm sixteen I'll drive."

"I can drive," Steve says.

"Yeah. Doesn't take a genius."

"You need a license," Paula says.

"Who cares," Steve says. "Nobody checks."

"Yeah." Nick jabs the tire with his heel. "All you have to do is get in this baby and drive. You got the keys, don't you?"

"Steve, don't get any ideas. You're going to spend an hour at the arcade, not more. Then, you're coming home."

His friend lunges at him, swerves away, and together they amble toward the street.

"Hey, how do I get out of here?"

Nick takes her arm.

Chapter 10

It's past five. His one-hour limit at the arcade often stretches to two or three. Paula dumps a can of kidney beans and another of tomatoes into a pot of sizzling onions. She shakes Tabasco sauce over the chilli and sits down to wait for the creak of the door, for Steve's cat-like entry and the sigh made by his breath as he pretends not to exist.

At six, she turns off the chilli. Six-thirty rolls by, then seven. He could have lost all sense of time in the arcade or– be unconscious behind a garbage pail. Paula stands up so fast, her chair falls backward.

Led gingerly by the street lights, she passes the block of row houses barely discernible in the dark. At the corner, she peers into the distance and lifts her arm. Somebody there? No. Maybe a single tree with narrow white branches reaching to the sky. Beyond the ricocheting headlights is the oblong mall glowing against the dusk. Probably the mall. There's a traffic light out there. When it's not solid red it turns into a confusion of red and green arrows. A little white guy sometimes appears on the pole to tell pedestrians to walk. Except most of the time, he's invisible. She's about to go home when two silhouettes coming from behind, slide past her. Following their conversation, she takes a chance and dashes across the boulevard.

Paula stumbles past the food court and past the weight of a glass door into the bowling alley. A group of middle-aged women wearing matching blue T-shirts watch as number eleven trots to the starting line and angles for a roll into the wide-open lane. To one side of the room, in a darkened alcove, arcade lights blink. Paula races straight into the bouncing lights. A computer screen liquid with the blood red of battle scenes surges up on her. She closes her eyes. Bowling balls smash against the pins in the outside hall. Closer by, gaming machines play their own ping-pong tunes. The smell of popcorn pervades. Arms outstretched, she opens her eyes and advances toward a board of pulsating football players. She bumps into the steel frame of a machine. Oh– sorry. The kid at the game station leans closer to the screen.

Ahead, another boy squeezes the sides of his console, pressing and thumping it softly

"Steve?"

A couple of boys move aside. She advances into the aisle. On both sides of her people are playing– Playing? Is that what it is? She bumps into one kid after another.

"I'm sorry. I'm looking for– maybe you know him. Steve Hor–"

"That's not my name."

Paula reaches for his voice– grabs a stiffened shoulder in the next aisle.

"Hey–" He's grasping a steering wheel, his eyes fixed to a glaring bull's eye.

"I'm gone, man." Another voice pipes up.

"Look what you did. You're ruining my game."

"Ruining? Do you even know what time it is?"

The machine rings as the eye shrinks into a lone bullet that zooms across a green horizon. In a split second a road snakes over the hilly greens. Blinking red, a little car pops up at a starting line. Steve holds his steering wheel like a race car driver ready to bash through. Paula pins her eye on the red car and loses it immediately in the irrational gullies that manifest themselves along the road. Minutes later, the computer begins to bleep and on a final long bleep, the concentric circles of a bull's eye spread their rainbow colours across the screen and swallow the car in their black pupil. Steve curses. Without hesitating, he reaches into his pocket and feeds the ravenous machine.

"Steve– it's enough."

But the shiny red car is already at the starting line revved and snorting to go.

"Steve, you have to follow the rules. When it's time to go home, you go." She touches his arm and gets shaken off. "It's just a game."

"You don't understand. I can't leave when I'm winning."

She can't remember if she left the chilli bubbling on the stove. Burned or not, he won't eat it. When he was small Louise ran after him with bits of egg and bread and tomato. Behind her back, Paula and Shelly tittered at her sort of motherhood. But maybe it wasn't that she spoiled him. Maybe she was spoiling herself as she played right along with him, covering her face for peek-a-boo, crawling behind him on her hands and knees. If she was at the arcade now, she'd throttle the car's engine and race it over the green hills. If she had enough money for the rapacious coin slot that is. And if Oscar wasn't around.

"It's been a while since I drove," Paula says. "I might like to have a try at this thing except the chilli's on the stove." Not knowing what else to tell him, she says, "I used to have a car. But your father drove it more than I did."

In the opaque brightness of the room, she can't see the shock of dark hair across his white forehead. She feels his breath on her arm, feels his eyes bore into her.

"You have change?"

"For what?"

"You can try." He edges over, making room for Paula at the wheel.

She slides onto the seat and for no good reason, opens her wallet. She has maybe fifteen minutes before the apartment building burns down. Maybe less. Facing the screen, she feels as if the car's rubber tires are on either side of her hips.

"We better go home."

"Not yet." Steve takes a handful of coins from her wallet and pops them into the slot. "Look straight ahead."

The road shapes itself in front of the little red car. The engine revs.

"Go on go on, drive." Steve jerks the steering wheel and the car leaps forward. "Take the wheel. Turn left, left."

The blinking red dot dives into the paving and vanishes.

"Left," Steve shouts.

But the car is gone. Paula wriggles the steering wheel till the vehicle leaps out of a gully, bolts onto a road and rises above a hilltop. Glass splinters and abruptly, the vehicle tumbles across the monitor like a wind-swept beach ball. A moment later the car morphs into its bull's eye and the machine shuts down. Paula wiggles the steering wheel.

"It's too late, you lost." Steve slams the side of the screen. "You didn't even last five seconds."

"This stupid game is stealing all your money. It's nothing like driving a real car. And how are you going to take driving lessons if you have no money?"

"I don't need driving lessons."

"Let's get out of here." She gets up.

The whole driving business makes her teeth ache. How she received her license barely able to place the car between two others, was a pure miracle. While Paula's little brother smirked in the back seat, their driving teacher urged her to go faster. Faster came the word faster– from the teacher to the examiner to her friends in the passenger seats. Oscar got his license on the same day as she did, practically by osmosis and took off in their father's car a minute after he tucked the official paper into his wallet. When it was Paula's turn to show off her newly approved skills at the wheel, her father took her by the hand and led her to the car. As long as he sat beside her, she managed to toddle around the block. He gave Paula and Oscar each a set of car keys attached to horseshoes but to Paula's silent relief, Oscar got first dibs. The thought of parking made her nauseous, the highway entirely dizzy. Vehicles emerged out of nowhere and in the wrong place and at what distance away, she couldn't fathom. She only knew that the road curved where it shouldn't. And that it moved like a renegade under her wheels.

"You may think you don't need driving lessons. But you need a license. If you want a license, you need the lessons. Those people who give out licenses want to make sure you're a good driver before they hand it to you." Paula yanks at Steve's t-shirt. "I don't know how you manage to play those games. That car nearly ate me alive."

"It's harder to drive on a game than on the road. The real thing's a cinch."

"You're really good with that machine."

"I'm practicing."

She yanks again and he begins to move.

Chapter 11

They have about twenty minutes to eat before the nightly phone call. Steve crumbles bread into his chilli and stirs the beans into a mass of inedible clumps. Allowing a polite interval, he removes his bowl from the table, dumps the contents in the garbage and pads into his room.

At eight pm on the button, Mariette Dumont always asks her grandson to pray for his mother. She then passes the phone to her husband who praises Steve for getting out of bed and getting dressed, for brushing his teeth and combing his hair as flat as his own. Mariette takes back the phone, checks on his health and presses on. She expects Steve to spend the weekends with them. She wants to know what he ate for dinner, if the vegetables are fresh, if the sauce is greasy, and if the water he drinks is filtered. Well practised, Steve knows what to say. At every meal, Aunt Paula provides a salad or two, a homemade soup and once, when he was especially imaginative, she offered him a compote of organic apples for dessert.

Mariette takes a breath and asks how often his aunt Paula washes his sheets and if is he sure the aunt doesn't use his towel. The Aunt Paula is a little odd. Her two blouses look as though they're forty years old, her baggy house dress from the rag bin. And why does that aunt of his carry a purse of leather so thin, it looks like paper? Is she so poor? And if she is, Steve should live with them. They have a nice bedroom for him and a big yard. In the unpolluted air of the south shore, he'll breathe free. Steve hears her gush on with the phone in his lap. He can recite her litany backwards.

On this first Tuesday in March, his grandmother mentions Easter. Too much homework or not, don't you forget, Easter weekend belongs to the Dumonts. He puts the phone against his ear about to tell her that he might have other plans but she won't stop jabbering. The family is looking forward to seeing him. And soon you'll be with us and, do you know how much whiter the snow is here and how and if only– and finally, *"Bonsoir mon beau Steve. Beaux rêves,"* she says, and hangs up.

Sweet f-ing dreams. Yeah right. No dreams. Only realities. Steve sees the image of his mother drinking coffee at the kitchen table, her stomach folded over the stem of the yellow tulip etched on her housedress. She's rolling pennies in brown paper. There's the thud of stumbling feet. He opens his eyes wide and squishes her out of his head. Useless pennies.

He takes the wad from his back pocket, unfolds it and lays seventeen twenties on the desk. Beside that, he places nineteen tens and alongside that, a pack of fives wrapped in an elastic. Over six hundred miraculous dollars. He reaches for an imaginary cash register and air pings the total sum, six-hundred-and-thirty-five point-zero-six. Following a fist bash of triumph directed to the moon, he makes a move as if to scoop it all up and get the hell out. But not yet, not so fast. At Easter, his grandparents will give him money. He backs away from the bed. One thing he knows is that more is better. A lot more. His orderly rows of bills are virtual crumbs compared to the huge expense of gas every second day, of food, maybe a pair of socks if his wear out. Crossing the country, he'll eat whatever is on special, even tuna if he has to. To sleep, he'll spread a blanket on the back seat of the car and stick his legs out the window. In Vancouver, he'll get a real good job, something in an oil field.

The map tucked in his other pocket is so soft and creased, it's almost see-through. And the green highlight that marks his route is just about invisible. Doesn't matter. He knows it by heart.

Mariette Dumont hangs up and redials. Excited or tense, her voice gurgles as if she's holding back a mouthful of spit. She's gurgling now as she tells Paula that Steve will be picked up as soon as school is over on the Thursday before Easter. She spits out a series of instructions in a language Paula can barely decipher. And makes her demand so far ahead of the date, Paula is sure to forget. She cuts short, gurgles *Merci*, and hangs up.

"No, legally no," Sharon says. "They can't take him without permission. But it wouldn't be right for you to tell them not to see their grandson. What difference does it make anyway? You don't do Easter."

"Easter shmeester. It's a long weekend. I was thinking of doing something fun with him."

"A weekend with Aunt Paula? Doesn't sound like fun to me. Don't annoy them, Mom."

Annoy? Paula hangs up, tiptoes down the hall and presses her ear to her nephew's door. Steve's mutterings are as public as they are intimate. He's counting. Clearly, the money he wasted at the arcade is eating him up. When the knob turns, Paula makes as if she's passing by.

"Oh– Steve. Taking a break from your homework?"

He stares.

"I know you're good with the math but it doesn't have to be perfect you know. As long as you get it done. And if ever you need help, I am around."

He scratches the down on his face.

"I can't read much but I can still help. You ask me any question you want."

"I got it done."

"Good. Then you'll want a snack. I've got a chocolate bar for you. Hey, how about a hot chocolate? And a chocolate sandwich. You're going to the bathroom? Go ahead, go." She gives his hand a little push toward the bathroom and rushes into the kitchen.

*

Steve wrinkles his nose at the sandwich and fishes the marshmallow out of the milk. He licks the marshmallow, sucks down the rest of it, takes a bite of the chocolate and then of the bread.

"Good, huh."

"It's not horrible."

She sticks her tongue out at him. In three months it's about the best thing he's said to her. And here he is– eating and wrinkling his face and sticking his tongue out at her.

Chapter 12

On the south shore, across the bridge, Steve's mother is everywhere. From the top of the driveway that leads to his grandparent's house, Steve hears the swish of her legs as they enter the vestibule and the slap-slap of her slippers on the floorboards. An odour emanates from the rooms– the dampness of aged wallpaper, of soup and garlic. Most powerfully, nauseatingly, it smells of his mother's skin, warm and sweet at the end of a hot day. Not even the Javel that clings to the sheets and towels can dislodge it. Her scent seeps out of the oddest places– from the radio or the water faucet, from window screens and radiators. And from nowhere, her floating voice drops off some piece of advice. He can't stand it. The precise tone of his mother's French syllables, even when somebody else speaks them, is like the tapping of her nail scissors on his eardrums.

There's one place to escape to. While the authorities decided where he should live, it was his only hideout. Within a half-hour's walk from his grandparent's stone cottage– a separate country for Steve– is a grove of pine trees that leads to the river. There across the river ice, he tramped for hours on his grandfather's snowshoes pushing the thoughts of his parent's death under the snow. He'd have slept under the pines, among the creatures who begin to stir in the four o'clock gloom if he were permitted to. To disappear in the darkness– such a temptation. He almost did but invariably someone came and took him back to the house. And now that the ice is melting, where will his refuge be?

Steve's grandmother buys him a collared shirt and slacks with a crease down the front. On Easter Sunday his grandparents drag him to church where they sit in an oak pew with his *Oncle* Marc and *Tante* Céline and their two girls. His grandparents crouch right down to the padded kneeler and bow their heads. Starkly white against the blue silk of her blouse, Mariette's face trembles. While they whisper prayers for their dead daughter, Steve looks at his polished brogues. He never had such a banker's pair of ornate wingtips. Below the knees, he's now a man. He stands on his toes and gazes at the arched ceiling painted a pale firmament blue. Fourteen-year-old Julie mutters her English at him while Arlette, on the far side, crosses and recrosses her legs. To keep himself looking busy, Steve sings the hymns and recites the liturgy till Julie switches her mumblings to her sister.

Before serving the Easter ham, Mariette gathers her guests around the dining table. She clutches Steve's hand and thanks God as she has every Sunday for over sixty years. *"Merci mon Dieu pour notre bien-être."* Thrusting down her head, she continues. "Remember my daughter Louise, who would have been praying with us today if you had saved her." Steve tries to pull away but his grandmother tightens her hold. "She was a good girl. *Jesus, gardez-la dans vos soins.* We pray that she too, has risen."

They serve themselves from a buffet laid in the hallway between the kitchen and dining room. Fourteen adults, some hard of hearing, are in the dining room filling their glasses. Julie, Arlette, and Steve sequester themselves at the kitchen table with two small children. Julie checks among the dirty pots on the counter and finds a couple of opened wine bottles, a bottle of gin, and another of scotch. She offers juice to the children, sloshes a mix of the alcohol in plastic tumblers and passes them to the teens.

Arlette gags, throws the rest of her drink into the sink and snarling at her sister, stalks out of the kitchen with her thinly coated plate of vegetables.

Steve has already taken two careful sips of the concoction. "It's not that bad. Tastes a little like cough syrup. I'll fix them." He smooths their drinks with hefty tablespoons of sugar.

Covering her mouth with her ring-adorned fingers, Julie begins to giggle. In the warmth of the kitchen, a blush appears on her cheeks. "I 'ave my Henglish class hevery day after school. Wit you I'm suppose to practice today. Dis is my 'omework."

"Homework."

"Yeah, dat's it. You suppose to live with Grandmaman. We don' 'ave a room for you an' dey 'ave a big one 'ere."

"I live with my aunt."

"Non. She cannot take care of you if she *aveugle*."

"She's not exactly blind."

"Yeah. She blind and she bump on de chair. *Maman* see hit."

"She's just clumsy. And anyway, nobody needs to take care of me."

"Yeah. Luc say she can 'ave a haccident an burn de 'ouse."

"That's ridiculous." He snaps his mouth shut and hears the clacking of his teeth.

Watching her reflection in the chrome toaster, Julie shrugs. Except for her huge eyes, she has the narrow traits of the Dumonts. With her pinky, she applies lip gloss to her pursed mouth and smacks her lips before going over them again with another glop. *"Luc est un avocat. C'est quoi en anglais?"*

"Lawyer."

"My fader give 'im one tousand dollar, even more, to get you from dere." She stretches her mouth over her teeth and squints at the toaster.

"He's wasting his money."

"I tink you like 'er better den hus."

"I don't like anybody."

Julie's talking fast, throwing her ponytail left and right across her shoulders. Steve has no idea what she's saying. Once in a while she widens her colt-like eyes and stops jiggling long enough to look after two small children, a boy and girl who belong to a divorced lawyer in the living room. Arm around each child, she carefully presents them to

Steve. *"Voici Yann et voici Sylvie."* Steve looks away. They're as slobbery as dogs. Julie turns them back toward his face. Yann climbs into Steve's lap. Each time Steve opens his mouth, Yann pops in a tidbit of maple candy, howls with delight, and pulls back his fingers. They continue the game till the adults call on them to search for tinsel-wrapped chocolate eggs.

While Julie charges around the house with the children, Steve gulps down his syrup and the rest of Julie's. It's hot in the room. Light as air, he has the sense of being suspended above the floor. He pours himself a glass of wine and swirls it in the warm plastic before sipping it. His nostrils pucker, his thirst still unquenched. Too tired to reach the sink for water, he scratches his itchy nose, has another glass of wine, and feels himself rise a little higher. He heaps his plate with ham and mashed potatoes, slathers it with gravy and begins to eat. He's been utterly vacant and hasn't even realized it till the food enters his mouth. The brown gravy tickles his throat. When the tickling refuses to stop he covers the puddle of gravy on his plate with another mound of potatoes. So velvety on his tongue.

Steve doesn't see him at first and then he does. The guy's salt and pepper head leans against the wall. He's watching him through the white wine in his raised glass. Steve grins. The guy has a name that begins with an L, that much Steve remembers. He tries stretching the L sound into some kind of word but the letter, strangled by his tongue, emerges in a guttural slurp.

"Remember me? I am Luc." The guy pushes the mass of soiled cups and plates aside and sits at the table beside Steve. "You had a little something to drink, I see. You know, the legal age is eighteen." He laughs. The little breeze that comes out of his mouth feels cold and soft at the same time. "*Excuse moi.* I am a lawyer."

Law is the profession his mother wanted for him. Steve can't remember if the guy with the L name is speaking in English or French.

"You're much too young to be drunk."

Steve tries to tell the polite man how not young he is but a boat rising from his stomach to his throat, veers on a wave and he finds himself vomiting at the sink. He wants to hide the stuff that bursts out of him. Too slow. In half a wink Julie is there, looking it over. A clump of acid shoots through his nostrils.

The L-man leads him to bed. He's so kind. "This drinking is coming from the house of your aunt, is it not?"

What does that mean? In his aunt's house, everything in the room is pink. In this place, there are shadows in the room and his mother is wringing her hands at him. Steve gets under the covers. Above him, the ceiling circles sluggishly around the light fixture. Snow trickles down forming a white mist above his head. Oh, winter again. He snuggles deeper under the covers.

"Your aunt gives you wine?" The dimple in the L-man's cheek winks.

Steve wants to make a joke too. He opens his mouth, nods at the snow and clacks his teeth. Through the window, the cedar hedge shivers.

"And what else? She must give you beer? And maybe, something to smoke?"

His head bobs all by itself, the L sound curling in the back of his mouth. Thank you. Thank you, Mr. L, he wants to say. He clacks his teeth and falls asleep.

Chapter 13

The night of the first seder, Paula sits alone at her table. Three sheets of matzoh covered with a dish towel are piled in front of her. She's poured herself a tumbler of wine. A big one. With one bite of matzoh and a sip of wine, she'll turn from Paula Horvath into Paula Shapiro. No easy performance.

She let part of her Judaism fall away with her separation from Shelly, marking the holidays with nothing more celebratory than a circle on the calendar. But this year, because she expected Steve to share Passover with her, she replaced bread with matzoh and prepared for the change in diet by running through the house with her spring cleaning, spraying floral disinfectant in the cupboards, shaking out clothing, jabbing at the recesses of each closet with her vinegar-soaked mop. A week later, she wrapped the last of the bread in an opaque plastic bag and hid it in the back of the freezer. At her private seder, she rubs her itchy hands and eats a hard-boiled egg along with matzoh topped with apple sauce. She drains her wine and feels spiritually renewed. Or simply drunk.

Despite the koshering of the apartment, and the sanitization, Paula sprints over to the mall on the second day of Passover and eats a full doughnut before remembering that she is a Jew by choice. She sweeps a napkin over the crumbs, gulps down coffee to make the doughnut disappear and cups her hand over her mouth to cover up the lingering evidence of yeast. Somebody greets her with a semicircular wave, so close to her nose, she feels it. The fortune teller. If that clairvoyant had real power, she'd be able to reverse the clock.

Marnie wiggles her skinny fingers at Paula. "It's so hot today."

"You must be looking into the future to find heat."

In the cool dusk of March, Marnie lifts her turban, loosening her damp hair. "I can hardly wait till the kids are back at school. Holidays kill me. Sometimes boarding school sounds good. You have two children. Right?"

"I have one. She's grown and gone now."

"Where's the other?"

"I only have one."

"There's another. I saw him in your palm."

"What don't you get? I don't have another. I only have my nephew with me now."

"That's him. How old?"

"Fifteen."

"He's maybe even noisier with his music than a little one."

"No. He's a quiet boy. He doesn't say a word. Doesn't even whine."

"They're all difficult when they're fifteen. For twenty dollars I give advice on relationships based of course on whatever medium you choose. Unless you choose astrology. That would be fifty for you and fifty for your nephew."

"You said twenty for two sessions."

"Twenty then. Twenty for the tarot."

Paula's hand tightens on her purse.

"So what do you want? The tarot?" Marnie fans herself. "All right all right. Twenty for whatever you want. Go ahead, choose. Health and politics often show up in the tarot. Maybe you're feeling tired these days? If you choose the tarot, I could tell you how you're feeling."

In the preceding week, exhausted and hyped by her cleaning spree, Paula hardly slept.

Marnie tugs at Paula's arm and pulls her to the booth. "Once I know how you're feeling, I'll be able to tell you what to do about it." She supports three children on the cards. Sometimes she makes them a comfortable living, sometimes she can't make the rent. She places a deck of cards in front of Paula. "Separate and shuffle."

"You think I don't already know how I'm feeling?"

"Paula. That's a simplistic comment."

What you get for eating a doughnut at Passover is a talking turban.

"Come on, Paula. My sixth sense tells me you have an important question to ask about somebody close to you."

Paula's fingers tingle. That fortune-teller can't know anything about Oscar. Except it was all over the news. Wrong information and no good reason given by anybody. Paula looks at the deck. Nothing in there can answer why he did it. Yeah but, why did he? She squeezes the cards, taps them against the table and begins her inexpert shuffling.

Marnie closes her eyes. Paula's grey skull rests in her mind's eye. She wills the top of the woman's thrust-forward head to open up and let her in. And wills the woman to open her mouth and list her illnesses. She wills a twenty-dollar bill to slide out between the zipper teeth of Paula's wallet and places itself on the table by her right hand. If not now, then by the end of the session.

"Tell me about your head. There's a solution to your pain in these cards."

"What pain?" Paula's wide shoulders crimp. "The only kind of pain I get is a pain in the ass."

"Well. If you're not interested, that's fine." Marie sweeps the cards aside. She isn't about to read for nothing. She's too tired. All weekend, teenage girls searched for love in her cards, each one demanding an original story.

"Fine. Just tell me what's in there." Paula unclips her purse and just as Marnie has predicted, a twenty-dollar bill lands on the table.

Marnie pulls her chair up and slides the bill into her pocket. "Is it the eyes?"

"You saw. My eyes are crooked."

"No, Paula. That was a guess."

"I have a form of macular degeneration, if you must know."

"You do. I saw illness in your head."

"Sure you did. What's the point of this exercise? You don't even know what interests me."

"I'll tell you one thing for sure. The cards aren't working for you today."

"What are you talking about? I paid."

Marnie shrugs. "Don't worry. I'll do something better for you. I'll read my heart's feelings for you and next week, maybe I'll read your Tarot." For the sake of atmosphere, Marnie turns on her crystal ball and swirls her hands above the globe.

"What is that? You studied marketing? I hope there's twenty dollars' worth of entertainment in this show."

"Yeah, yeah." Marnie takes Paula's hands and closes her eyes. This big woman is as broad as they come, a load of impermeable flesh and muscle in her back. But the cap of greying hair is thin, her skull likely porous. Marnie concentrates on the point between the forehead and the hairline. And already, Paula's thoughts are uncorked and ribboning out.

"Shall we talk about your eyes first?"

"No."

"Don't you want to know if there's a cure?"

"There's a cure?"

"I'm not a doctor."

"What good are you if you can't answer a simple question?" Paula sees the turban stiffen. If that's possible. The clairvoyant's face is featureless against the light of the globe.

"If you're not satisfied, you may leave."

Paula bites her lip.

"Shall we proceed?"

"Fine."

"Now let me tell you what I see. You're able to see some things but not everything. Do I have this right?"

"Hey– if I'm the one who has to answer the questions–"

"Pay attention please."

"There's no cure."

"Cure, no cure, doesn't matter. Your future is moving into brightness. There will come a time when you will see far better. Last week I saw this in your palm and today I feel it in my heart."

"Do you know about my brother?"

"We need to talk about life's affirmations."

"You don't. You don't know anything."

"Some people don't believe a word I say. They create cages to crouch in. Don't do that. Now. Close your eyes."

Paula's eyes close automatically. She feels as if she's being enveloped by something cozy– some kind of blanket. Maybe it's a catch-up on her broken sleep.

"Now tell me," Marnie says

Maybe Paula's mouth stays as open as her thoughts unfurl. Maybe not. Maybe only her skin speaks.

There are two white coats. One is worn by a balding man and the other by a man whose straight bangs hang over the metal frame of his glasses.

"Yeah– doctors. One said I should wear glasses and the other said not to bother. Now there's nothing but fuzz in there."

Her brother runs by. He laughs, throws a ball at her and tells her to practice her catch.

There he is again, running back and forth, shaking his piggy bank. Practice, he calls. Don't forget to put a quarter in the bank.

"My brother's running away."

"Away from you?"

"I don't know."

The piggy bank is on the grass. It is an actual pink pig, ceramic, a cork plug in its mouth. Paula wants it too but it bounces into the clouds and disappears. Paula yawns. Oscar is gone and so is the pig. Paula is sitting on a sleepy chair. A woman in a turban strokes her hands.

Marnie searches for the so-called fuzz in the woman's eyes. Her vaguely green irises appear loosened from their eyeballs, the green floating like hats on white water. No wonder she can't see. She's not fixed to anything or to anybody, isolated on her own lagoon. Paula shouldn't have invited her in so deeply. If Marnie ever sees death, and this is rare, she sees it in a person's eyes. One silhouette, then another crossed over it, lie dark in the big woman's pupils. Paula's fortune comes from somebody's death. Her life will be long but these cadavers, supine on her brain, are suffocating her. She carries them on her back and forever will. One of her life's break-ups possibly. Marnie doesn't know. It doesn't matter. Death is in everybody's future. It isn't her job to dispense the absolute. She lets go of the woman's hands.

"Get rid of bad memories," Marnie says. "We all have burdens. We don't need to carry them around all day."

"What does that mean?"

"Travel light." Marnie draws a suitcase on a sheet of paper, then an arrow pointing to it, and above that, writes the words, Dump the Baggage. She holds up the diagram.

Paula laughs.

"Not bad. At least you have a sense of humour."

"You're hilarious."

"Good good, that's very positive. Now. If you're open, and you're willing to receive it, your luck will change."

"Oh yeah– my eyes will open–" Paula sings out. "And they will seeee."

Marnie shakes her head. This woman is giving her gas. "If you want something good to happen, it's your responsibility to work on it."

"Who says I don't?"

"Fortunately, you've run out of bad luck." She peers into Paula's face. "I think you're at the tail end. The way it works is, you get your allotment of good luck and your allotment of bad. I'll give you an example. Some actors are lucky, right? They're famous. They're rich."

Paula waits.

"All of a sudden, their kid gets murdered or they get Parkinson's or their wife shoots some guy in a parking lot. Did you ever notice that?"

Impossible not to notice. The surreal lives of famous people in despair are constantly featured in the news.

"It's always more bearable if luck comes to you in a mixed lot, the bad with the good," Marnie says.

"Depends on what you mean by bearable." But– everything is bearable. No choice but to bear. Paula catches a muddy glimpse of the clairvoyant through the narrow side slits of her eyes and makes a silent wish for Steve's happiness and her daughter's good health. Might as well wish for the cure while she's at it. And why not for a million dollars?

The clairvoyant turns off her crystal ball, looks at herself in its glass and readjusts her turban.

"I don't care what you say. I'm not a lucky person," Paula tells her.

"It's all relative. The boy is your happiness but he comes from your misfortune."

"He's not such a joy. The kid won't eat."

Marnie shrugs. "Our session is over now." She gazes toward the mall. "Thank you."

"But—"

"Thank you. Please come again."

Paula gathers her coat from the back of the chair. She does not see the fortune teller's folded hands, or the way her mouth is drawn in fatigue. Nor does she see the storefronts as she passes them, nor the pedestrians she bumps aside. In front of her eyes is a wet blur. Slurping at her ghoulishly, the television parade of her misfortunes and afflictions marches ahead.

Probably she brought them on herself. But what was she supposed to do about Oscar? Give him money she didn't have? Maybe a kiss on both cheeks or better yet, a giant slap across the face. She should have shipped him to a psychiatric hospital, to a prison cell with yellow walls.

She stops in the middle of the aisle, grabs a clump of hair in each fist and pulls till her scalp feels as if it will detach. She'd deserve it too. She hadn't known how to cling to her portion of good luck. And didn't recognize it even when it pulsated with joy. It was she who asked Shelly for a separation. Because they could not agree on how to bring up a thirteen-year-old? They blamed each other when the girl watched hours of TV or brooded into the telephone or left her shoes lying in the doorway for Paula to trip on. All of it so incidental, tolerable to anybody but Paula. Still, that she was the only one who ever washed the dishes was simply too much. Too much and nothing at all. She should have let them pile on the counter. She should have ignored the crusts on the forks, the greasy puddles in the sink. She should have watched TV with her family. Travel light– whatever the heck that means.

Dirt caused their last wrangle. Dirt, dirt and more dirt. All of Monday she had scoured. And in came Shelly from work. He tossed his jacket on the couch. In the kitchen, he poured canned tomato juice into a glass. He cut a lemon in half and squeezed part of the juice into the glass, part onto the counter and after swirling his ill-contained mix with a teaspoon, deposited the dripping utensil on the edge of the counter. A thick red drop landed on the floor. Paula's intestines knotted. From the pit of her stomach came her voice. "Do I look like your maid?"

Mistake. She should have taken a breath, washed her hair instead of the floor. But no. Her face hot, she bent to her knees and wiped not only that sanguine drop of tomato juice, but most of the floor, the cupboard doors, the entire seam between the counter and the wall tiles. She dropped her rag in the sink and went on to dish out a dinner of roast chicken and mashed turnips and a salad as tired as she.

"Those turnips stink," Sharon said before she even got to the table.

Shelly bit off a piece of chicken and poked his fork at the salad.

"I-am-not-eating-that," Sharon declared.

While Paula glowered, Shelly grinned at his daughter and with his fork, began to shape the turnips into a cone. "Mount Everest."

"Looks like an ant hill."

"Volcano." Furrowing his knife in the turnips, he created a tunnel in the ant hill. "About to blow."

Sharon topped his volcano with a drooping lettuce leaf. "Boom."

They burst into laughter.

Paula could not recall precisely what happened next, how her chair smashed into the wall, the plate of turnips right behind. She and Shelly screamed as if the earth had erupted. And while Sharon sat crying with her fist in her mouth, Shelly grabbed his keys and rushed out of the house.

Ultimately, their decision to separate was made for Sharon's sake. For her, they sold their house and divvied up their goods peaceably. For her, they smiled and joked and hugged and cheek kissed.

Paula took all the furniture and moved into an apartment close to public transport. Alone on the bed, she lay splayed across the entire mattress. Free from his weight, she slept placidly beneath unruffled covers. But every night, no matter how calmly she started off, a light invariably flickered in the deadpan highway of her mind and awoke her. The only way she found rest, was to keep to her side of the bed where Shelly was not. The other side, as bare as it was, would always be taken.

Paula became too worn out to tolerate Sharon's music, her strewn clothing, her long hours on the telephone. From the moment she came home from school, Sharon made demands. Within weeks some of Sharon's clothes stayed in her father's condominium and soon after, every single pair of her shoes. When her stereo moved from the apartment to the condo, it was clear that Sharon was living with her father and visiting her mother on weekends. Then there were weekends when she did not come and holidays that were more fun elsewhere.

Chapter 14

Steve's legs hang off the edge of the bed. Seated on either side of him, Mariette and Réal say nothing while he blinks himself awake. He did something wrong but doesn't know what. When he finally opens his sticky mouth, his head wobbles as if his neck is spring-loaded.

"Am I sick?"

"*C'est le monde qui est malade,*" his grandmother says.

Ya, it's a sick world. That much he knows.

"*Qu'est-ce-qui t'arrive*s, Steve?"

Oh– he had something to drink. So what? The whole effing world drinks.

Question after question, they won't shut up. They don't understand what's become of him. Something to do with who he's seeing and where he lives. His Aunt Paula, what are her rules? What does she ask of him? She lost custody of her little girl, isn't that so? With her disability, she can't possibly care for children. Her clothes look unwashed. Her nails– we don't want to mention it, but honestly, we couldn't help but notice the dirt-encrusted underneath them. Tell us the truth now, is she quite normal?

He cranes his neck to ease the weight of his head. They're always asking something, asking, asking. Again, his grandmother says, *Tu caches quelque chose*. Hiding what? Man, everything in the room is visible. He's in their choice of plaid pyjamas, his bare feet curled in the draft of the old house. Hiding? He crosses his arms over his chest. Under the pyjamas he's naked.

His grandmother releases a grunt as she slides off the bed and leaves. Réal hands him his clothes.

"Steve– *Tu est le fils de ta mère*. Make us proud."

Steve stops his unbuttoning. "I know."

Réal Dumont looks at a spot on the floor as Steve dresses. "At your aunt's house, how do you spend your day?"

"I go to school, man."

"Steve, you must tell me, *grand-père*." He waits for his grandson to pull his socks on, then lifts his eyes. "And after your school. What do you do?"

"I don't know. Homework?"

"And when the homework is finished. You play with friends?"

Steve shrugs.

"Maybe you have one good friend?"

"Ya."

"Who is this boy?"

"Nick."

"Neek," His grandfather repeats.

Next, he'll want to know about Nick's parents and his grandparents and the name of the garbage man who passes in front of the house.

"What do you do with this Neek?"

"I don't know."

"You have a little beer sometimes?"

"No."

They hear Mariette calling them to breakfast.

"Baseball?"

"We don't do anything. Just talk."

Mariette calls again.

"Where you talk?"

"Nowhere. School. Sometimes we go to the arcade. That's it."

"Ah. Arcade. Steve. This arcade is a place for gambling. Your father, maybe he gamble."

"He didn't and I'm not like him anyway." Steve looks at the mirror facing the bed. The sombre eyes of his grandfather regard him. Mariette clips down the hall. "I'm a Dumont," he says loud enough for his grandmother to hear. "That's me. Steve Dumont."

His grandfather pats him on the back. He reaches into his pocket and passes him a pink bill. A little something for Easter.

Steve is eating a ketchup sandwich in his room. On Passover, his aunt doesn't let bread into the house. But if she can't see the stuff, it doesn't matter. Sometimes Paula's a Jew and sometimes she's not. Obviously, when she hides from bread, she's Jewish. Otherwise, she's too busy cooking and cleaning and pretending to love him to be anything. She says she doesn't believe in God but in prayer she does. But if that's true, she wouldn't keep saying, Dear God every time she looks at him.

Not that it means anything. People blather those words even when they aren't praying. His mother was the biggest blatherer of all. *Mon Dieu, Mon Dieu, Mon Dieu* she kept saying. That's the way women try to fix their problems. They mutter the two words without even praying– they only think they're praying. Then they wait for the world to adjust itself. Prayer, the one that's real, has a kind of foreign sound because it used to be in Latin. Now it's in all kinds of languages but not comprehensible ones. And not in any that work.

Steve opens and closes his fist. He never prays for anything. The only thing he wants is to make enough money to get the hell out.

He unfolds the list– pages of loose leaf divided into three columns. On the first column is the date and on the second, every cent he ever collected. The third row summing up his expenses, is marked up with warnings: Asshole!! Dumbass! Idiot!!! On the next line he prints, April 7– $50. –Good take. Don't waste it if you really want to get outa here!!!

Paula passes her mop under the couch to the staccato rhythm of the Rolling Stones. All afternoon she turned her music on and off, worried that Steve's homework would be disturbed. Now, late in the afternoon, the blaring speaker is so loud, neither of them hears the doorbell till the song finishes.

"*C'est l'facteur*," the postman shouts.

Paula searches for the button that shuts off the CD player and answers the door.

The postman tucks plastic boxes of audiobooks into her hands and closes her fingers around an envelope. *"Pour vous, madam. Post certifier. Signer ici."*

Paula signs where his finger points, shakes the envelope and closes the door. So much paper enters the house– thin newspapers offering up neighbourhood gossip– coupons and circulars that entreat her to buy– useless information demanding to be read. She piles every scrap of it beside the toaster and there it lingers till most of it becomes irrelevant. Once in a while, she mislays unpaid bills and beige government envelopes in the pile till the recycling box swallows them all up.

At the kitchen table, she slides her magnifier across the certified mail. The thick texture of the paper alone gives it a sense of solemnity, not to be ignored. So sure of itself is this envelope, that her name appears embossed above her address. She shakes the envelope again as if rattled, it will talk, then plunks it on her bedside table. Later, honey. As the Rolling Stones get another turn to shout, she continues her mopping.

For dinner, they eat matzoh pizza and watch stupid comedies on TV. Steve turns sideways to the wall each time he laughs. Paula cavorts around the living room during the commercials joking about the jokes till Steve joins in, making a show of gagging on his drooping tongue.

The TV jokes end and Steve shuffles to his room. Paula settles into bed and waits for Steve to sleep. She's familiar with his routine, hears his voice through the wall, can almost see the curve of his cheek by the desk lamp. Every night he reviews his math. Whenever she cleans his room, she dusts off the orderly row of math books on his desk. He loves numbers. The wall between them barely exists.

For more than an hour, the envelope lies under Paula's pillow pleading for Steve to bend his knees and fold into sleep. At last, there's a thud in the next room— an arm or leg against the bed then nothing, silence. Paula's neck gradually loosens. She rips the envelope and pulls out the folded sheet of paper.

There's a row of unreadable names on the letterhead— accountants or lawyers, maybe dentists— doesn't matter. The thing looks like the peevish demands of a bill collector. The typescript on dusky paper is unreasonably thin. That's enough to almost make her crumple the letter in frustration. And the words, in English fortunately, are long, mostly multisyllabic. Paula focuses the bedside lamp over the letter and begins to drag her magnifier over the page. Though it's all of two paragraphs, it takes her a good half hour to get through it. At one point in her life, she read a book a day, three hundred pages in a blink, and not the easy stuff. Well— not really. But she could have if she only sat long enough. Okay so maybe not. Books, she never held long enough to actually read. But magazines, yes. She used to lie in bed with the pages opened to makeup and fashion, to glossy reds and greens, to paragraphs that basically said what she already knew, why bother with them? So she didn't. She had enough obligatory reading to do at school, enough to make anybody blind. Maybe her vagueness of sight started then. Or earlier, but she can't remember. She can't precisely say when a bush planted itself in the middle of her eyeball never to be cut down.

Her neck is cricked already and not because she's bent over the magnifier. The first words in front of her are distinctly ominous– Madame, we have been mandated by Monsieur Réal Dumont and Madame Mariette Claudel to– What the hell do they want? –request the custody of their grandson, Steve Dumont-Horvath– She gradually deciphers the words but the rest of it, understanding the message, is a maze. –It would be in Steve's best interests to live with his grandparents. The Dumonts live in a safe and stable home. Steve's living situation would be significantly improved in the countryside where their spacious home is located. We urge you, Madame, to consider before all else, the well-being of your nephew. Should you not proceed amicably with our request, further actions will–

Stable home? In his best interests? So it's a lawyer writing. She reads the letter again. On the top corner, it says, *Without Prejudice*– because the lawyer knows perfectly well that the Dumonts are the most prejudiced people on the face of the earth. As if she doesn't care about Steve. As if she makes him walk barefoot on nails. The moment the old Dumont lady entered Paula's home she sniffed, her big snotty nose aimed at the ceiling. A cup of coffee those people wouldn't have with her. They think she lives in squalor, that she spits in her mugs. Prejudiced through and through.

She presses her nose to the paper. It smells vaguely of a nauseating cologne, too sweet to be sincere. She'll give that lawyer such an ass-kicking answer, his head will spin. He isn't the only one who can write a letter. She'll go to the law library. She'll study the precedents. He'll be cringing in his boots just to glance at her response. Big shot lawyer.

It's just a matter of getting a few documents together. It isn't as if she's completely uneducated. She had two years at McGill. And the library's open to everybody. She stabs her fist in the air. Nine a.m. she'll be at that library door. All she has to do is walk in and find the right book.

As long as the books on the shelves are at eye level and she doesn't have to stand around like an idiot, unable even to read the titles. Her jaw tight, she feels herself about to tear up the letter but holds back. That lawyer isn't worth the trouble. She'll sleep off the entire absurdity, and in the morning, things will look far different. In time, that silly letter will disintegrate all by itself.

Chapter 15

All night Paula grapples with the lawyer's demands, seeing herself argue her case brilliantly in front of the bench to an applauding slew of judges. To an uglier dream later in the night, that loser of a lawyer slithers under the doorsill of her apartment and snatches Steve off to the vicious grandparents. She awakes hyperventilating, the lawyer's letter wedged in the crook of her arm.

She stumbles up from the bed. In sunlight that stretches from wall to wall, she shades her eyes and crumples the letter. Bye-bye. She's already forgotten the name of the lawyer, Luc What's-His-Name. And if she wants to, that is if she really wants to, she can simply call up that Luc the lawyer guy and tell him, How dare you imply, no, insinuate, that I am not capable of taking care of my nephew? How dare you? Just because I don't see as perfectly as you. Just because I don't own a house on a weed-free lawn— just because I'm a Horvath. She stalks to the kitchen, stuffs the shreds of the letter into a pickle jar damp with brine, tightens the lid, and shoves it to the back of the cupboard. Then she dials Shelly— not that he'll be of any use but she has to tell somebody about how she had to sign for some random envelope without even knowing what the heck she was signing for and how next time, "I'll jab the pen into the postman's eye rather than accept it."

"Just shoot him with your handy pistol. It's faster."

"You have any better ideas?"

"Tell them you couldn't read the letter."

"Are you kidding? You want them to call me an idiot?"

"You're visually impaired. It's a perfectly reasonable excuse."

"That's exactly what they want. They'll say I'm too handicapped to take care of him."

"That would be illegal."

"You bet it's illegal."

"A lawyer wouldn't send you an illegal letter."

"Lawyers are tricksters. You know it too." She hears his radio sing. "You're driving?"

"Paula, the fact is, his grandparents do live in a positive environment. It wouldn't be so horrible if the boy lived with them. They could send him to a good private school and get him psychological help."

"Thank you so much for your lousy advice. Spare me. Please. And by the way, you shouldn't talk on the cell and drive at the same time." She slams down the phone.

Psychological help nothing. Steve needs to enjoy himself. He needs to live. She strides to his bedroom and swings open the door.

He's shuffling about in his pyjamas. Some internal alarm wakes him each morning but rarely brings him out of the room till Paula pitches her high-voiced *Good morning* at his door. "You're still not ready? Do you know what time it is? The beginning of school has come and gone. Get dressed and get going."

"*J'ai même pas mangé.*"

"You'll take a sandwich."

"I'm sick today. Feel. My forehead's boiling."

"Boiling nothing. If you don't go to school, they'll take you away. They'll put you in the suburbs with your grandmother. She'll make you get up at six even on weekends."

He scratches the down on his face. He looks like he's fifteen going on three. Maybe the lawyer wants her to be tough with him, maybe soft. She doesn't know what the heck they want.

"Well. It's almost lunchtime. We might as well have a decent breakfast. I'll bet that grandmother of yours doesn't make hot chocolate with marshmallows."

"She makes boiled liver." He lets his tongue hang out of his mouth pretending to gag, mimicking his joke from the night before. "Coffee," he grunts.

Paula is sure the grandmother doesn't give him coffee.

They have French toast and two pots of coffee and listen to the rock station that Steve understands. Sheltered by the resounding music, they take all the time in the world over breakfast.

"You won't tell your grandmother about the coffee, will you?" Feeding coffee to minors might be an arrestable offence.

"I don't tell my grandmother anything."

"It's just as well."

Steve angles his dirty cutlery on the edge of his plate. He glances at his aunt and turns away. "You keep looking at me."

"I'm kind of worried."

"What for?"

"I don't want to lose you."

He shrugs, stares at his bare feet. "I'm not going this very minute."

"Going where?"

"Vancouver."

"What's in Vancouver?"

"I don't know. There's the beach."

"You don't have to go all the way to Vancouver to get to the beach. There's all kinds of water around here."

"It's not the same thing."

"So. As soon as you turn eighteen, you'll jump into that car and drive away?"

"Sixteen. And a couple of months to get my license."

"I thought we were friends."

She can't keep children close even when they're obliged to stay. Her own Sharon had run away to her father and only visited for a taste of Paula's chicken soup. The girl would eat and leave.

"Yeah. We're friends."

He looks back at his toes and wriggles them. Paula has the sense that he's about to bounce up on those muscular legs and run.

"I have a driver's license," she tells him. Every renewal she pays. They never ask if she can see anything.

"How come?"

"I used to drive, you know. It's true. I really did."

"But you can't drive now."

"You never know. I'm waiting for the cure. The fortune teller at the mall says my eyes will improve. I swear to God. That's what she said."

Paula widens her eyes and ogles him. A splendid flash of clarity brings Steve's dark hair into focus. She looks around the kitchen and thinks she sees hairline cracks in the white linoleum. The silvery gleam of the kettle appears brighter than usual. Suddenly the dishes in an open cabinet become visible. If she gets closer, if she turns her face, she'll likely notice the crumbs on the counters. She shuts her eyes. It's not wise to see dirt. No peace in that. Still, perfect eyesight would permit her to see her nephew's concentration. She'd see how people feel. Whether they're sad or happy, she isn't always sure. She peers into Steve's face. He's telling her something. She sees expectation in the tilt of his mouth. And trust, for a change.

"I'm ready to go if you are," she tells him. Steve chuckles into his shirt.

"I'm not joking."

Eyesight doesn't have to be absolutely perfect to get things done. To look at her, people have no idea that she's impaired. "You say the word, and we'll go."

"Where?"

"Vancouver. I'll drive you."

Chapter 16

The moment he spots Steve, M. Brosseau's jowls droop. "I didn't get your last two algebra assignments nor your geometry problems. If you can't get them to me by this afternoon, *you* will be the problem." He straightens his six-foot frame to pillar proportions. "I'll be at my desk at 15:15. Just for you."

Steve slips into the class and takes his seat. The students titter. Brosseau faces the blackboard and begins to chalk equations. Steve watches the numbers with what he hopes looks like interest. His face is so stiff, he stays rigid when the number four flips over and there, in front of his face is his mother lining up cards on the kitchen table. It's a film with a soundtrack —His father's, *I can't bear it,* the crashing of chairs, of footsteps, his own thumping up the stairs, shoes tumbling past him. On rolls the footage— the torn braid rug under the kitchen sink, calendar dates on the fridge crossed off neatly to the day. And fading on Louise's housedress, the cheerful yellow tulip flipping him the bird. Steve refuses to endure it. He reaches out to turn off the tube.

"Steve, what is your answer?"

Steve brings down his hand. He's in the classroom. The squiggles on the board are just numbers.

"42," he calls out.

"Wrong. Think harder."

He does. Much harder. The moment the images reappear, he shoots at them with flaming bombs, smashes and flattens, torches the wispy strands of his mother's hair as it falls across his face, blocks the rasp of his father's voice with a hammer blow to the back of his head. All gone. He figures out the correct answer to the equation. Not fast enough. The next math problem and the one after are already on the board.

Nick draws cartoon faces of Brosseau on loose-leaf, spears it with his pencil and passes it to Steve, a note scrawled under the teacher's strangulation tie.

–Doing anything this afternoon?

–Driving to Vancouver. Want to come?

–Are you supplying the snacks?

–Sure. Chocolate sandwiches wrapped in algebra loose leaf.

Nick snorts. –Sounds delectable. What about Brosseau?

–Who cares.

Three more minutes of class. The bell rings. Steve runs past Nick, past his next class, runs around the school circle. Around and around– no place to squeeze into. No place to hide. He passes room 123 and backtracks. The door is partly opened. Boneti told him to go in. Just go in. Go. But right now, he's too busy fighting the advances of his throbbing memory– the crashing of chairs, of footsteps, his own big feet thumping up the stairs– the *I can't bear it, I can't bear it, I can't–*

and his mother's *Os-car, Os–*. He shakes his head like somebody flapping a mop to get rid of the durst. As the last bell screams, he scoots past the guidance counsellor's office and into the bathroom.

The lock on the only stall clicks. A door beside the urinals is cracked. He opens it and steps in. The conflicting smells of urine and mint disinfectant rise from the two buckets along the wall. A stringy mop rests in a pool of water over a metal grate. So it's a broom closet. A rush of water clears the buzz in his ears. The guy's washing his hands. Good job. Steve waits till he hears the guy beat it out of the washroom, upturns a bucket and sits on it. Water sloshes down the drain. He opens his binder. Not a big deal. The geometry's been done for ages. In the light dulled by the mustard tiles that line the walls of the enclosure, he scribbles the answers to the algebra problems.

Steve and Nick meander out of the school. For a while they kick at a wedge of grey snow, the very last of a grand hill deposited by snow removal trucks. In a few days, rain will wash away the polluted residue of winter. Spring, peering wetly above the buds, will arrive.

"So, what about Brosseau?"

"He can wait."

"Yeah, man. Let him wait." Nick kicks up granules of snow into a spray and watches the descent. "Need anything from your locker?"

"Like what? Books? Don't make me laugh."

"Yeah I'm with you. But my dad'll kill me if I don't bring home a book. As long as the old folks are happy, everything's cool."

Steve shrugs. "Doesn't matter to me. My aunt wants to take me to Vancouver."

"Oh yeah? That was a real question back in class? Like when?"

They wander back into the school.

"Like now."

"Yeah right. When is she really taking you?"

"Are you kidding? I'm not going with her. No way."

"Yeah. I make it a policy not to fraternize with anybody over nineteen. Once a person crosses into the two's, they move into the dullness range."

Nick fills his backpack. He high-fives a couple of the passersby and grinning, flips some of them a friendly, waggling bird. "Does that mean you're going?"

"Maybe on the weekend."

"Not with your aunt."

"Of course not. I've got the car and I have money. Want to come?"

"Sure."

"Great."

"Yeah but not right away. It's my cousin's wedding in a couple of weeks. They'll kill me if I don't show."

"We can wait two weeks."

"No rush, right? I'm dead if I miss my mother's birthday."

"No rush. I'm still practicing my driving at the arcade."

The boys shuffle off down the hall. The math teacher's door stands ajar. Nick hesitates before it but Steve has already gone ahead. The math teacher is only one among many. All the teachers want to see him after school. As if he has time to waste.

Chapter 17

Sharon puts off her usual Thursday dinner visit till the next day and keeps cancelling. By the time she kicks her boots off and slings her coat into an armchair, Paula is completely disoriented.

"What's for dinner?" Sharon checks out the kitchen and sees nothing simmering on the stove.

"Fruit Loops."

"What happened to the salami sandwiches?"

"That's lunch."

"Good thing you only feed him nitrates once a day."

"I didn't think you were coming."

"I called you this morning."

"Forgetfulness is one of the symptoms of menopause." Paula can't remember what the rest of them are. She settles in at the kitchen table, reluctant to move. If only dinner could rustle itself up without her intrusion.

"Where's Steve?"

"At the arcade."

"You let him go there?"

"Think I should lock him up?"

Sharon looks inside the fridge. "There's nothing in there."

"Everybody thinks being a guardian is a piece of cake. It's harder than being a mother."

"Not even salami."

"And then you get a big shot lawyer's letter full of mumbo-jumbo."

"I know."

"Who told you?"

"Dad."

"Of course Dad. And on whose side is he, your precious father? Theirs. That's whose."

Sharon fills a glass with cold water and drinks it. "I have leftover chicken at home."

"And that boy to keep you company."

"He's studying his physics."

The boy Paula's met exactly once, plays raucous salsa CDs to which he and Sharon could jig while the physics problems wait. "He's more fun than me."

"Mom–"

"Do you know what your father said?"

"Not to worry?"

"He told me that Steve is better off with his grandparents. Like he even knows."

"He just talks. He doesn't mean anything."

"He meant it."

"Should we order pizza?"

"Are you listening to me?"

"Mom. You're getting stressed about nothing. It costs all of fifty bucks to send a lawyer's letter. And it's worth about zero. It's all fakery. If they want to become Steve's guardians, they'd have to prove that you're lousy at it. Unless he's on drugs and everybody knows about it, or failing school, what's there to prove?"

Paula peers at the clock and sees the big hand pointing urgently to the twelve. "What's the time?"

"Six."

Sharon knows something about the law and could have gone on but Paula shoves plates into her hand. "Set the table."

Steve has a school night curfew of six p.m. and is utterly obedient. She's done a good job with that. Each night he steps into the house a few seconds past the six o'clock dong as if a ringer is actually reverberating in his ears and he's about to turn into Cinderella or the pumpkin if he's late. Right on time, he places his shoes by the doormat, pauses at the kitchen long enough to grunt at Sharon and slides into his room.

"Was that hello?"

"We're working on that."

"Great." Sharon picks up the phone. "What doesn't he like?"

"Everything."

"I'll order mushroom. They don't show under the cheese."

There's not enough money in Paula's wallet for the pizza. While Steve hovers by the kitchen door, she searches her pockets.

"You have anything to make a salad with?" Sharon's back at the fridge.

Paula spills her change purse onto the table. "See any dollars in there?"

Steve feels inside his pockets. His father kept his tips in the fridge for safety, in a metal coffee can. Before the end of the week, every bit of clanging change was eaten up.

Sharon rolls her eyes. "Don't tell me you have no money."

Steve clenches his fists around his bills.

"I couldn't get to the bank."

The pizza boy shows up and Sharon pays.

"I'll write you a cheque."

"Mom— don't worry about it. It's my treat." Sharon folds up her glasses and tucks them under the rim of her plate. She flips back her hair and picks up a slice of pizza. "I'm not supposed to say anything but I'm translating for a kid who's about your age. He's accused of beating up a handicapped woman."

He turns away. Though he doesn't want it, Steve eats their food. "Did he do it?"

"Somebody did. I don't know what the world's coming to. I don't think I can stand this job much longer. I'm sending applications to Toronto."

"What about Eli?"

"Him too.

"What's so great about Toronto?"

"Everybody I know is moving there. That's where the opportunities are."

"Spare me."

"Eli can't stay here anyway. His French is crappy."

"He speaks fine. I heard him."

There's a litany of telephone solicitations. Paula's first words on the line are, No thanks. No. But on the third call, she says, Yes. Of course. I hope everything's all right. Tomorrow. Three p.m. We'll be there.

She hangs up. "Steve?"

Sharon puts her plate in the sink. She washes her hands rubbing dish soap into every crevice of her palms, and inserts a pair of contact lenses into her eyes.

"Steve, that was the principal."

"Oops." Sharon raises her eyebrows. "Gotta go." She sweeps her purse off the back of the chair, grins at Steve, and clatters off.

Steve raises himself from the chair.

"Sit."

He's half-arched, ready to bounce. A wedge of pizza sits limply on his plate beside a mound of mushrooms.

"I said for you to sit." Paula owned a dog before Sharon was born. "Are you in trouble at school?"

He looks at his feet. "No."

"The principal told me there's a problem."

He shrugs.

"Is there?"

"I don't know. Could be."

"Ah. Could be." His aunt slides the dark pupils of her eyes to the side of his face and towards the wall. "Now what does that mean?"

"It means nothing."

"Right. Nothing. Well. Tomorrow we'll see about that. We've got an appointment with the principal."

Steve picks up his plate.

"You'd better get your homework done."

"It won't make any difference."

"What does that mean?"

"Nothing." He slams the dish into the sink along with its debris and strides past her into his room.

Kids. Paula clears the rest of the table and places Sharon's glasses on the counter. Sometimes the girl's head is in a closet. Just a few months ago she lost a brand-new pair. They're all alike. Their moods. Their tempers. Too bad for them. Tough bananas. Bad stuff or not, there are rules to follow. Paula should have made things clear to the boy from the start. If her brother was brought up with rules, he'd have been a different sort of adult. her parents tolerated all of Oscar's pouts. Well. It won't happen here.

She throws open the door to Steve's bedroom and switches on the light. His bed is unmade, his clothes strewn everywhere. She steps around his school bag and trips on a running shoe. Where in this other world of littered paper, this wasteland, is he? Not four days ago the room was clean, everything in order. She was in it herself with a broom and a mop.

"Steve?" She holds her breath and counting to ten, shakes off her ridiculous panic. There are no knives in this room. "Steve–" He is, must be here.

A quick breath sounds from the bed. She swallows, sits beside a heap of clothes and tickles the wedge of sheets. "Got you."

He shrugs her off.

"If you want me to go away, you'll have to talk." She settles in against the headboard.

Steve slides to the opposite edge of the bed.

Paula stretches out her legs. "My little finger tells me you've been up to something. There's no principal in the world who's going to call the house for nothing."

"I'm not two. Christ."

"You're acting like you are."

He's wet with perspiration, overheated by the blankets. He wants to tell her to get off his bed except it isn't his.

"At least tell me what you're angry about." She tugs the sheets away from his face and touches his cheek. "You're crying."

"I'm hot, damn it."

"Stop swearing."

"I'm not." He rolls off the bed.

"Have you been smoking?"

"Me?" He almost laughs. People are always asking stupid questions.

"I'm not talking about cigarettes."

"I wouldn't waste my money on that crap."

"No?" Her temples pulsate.

He can almost feel her putting thoughts together and arranging them into a trap. He grinds his teeth. And doesn't say a word.

Chapter 18

They take the two chairs angled perfectly for an inquisition and the principal starts in on an endless story about some kid and all his should-haves and could-still-be's, if only he was more this and more that. He goes on lecturing for about an hour, his moon head as starkly polished as the top of his grim desk. You'd think he's in front of a blackboard giving a History lesson except that he's talking about *him*. And the *him* is Steve-full-of-faults – how he skips class and ignores the teachers, how he never does anything he's supposed to. How he acts like quite-an- independent off on his own track. The wrong track. Rickie doesn't exactly say that he's stupid, but Steve feels it. The next sentence, the one that says, there's something wrong with this kid, is on the tip of the man's tongue except he sucks it up, leaving all the telling in his swollen cheeks. As he opens and closes his battery-operated mouth Paula leans over her purse, all the way over the guy's desk, practically in his face.

"But every night he goes to his room and sits at his desk. He writes and writes. Don't you, Steve?"

They look at Steve and wait. He's supposed to say something but his jaws are so clamped, he can only nod.

Rickie aims his bald spot at the flat grey hairs of Paula's scalp. "Every one of Steve's teachers has expressed concern. He does not hand in his assignments. He does not take part in the class discussions. Steve, if you do your homework, as you say, where is it? There is no homework. No assignments handed in. Nothing. Right?" Eyes wide on Steve, the glaring moon head finally shuts up.

Sometimes there is, Steve wants to say. In that pink room there are papers everywhere— math problems all resolved and crumpled up– research notes placed neatly in binders or jumbled under the bed. He rather likes finding facts and copying out the information. Somewhere between the pink walls are a couple of completely finished essays, as neatly block-lettered as typewriting. Or if not there, then in Paula's recycling box, or maybe on a bench at the shopping centre.

Paula eyes the wall beside the principal. "He gets library books."

"You like to read?"

He does, but has no time for it what with all that homework to labour at. He only has time to practice his driving at the arcade and with a few bets, raise money for the trip. That's it. Raising money takes hours of time. He has no choice. Without cash, he's nothing.

Rickie arches his neck as if he's about to leap at him. "You're fifteen years old. You may not know it, but the best time of your life is now. If you want to succeed, you'll have to buckle down. A couple hours of study a day, you'll be on top of the world. Got that?" He narrows his eyes. "Boy. I can tell you one thing. And this is a guarantee. If you don't get to it, you'll have to repeat your year. Is that what you want?"

Steve shakes his head. He does get it. You're supposed to show you agree.

Mr. Rickie stands. Trying to make eye contact with her flickering pupils, he takes Paula's fingers and squeezes them. "Thank you for doing what is necessary. I'm sure that from now on, Steve will be diligent."

They walk the long way home passing narrow little houses, one abutting the other. In some of the gardens, tulip heads are stiffly alert to the sun. Bright days to come. Protected by two pairs of sunglasses, Paula stares at the ground away from the glare. They stop at the fruit store and its adjacent bakery. More time taken from house and homework yes, but it's important to do the necessary. To buy food, walk, place her hand on her nephew's shoulder.

"I can help you with your homework."

"You can't even see."

They buy cheese danishes and the first of the season's peaches.

"You're really smart. You'll catch up fast."

He swings the bags as they wander.

"I can help you organize"

"There's nothing to organize."

Paula unlocks the door to their immediate clutter and the smell of old shoes. Only a couple of days earlier she had vacuumed.

"Want anything special for dinner?"

His shoulders lift and drop, his usual impassivity. Outlines she sees well, the way a person walks, the structure of a body. Steve's face is a blur. But muddy faces, she's used to. There are other ways to figure out a person's expressions. He seems happy when he eats. If he eats.

"Let's see. What do I have in here?" She ruffles through the contents of the freezer. "Are those hot dogs?"

"I don't know."

"You know what? There's protein in cheese danish. And probably in ice cream. Sounds good doesn't it? Ice cream and cheese danish it is. And peaches just for the fun of it. Now set the table."

Over the ice cream, Steve cracks a few jokes. None are hilarious but out of relief, Paula whoops and keeps on rewarding him with her guffaws. They're laughing so hard, they ignore the phone until the ringer stops, pauses, and begins insisting a second time.

Pressing her hair flat against her scalp with her two hands, she says, "Boy. You want to be on top of the world? Keep eating ice cream and in no time you'll be ten feet tall." She thrusts her head over the table like the bull principal. "It's for you Boy. You get an A plus for answering the phone."

"But he's a basketball player," Steve mimics. "And I'm coming to see all his games and if you kick him out of school, how am I going to sit in the front row and eat ice cream and clap?" He tilts back his chair and picks up the receiver. "Residence Horvathium."

And sure enough, just as Paula promised, a familiar voice says, "*Allo, allo?*"

"*Oui?*"

"Steve? *C'est tu toi?*"

"*Oui.* It is."

"*Bonjour cher, comment vas-tu?* And school? How is it going?"

He can't remember who the man is, though for sure he knows the voice. It's so polite, so kind. Well educated, his grandmother would say.

The man says, "Study hard and pass your aunt to me."

"*Un moment s'il-vous-plaît.*" Steve holds the phone out to Paula.

"*Mme Horvath.* I am Luc Richard. I am sure you received my letter by this day. All this time we are waiting for your answer."

"I can't talk right now."

"Ah. The young man is with you. The Dumonts want only what is best for him. I am sure you will agree with them. The fresh air by the river is good for children who are growing so fast."

"Listen—"

"No no please, you need to say nothing for now. I only want to make a contact with you. I am sure you will agree, Mme Horvath, the *environnement* is more important to the young people today than is the family. Where you live, it is well known that the drug problem is large. And it is well known too of the gangs in the area of your *appartement.*

And you will agree of course, that Steve is delicate right now. He needs a good *atmosphère* to grow straight. Maybe already Steve is drinking a little bit. And maybe his schoolwork is suffering. If you are thinking like a mother, Mme Horvath, you will like him to live in a place that is safe and healthy. You will want him to be excellent at his studies and to move on to the *université*."

"Look–"

"Mme Horvath. I need nothing from you at this minute. Please think of the best for Steve, and we will be in touch in a few days to make the arrangements. *Bonne fin d'journée*."

"Hang up." Paula passes the receiver to Steve.

"Was that guy Luc?"

"You know him?"

"He was at my grandparents' house."

"He's a lawyer." Paula squeezes her hands together. "And you know what? Lawyers charge by the second. The more they talk, the more they get paid."

"Yeah but, what does he want?"

"Doesn't matter. You better get your homework done." Steve reaches for the dishes.

"Go right now. I'm serious. You get it done."

He's a good boy but she's sure he hasn't heard a word she said. She should have helped with his studies, not that it would have made any difference. Her French is useless. She can barely add and subtract and can't read in any language. She fills the sink with soapy water. She can't answer the lawyer's letter, can't use a computer, can't write a legible note. About all she can do for Steve is show him how to wash dishes. She can almost hear the lawyer's jeer –You can barely see his face, never mind what he's doing back in that room. She throws the wet dishcloth at the window. That lawyer guy knows nothing. Just because he gains instant information just by opening his eyes each morning. Just because it's automatic for his brain to form and articulate his thoughts. Especially stupid ones.

Imagine that, instant knowledge with a glance. Free for others. Not for her. She rubs the roots of her hair till they tingle. Enough self fucking pity. With one glance from her, he will crumble.

She makes her way towards Steve's music and swings the door open.

He's at his desk, a paper spread in front of him. On the floor, pages flop from open binders. He's thrown everything off his desk– or dropped them by accident.

"Everything fell?" Steve smiles. "Yeah."

The spine of his math book is broken. He's supposed to have cleaned up his disorder. But it's worse, far worse than the day before.

"What's that you're studying?"

"It's a map."

"It's homework, right?"

"Nah."

"Is there something about the school you don't like?"

"It's overrated."

"Steve. Do your homework. Now."

She strides away to the kind of scrubbing that wears the daisies off plates. As she wipes down the counter, Sharon's glasses skid off. Paula scoops them from the floor and onto her nose. The light in her sight seems brighter. She takes a couple of steps backwards to view her white table. Like in an advertisement for detergent, the melamine surface is whiter than white. Even the fake marble counter gleams, no longer scratched. She removes the glasses and compares her vision with and without. Possibly the glasses can be of some use. She isn't sure. What she sees, what she doesn't, often confuses her. She sometimes sees objects that are not there– a kitchen table, oranges in a bowl, perhaps a crawling baby, or a chair haphazardly placed in the middle of the room. And in spite of all those made-up images, for-real items that are blatantly in front of her nose, are invisible. She places Sharon's glasses on the windowsill, takes a breath, and rushing down the hall, bursts into Steve's room.

He hasn't budged from his desk.

"What's that map about?"

"Canada."

"What do you mean? The provinces?"

"A road map. Look," he takes her hand, places it on the paper and traces her finger along the bold red line of the Trans-Canada Highway going far west into Vancouver. Canada is creased, almost worn through.

"Maybe you'll want to study geography in university."

"Bad idea."

"I think you should be in the English stream at your school. Maybe it's too hard in French."

"It's not hard. It's just boring."

"It could be a lot more fun in English."

"It's not fair to be so bored. All day long I sleep in those classes."

"We'll tell Mr. Rickie to put you on the English side."

"He won't. It's against the law."

The radio constantly buzzes about how the province is close to becoming an independent country and how all English people will be obliged to speak only French. She knows a few words of the language and here and there, can use it in a pinch but probably doesn't know enough to survive in an entirely French country.

"What's not fair, is being forced to study in French," She tells him. "In any other province, you can choose the language of your education. In the whole world I'll bet you can."

"Ya. Even in China."

"You're smart. I'll bet you'd do brilliantly in English."

His shoulders lift and drop.

"Why are we staying here anyway? We could just pack up and go."
She feels her heartbeat. Maybe she's just talking but she isn't about to
stop. And maybe she's serious. "You still travel light don't you?"

"Ya."

"Good. Let's get going then."

He leans over the desk to face his map. "Where are we going?"

She tosses back her head. "Didn't I already tell you? Anywhere you
want."

He places the tip of his finger as far west as the rim of the paper.

Part 3
Trip to Nirvana

Chapter 19

Steve writes lists and laughs and pulls Paula into his room. She's never seen him so light. He faces her to the wilted Canada and she becomes student of the map and he, the teacher. Here is Kingston, then comes Toronto and then Sudbury. The eraser end of his pencil dabs at Winnipeg, Saskatoon and Regina, the little towns of Swift Currant and in Alberta, Medicine Hat because he likes the names. He points out Edmonton and Calgary and why not see Banff while they're at it? In British Columbia, they'll have to stop at all the towns with the cool names: Golden, Revelstoke, Salmon Arm, Kamloops. There's many more but you can't stop everywhere. Before they know it, they'll be in Vancouver, British Columbia, all the way to the edge of the Pacific coast. The ocean. He taps the blue waters on the map with his pencil and proceeds to fold it.

The whole idea of meandering through their unknown country in a rusted cab makes Paula's skin taut. But tomorrow's another day and there's no harm in a little fun. The moment Paula's about to say, All right! Let's go to the mall for a hot dog– Steve slams his fist in his palm and says, "It's all set. Six a.m., we pick up the car." Though her flesh tingles quite painfully, Paula flickers her fingers in a gesture that seems to agree with Steve's every word.

*

They forget to set the alarm and awake in the midst of rush hour. Their second coffees drag into late morning. Only after the coffee pot is completely drained do they begin a haphazard gathering of belongings: Two unzipped duffel bags bursting with clothing, a couple of towels, a dictionary, a cardboard box of shoes, maps, cutlery, a kettle, and a blanket. To that Paula adds a jar of peanut butter, bread, cookies, fruit, and Monday's leftover pizza. Their desultory luggage lies ready at the door. Three times Paula checks her wallet for her license. By two they're ready to go except they don't want to faint from hunger. Paula fries up the three lonely eggs that remain in the refrigerator and they eat that, along with the pizza. Steve's radio station keeps him strumming on his mind guitar till supper time and Paula decides that even with years of driving experience, anybody with half a brain wouldn't start a long trip on an empty stomach.

Except that Steve is ready. "Let's go," he shouts.

"It's rush hour."

"Around here it's always rush hour." He dangles the keys at her nose. "I'm going without you." His face in the doorway is pinched, his ankle-high runners huge. Paula doesn't understand how he gets anywhere with his perennially unlaced shoes, how his wide pants don't fall off his hips. He looks down on her, a full head taller than she.

"Are you kidding? There's too much traffic now."

'Bye-bye." He slaps on his backwards baseball cap and turns.

"Alright alright. But we still need to get our stuff over to the car. You don't want to start shlepping now, do you?"

"I'm getting the car."

"What get? No sense bringing the car over here if you can't park it."

"There's a space right in front of the door. We could have left it there all week except for Tuesday afternoon."

"Isn't it Tuesday?"

"Wednesday."

"What's the rush? We can go tomorrow, early in the morning, just like we said."

"See you in a few years." He pivots on his heel and strides out the door.

"Hey— hang on." Squaring her sunglasses on her nose, Paula hooks her purse on her arm and runs after him.

The early evening sun is waning already. Steve paces the length of the three residential blocks to the parking lot, Paula trotting behind, her face angled to the pavement. At the stop light, Steve looks back and waits. Together they cross the street. Had she seen the grim despair in his down-turned mouth, she'd have hooked her arm through his and turned them around. Instead, they proceed through the deserted parking. The mall is closed and vacant. How the cockeyed carcass of the Malibu remains here, its nose pointed glumly at the pavement without being towed away, is really a wonder.

Steve unlocks the driver's door. Handing him her purse, Paula sets her foot in the vehicle.

"You're not driving."

But she's already buckling on her seat belt.

As Steve gets in on the other side she holds out her hand for the key, feels the horseshoe in her palm and grasps it tightly enough to feel the resonance of pain. She concentrates on it. It feels okay, her existence as a driver confirmed.

"What are you waiting for?" Steve takes the keys from her hand and inserts one of them into the ignition.

"I'm thinking." Her hands slide wetly on the steering wheel. She wipes them on her pants. She knows enough to turn the key in the ignition but can't remember if she has to press the gas pedal at the same time. She's hot. Though the car is not engaged, she hears the beating of desperate wings in the motor. If she can get going now, it might be alright. The sun is low enough in the sky to be a friend. But if they sit in the car too long without moving, the light of day will dim so quickly, everything around them will turn into mud. And in that darkness, she'll be completely blind and they'll be obliged to sleep in the parking lot.

"Maybe we should do this in the morning. It'll be dark soon."

Steve slams the dashboard with his fist. Clattering, something slides off. "What do you mean dark? It's a four second drive to the house. Listen. I can drive this baby. My da–" He swallows, quiet for a moment. "Sometimes he let me drive."

Like the silent patrons of a movie theatre, they look at the trees through the windshield. A two-minute film.

"Something fell."

Steve rummages on the floor. "Glasses."

"Sharon's I'll bet you. The new ones." Paula grins. "She'll be thrilled." She blows on her wet palms. "Maybe it's a lucky sign." Marnie the clairvoyant would insist that it is.

"Start the car."

"Give me the glasses."

The outside light is perfect for her, clear without a hint of a glare. Wearing Sharon's glasses, she can see the length of the curb alongside them. And she's not dizzy as long as she doesn't move her head too quickly. She tilts her face and sees a car close by on her left, possibly in the next parking spot– moving or still, she doesn't know. She didn't notice its arrival, did not hear it, not its wheels or its motor, or the door as it closed. She tries to roll the window down then remembers that she has to start the motor first.

"What are you waiting for?"

"There's a car right beside us."

"No car. Zero nothing."

She closes and opens her eyes. It must have gone by. "Where's the key?"

"Crap. It's in the ignition."

"Oh yeah."

"Go already. Turn the key."

She feels for the metal and twists her wrist in that one movement that will start a trajectory that can't be altered. But as inept as ever, she only elicits a dry click of the ignition. Smiling, she turns to Steve. "It's not working."

"It works. Tony rebuilt it. New transmission, new everything. It–" He stops. Paula sees his tongue in the gape of his mouth. "Oh my God. Don't tell me you didn't put on the brakes."

"Isn't it the gas?"

"The brakes for God's sake."

"Alright, the brakes." She keeps smiling, her face numb.

"Right-foot-on-brakes. Go on, right-foot-on–"

"I know," she mutters through her numb teeth. And with that, she presses the brake as hard as it will go and engages the engine with the key. It starts.

"Now put it in drive and go."

She peers at the lever.

"You don't know what you're doing."

While the thrum of the anxious motor beats inside her veins, the sun is receding. She grabs the gear shift, loosens her teeth and shakes out her left arm. "I know exactly what I'm doing."

It's only a matter of finding the right slot on the gear shift. For that she has an instinct. And a driver's license. Heck. Her brother was a cab driver. It's in the genes. She owned a car and was perfectly able to persuade it to lift its blue haunches and toddle around the block. She tugs at the shift. You can't forget how to drive. As long as somebody sits beside you. And you don't have to park.

"Pull the gear shift toward you." Steve reaches over and changes gears. The car jerks. Paula slams her foot on the brakes. Now that's instinct.

"Aunt Paula—"

"What?"

They sit in silence, Paula's leg clenched over the brake. The sky is a little darker.

"We have to go now if we're going."

Paula eases her foot off the brake. The car rolls ahead. She has no idea where they're situated. On the open asphalt there are no borders for her eyes, no landmarks. Somewhere is the entrance to the road. Steve grabs the wheel and the car swings right. She brakes. A row of cars whizzes past.

"They're miles away."

"They're fast."

"You need to get closer to the exit."

"I just need to find the curb. I'll follow it."

"Maybe you should practice."

"Alright. Good idea."

Inch by inch, the car waddles toward the exit. "Pretty good, huh?"

"Look. There's a stop light. Can you see it?"

"Can I see it? What kind of question is that? I've got glasses on, don't I?" She sees something of a glint in the distance.

"Alright. Drive till the light and when I tell you to go, you'll make a right."

Paula lets the car advance with its own brain, her foot above the gas pedal.

"Don't turn." Steve straightens the wheel. "Keep going. Go. Get your foot off the brake."

They pull up to the traffic light and stop. A second later the light turns green. Paula feels Steve's breath on her cheek.

"Go on. Turn right now. Hurry up."

Behind them a horn blares. Her heart beats in her acidic mouth. "Go, go, go. You're clear," Steve shouts.

Three blocks to the house. Endless. Cars wheel past them honking out sermons. And there's the house, finally. They lurch to a stop. Paula jiggles the gear shift, pushes it to park and turns the motor off– all this without a thought as to how it should be done. As if by agreement they burst into applause. And while Paula keeps clapping, banging out the shakiness in her hands, Steve plays bongos on the dashboard.

They're hungry again. Paula boils what's left of the potatoes and they eat them slathered in butter. Except for a few slices of bread and the obligatory jars of mayonnaise, mustard and ketchup, the fridge is barren. Steve loads up the car while Paula cleans up, though why bother? The May rent was just paid and when the next cheque doesn't hit the landlord's mailbox on the first of June, he'll be knocking on the door. By mid-month he'll be in with his key. As far as Paula's concerned, he's welcome to everything, every dish, every doodad in her collection, every single paper in the pile that never dwindles.

She ambles around her living room peering at the photographs– passages in her daughter's life– black robed on graduation day, her first lost tooth. She picks up a picture of Sharon balanced on her first two-wheeler, kisses it and returns it to the table. As if Sharon was not his, Shelly had scrawled, *Paula's Girl* on the back of the photo. She appeared to be entirely Paula's creation, her grey, Horvath eyes as opened and lit as her mother's had once been. But with each additional year, Shelly's pull on the little girl strengthened. Sharon's face grew longer, her nose narrower. Unable to see past her nose, she wore glasses. And– in parade with her daughter, Paula's drooping eyelids began to reconfigure her own face. Mother and daughter became wholly similar and wholly different.

Paula has no need of pictures. She closes her eyes and conjures up the bright, unblemished images encrypted in her memory. There's her four-year-old Sharon squinting at the sun, her small defiant arms crossed over her aqua bathing suit. Every nuance of colour in Paula's memory glints like it would in a photo. No longer can Paula see and recall the blue tones of today's sky. The mixed shards of green in grass have become indecipherable, forever blended into outdoor carpeting. And Sharon– is now a blur. Memory will have to remain Paula's willing companion, abler to recall what she can no longer perceive.

She circles the room again, feeling the walls as she passes. If she chooses to stay and fight, the lawyer will take one look at her face and automatically assume that nothing is in her brain. Her faded eyes make her look dim. And nothing intelligent comes out of her mouth when stress eats her up. She'll lose the vocabulary needed to support her cause. The collection of dictionary words that used to slip into her speech stayed behind in the books she no longer reads. Her thoughts are now an amalgam of TV speak and the superficial chitchat of neighbours. She'd never be able to research, from irretrievable print, an argument in her favour that makes sense. No way. In the muddle that's become her brain, the use of logic is impossible. The further she runs from that lawyer, the better.

Chapter 20

They sleep one more night on the unmade rumple of their sheets. At six A.M. Paula jumps out of bed to the alarm's insistence. She heads to Steve's room.

He grips the blanket over his face.

Drunk with resolve, with the electric pulse of adrenaline, she shakes him. "Hey, we're ready to roll."

He shoves his head under the covers.

Paula leaves and ransacks the kitchen cupboards. She finds a pack of cookies she never knew existed and comes back with bribery. "Cookies." She tucks the cellophane package under the blanket. "Chocolate."

"Leave me alone."

"Come on cootchie-coo, let's go." She tries to tickle the soft fuzz of his chin.

He stays wrapped in his cocoon. "I'm not a friggin dog."

"Who said you were? You're a map man. You're the navigator."

"I'm not going."

"What? You changed your mind? I guess you want to write an essay."

He stays compact under the blanket.

"Fine. I'll go by myself. You just stay home and write essays about–what is it? The Hundred Years War, I'll bet. A hundred years of essay writing."

The hump doesn't laugh.

"Well. Whatever you want is fine with me. We could be on our way to Nirvana. Or you could be in school facing the next detention."

"I don't care."

She sits on the edge of the bed leaning into his back. "Going out West was your idea."

Scowling, he throws off the blanket. Pink lines of sleep are creased on his face. And the red lines of rage. "If *you* drive, it'll take us a hundred years to get anywhere." His breath is musty. He has the unfortunate habit of ignoring his toothbrush.

"I can't help it if I'm the only one with a license. You don't want the police to stop us."

"I drive better than you. If you drive too slow they'll put us both in jail."

Or in a mental institution.

After driving school, she never again put wheels on the surface of a highway. Speed at her own hands terrified her. The only driver for the Malibu, if they hope to get past the mall, would have to be Steve. But then, they might put her away for inciting a minor. And while she clangs at the jail door, Steve will have to do his homework without her salami sandwiches, jabbed in the back by the principal's drill finger.

Or he'll end up across the river with guess who, obliged to breathe the countryside's stifling air.

"Alright, fine. Stay in bed if that's what you want. The whole idea's stupid anyway." She feels herself swallow. "We shouldn't go. And maybe, clean air would be good for you."

"It's my car." He's staring at the ceiling, his hands crossed under his head.

A caffeine headache descends on her right eye. Her nose is full of mucous. "We can't just drive across the country."

"Are you calling me an idiot?"

"I'm not calling you anything."

"Well I'm not an idiot. And for your information, I'm an excellent driver."

"I didn't say you weren't."

"Fine. I'm driving." He throws off the covers and bounces out of bed.

She's about to tell him, No way, we can't– but she's too sluggish to open her mouth and if they don't get away soon, the Dumonts and their lawyer will flail Steve's best interests at a judge and proceed to pluck him away from her.

"Brush your teeth," she demands.

Paula stirs instant coffee into a cup of faucet water for a last boost of energy. They eat half the cookies and load up the car. In the driver's seat, Steve considers the map one more time. A milk truck cruises the street stopping here and there to deposit dairy cartons on front stoops. Paula hasn't seen such a service since she was a girl and here, right on her own doorstep is a truck and a, *Bonjour Madam* from a smiling driver who holds out two pints of chocolate milk just for them. Why leave such a lovely street? Everything they need is here. They can sit in the car for a while, munch a few more cookies in their cozy huddle then go back to the apartment. Once they're home, she'll sit with him for encouragement while he catches up on his schoolwork. Just by her being there, he'll become confident. And with confidence comes success.

But in a matter of seconds Steve gets the car in gear and rolls onto the bumpy asphalt. There's not another moving car in sight till the Malibu scoots around the milk truck and onto the main drag. He slides the car neatly between two vans and shoots a dentist's smile at the windshield. Paula squeezes her purse, an anvil against her stomach. Hardly breathing, she doesn't say a word except for, Slow down, you're too close, and, Oh my God. Otherwise, she's absolutely quiet. Any sound could disturb his concentration. They swing onto the service road of the Decarie expressway, the car screeching in objection. Paula swallows back a sour wad of half-digested cookie.

Steve's shoulders are as high as his ears. At every red light, Paula-the-broken-record asks if he's okay.

"I'm fine. Stop asking."

*

The service road is blocked by parked cars on two and a half discordant lanes of aggressive traffic. By some miracle, Steve lines the car up behind a garbage truck. Every few minutes it stops, loads up with trash, and moves ahead. Steve puts on his flashers. Nobody's nice enough to let him pass. The car is going so slowly, it wobbles. Come on, please. If he doesn't get onto the expressway soon, he'll have to turn around and go back to his bed. The whole damned world is rude. Through his concentrating teeth he mutters, "Shut up." at the honking drivers. He smacks the horn and immediately, a space opens. The Malibu lurches into the next lane and just as suddenly, into the next.

The mob presses him onto the expressway, part of their ant colony, part of their great movement, there's no way to get out of it, no way to change his mind. He jets down the ramp as fast as the avalanche behind him and into the oncoming traffic. With a screech, he shoots into the centre lane and within seconds, into the extreme left, up the ramp and onto the highway. West on the Trans-Canada Highway, west to the other side of the country.

How he found his way is some miracle to Paula. Miraculous too is how he waited while the traffic whizzed by, so sure of himself and how he gunned the motor till the car landed right between the white lines, just like the little red car at the video arcade.

He stays on the right lane going easy. They've stopped swerving. His shoulders drop. Glancing at Paula, he grins.

"Watch the road."

"I am."

Paula catches sight of what she can, the glimmer of fenders on either side of them and little else. They're already in the suburbs surrounded closely by interweaving cars. Cement buildings line the road like icons marking the way. As they push past cavalcades exiting the highway, the buildings fall off the landscape. They cross a bridge onto open road cutting through farmland and bush and spruce forest. Steve is going too fast but she doesn't say it. As they bear down on the vehicles ahead, he guns the motor till the car holding them back switches to the next lane. This is how he drives, speeding and slowing down for reasons Paula can't see. There are long stretches between exits. Still wired tight, his eyes rigid on the cement ahead, Steve turns on the radio. He begins to fiddle with the dials.

"I'll do it. You want music?" Paula finds a music station that becomes spotty a few meters later.

"No music?"

She turns the knobs. "Doesn't look like it."

"Crappy radio."

The only station with a clear signal is hosting a call-in show for referendum ranters.

–Let me tell you, Sir, it is not possible for us to live as a minority in this Canada of Anglophones. All these people who take their hat off to the Queen, we have no interest in that. We have the right to feel at home in our own language, doing business, running our municipal affairs– The man's accent is distinctly French.

–But isn't it true, Monsieur Rancourt, and most of our listeners agree. Agree or disagree, please call us at 1800-why-jinx –that French is already the principal language of Quebec?

–You know very well that as long as we do not gain our independence, there is always a risk. French is difficult. Young people today do not want to work hard. With the Americans also on our back, they will go to English. And the Allophones also. They have no interest in the French culture. They live in their own *petit village*. And–

–Thank you for your call. Now. The question is: Will Quebec be better off as a sovereign state? Or will it–

"Who cares."

"You. Even if you're perfectly bilingual. You're already not allowed to study in English. They probably won't even let you talk in English if they get what they want."

He dials in the slurred tunes of a rock station and rolls down the window.

"Close the window. It's cold."

"Nobody's telling me what to do." He rolls up the window.

"They won't just tell you. They'll turn it into law. It's a good thing we left when we did.

There's already an English parade going down the 401. At least we're not last in line."

"How long have we been driving?"

Paula brings her watch to her eyes. "An hour maybe."

"I'm hungry."

"I've got chocolate milk. But you shouldn't eat while you drive."

"I can eat a cookie."

"Maybe we can stop at a Tim Hortons for breakfast."

"Come on. Just a cookie."

"I don't know where they are."

"What about the milk?"

"That's too complicated."

"It'll go bad if we don't drink it."

He snatches a few sips while Paula holds a straw to his lips. When he finishes his milk, he checks his rearview mirror like he'd seen his father do and passes to the middle lane. "That's better."

"It's not."

"You can't go all the way out west in the slow lane." He rolls down the window.

"Slow down."

He does not and there's nothing Paula can argue with. He drives as straight as an arrow, the nose of the Malibu as far up as it will go. When she and Shelly took driving vacations, the routes were long and the wind rushed through the open windows of their car. They aimed for speed. The sooner they got there the better. Any vacationer she's ever spoken to, talks about getting to their destination as if time spent in the car is as necessary and wasteful as tooth flossing. But every moment in the car can be counted as part of the holiday pleasure. There's something to be said about being buckled into that seat, the radio covering you with its music, time and its obligations left behind.

Paula begins to croon. The trees and grasses swing by too fast for her to keep her eye on the landscape. Every sign is unreadable, the cars alongside reduced to a swoosh and a shock of wind. She feels her weight pushed backward against the seat. She knows the words to many songs and closing her eyes, belts them out without embarrassment.

The car hurtles forward. Again it picks up speed and bears left. A horn screams. A van close enough to kiss the Malibu zooms by as the little car swerves right, left– then back to the middle lane. Paula screams.

Wet with the shakes, Steve slows down.

"What happened?"

"I didn't see him."

"You're supposed to look behind you."

"I looked. He came up from nowhere."

The Malibu crawls.

"You'd better get to the slow lane."

He puts on his flasher but can't move. On both sides, cars speed past. The Malibu crawls on, quivering in the wind swerve of passing cars. Eventually– fifteen minutes later? An hour? Three? There's a space on the right.

Paula turns to look. "I think you can go."

"There's a car."

"It's far." But she doesn't really know.

He jerks the wheel into the right lane.

"Let's stop at Tim Hortons."

He passes the exit for the coffee shop.

"You'll need gas."

Yeah, probably. At the next exit he'll get off as long as it isn't too busy. But it is busy. It always is.

"Is this an exit?" She keeps asking the same question.

"Maybe."

"Put your flashers on."

"We're not there yet."

"As soon as you can."

The exit ramp opens for him, the Tim Hortons a couple of meters ahead. For a second he shuts his eyes. He's on the ramp, rushing in, the curved red lettering of the Tim's suddenly beckoning.

"Where are you now?"

"Near the parking lot."

"Go in, go."

"There's cars."

Somehow he forces the Malibu into the lot and slides neatly between two yellow lines. He brakes, puts the car in park and begins to tremble.

Bagels, coffee, donuts. They're hungry, in fact ravenous. In the bright light of the Tim Hortons, Paula feels her stomach loosen for the first time in hours.

She closes her hand over Steve's fist. "Slow down. If we eat too fast, they'll make us leave before we're ready."

"I'm never leaving. I love this place."

They finish their donuts and she buys another round. It would be fine to sit at the formica table and never move.

Steve pretends to strum a guitar, bopping to the music in his head. "When we get in the car we'll get a station with a blowout sound. It's great when you have music to drive to."

"Steve–"

He makes the sound of a high chord. He doesn't know how to play an instrument but is feeling powerful enough to play anything.

"You're not driving."

"Yeah? Who's driving? You?"

"I'm the only one here."

"You won't even know how to get us out of the parking lot."

"If you navigate, we'll be fine."

"It's my car."

"Steve, you almost killed us."

"Of course I did. That's because I'm a Horvath." He smirks. "And so are you."

It becomes embarrassing to buy another donut and just as much of an embarrassment to sit in front of their drained coffee mugs picking at the crumbs. In the end, they shuffle over to the car and circle it till Steve, first to stand directly in front of the driver's side, shrugs and gets in. To bolster his self-esteem, Paula sits on the passenger side and buckles up. As long as the car is hobbled by the limits of the lot and gas alley, Steve can be allowed to drive.

"Alright Steve." She's the adult. "You fill up and I'll take it from there."

He noses up to the fuel bay, pumps in the gas and without fussing, pulls out of the station to halt beside a grass strip for the switch.

Paula adjusts the seat so that she's almost smack against the windshield, the better to see with, my dear. She shifts her leg back and forth from the gas to the brake pedal and decides that she would have to see a little less if she's ever expected to manoeuvre.

While Paula jolts her car seat back and forth in search of the perfect distance to the windshield, Steve leans against his door, one hand cupped over his eyes. "Are you finished?"

She clicks her chair into a final, disagreeable spot.

"Let's go already."

"Don't rush me." She puts on Sharon's glasses and fits her sunglasses over them. The fortunate light of day is clear and shadowless.

"No rush. You like driving in the dark."

Daylight will last another four hours, maybe. She starts the car and gradually, takes her foot off the brake hoping the car will roll along all by itself at least till they get onto the entrance ramp. It doesn't budge.

"Let's go."

Paula presses the gas till the Malibu lurches. She slams on the brakes.

"Horvath," Steve mutters.

This time she barely presses the gas pedal and sure enough, the car starts softly. They proceed toward the freeway. "Any cars?"

"You're okay."

She is. She has to be. On her right she sees a black line of asphalt and beyond it a strip of green. There they are, on the freeway. Directly in front of her is a clear space and just past that, dark blobs that waver, cars probably. Sometimes they're visible, sometimes they disappear altogether. Motorists jostle the Malibu as they pass with their burst of wind. No problem. As long as she follows the edge of the road, as long as she drives slowly, they'll be okay.

Steve reads the road signs. Sometimes she understands what he tells her. Mostly her heart beats too loudly for her to hear.

"You've got to speed up," he keeps shouting.

He's always in a rush, too young to understand the way it has to be. Sharon too had unreasonable expectations of her.

"How far is the car up front?"

"You can't see it?"

"I do."

A grey splotch floats above the pavement. But she can't figure out how close it is. She slows a little more.

"It's miles away. God– someone's going to kill us."

The Malibu sways. It has a brain this car. She barely touches it with her foot and it goes off on its own.

Steve grabs the wheel.

"Stop– what are you doing?"

"You were moving into the other lane."

"I was not." Not her. It was the car sliding all by itself. Paula grips the wheel. "Let go. I've got it." She leans forward as far as her arms will allow and peers through the windshield. Ahead are the cloud shapes of cars. She turns her head to the left and catches the glint of a fender. Or maybe a mirror. She remembers from her driving days that if you follow the car ahead, you don't have to think about how to turn the wheel. She forces her eyes to open wide and when they hurt, she blinks very fast and opens them again. Once more, Steve's hand is on the steering wheel.

"We have to get out of here."

*

Steve blows the clamminess off his free hand. As soon as an exit comes along he'll lead her off the road though the exercise is futile. He's destined to die. He sees that now. She hangs over the steering wheel just like Oscar had, her chin set like a mallet. His aunt is a copy of his father. Busy looking for fares, Oscar used to cruise along the curbs barely touching the gas, just like her. If the car moved at all, it moved on fumes alone. Didn't matter if he held up traffic or who he held up. An ambulance could be honking behind him for all he cared.

Steve deserves to be punished. He was impatient with his mother, often rude. He shrugged her off as if she was a dirty shirt. He hadn't realized she could disappear. Horvaths are like that. Maybe Paula doesn't mean to kill him. Maybe what that word *destiny* means, is that he deserves to die.

Chapter 21

Gone are the friendly fenders that led the way. Ahead, the road is a uniform grey. Beside her is Steve the navigator pressing her to go faster. She doesn't dare blink, her eyes so wide they burn like a stove top.

"Go faster."

Stiffening her calf muscles against the gas pedal, Paula obeys. She drives with her ears, with her heartbeat. They stagger forward. Faster. Get to the exit wherever it is.

"Three more kilometres," he says. "Go faster."

Threatening dusk coats the sky and still there's no exit. The borders of the highway are no longer visible. Paula's back aches. Darkness will soon sheath her in blindness. She drives on. Six days of it, a year, a century. The oppressive flare of an approaching vehicle bursts into her pupils. She blinks continuously, itchy tears gathering large and luminous in her eye sockets.

Steve jerks the steering wheel. "There's the exit. Go."

Through a watery glitter, Paula bumps onto the ramp. While he steers, she pulses at the gas. Gasping in unison Paula and the Malibu jerk onto the service road. Or do they? For just a second, her eyes shut.

"Hey–"

The Malibu screeches.

"God– don't stop here." Steve jiggles the steering wheel.

She turns her face and sees a bank of grass on the right side of the road. More driving. No end to it. The Malibu edges toward something– the grass or a barrier in the middle of the concrete or the rock side of a mountain. Paula slams on the brakes.

For a few minutes Paula falls asleep. Perhaps they both do. Her foot is clamped over the brake pedal, her toes cramped. She looks into the windshield. Oh. Her sight is better than it was in the apartment. Who'd have thought? Must be the drive. Maybe all these years, it was only a matter of exercising her pupils or retinas or some other part of her perverse eyes. The fortune teller was right.

She smiles at Steve's limp torso. "We're in Ontario, I'll bet."

He's crumpled in his corner, his face covered by the sleeve of his sweatshirt.

"Steve," she nudges him. "We crossed the border. We made it."

"We're in the middle of nowhere."

If she saw his reddened eyes or the streak of tears on his cheek, her optimism would vanish. She's lucky in that respect. Her situation allows her to view neither dirt nor sadness. Fear exists only in the bottom of her own heart. And probably, the fortune teller would tell her to swipe her palm over the left side of her breast and abolish it.

"You see any hotels around here?" Trees outline the vacant road. "I'm sure we'll find one if we drive a little further. I'll bet there's one just around the corner."

"You're not driving."

The neon lights of a pink motel beckon them. Steve brakes at the entrance of the parking lot and allows the Malibu to tilt in. He parks haphazardly, relieved just to stop. They're fifty meters from the exit.

At the desk, Steve rings the bell twice.

They hear him before they see a little young man scurry in from an enclosure behind the desk. "Welcome, welcome." His smile stretches his mustache into a horizontal line. "You would like to check in?"

Paula wants to ask the price of the room but is too tired to talk. Her eyes are closing.

"We have very clean rooms. Non-smoking? Yes?"

Steve signs them in.

"I am Khalif." The guy points to the plastic nameplate attached to his white shirt. "We have here almost a full-service motel. In the morning-time there is muffins and coffee at no charge. Please help yourself between six o'clock and ten o'clock any time." He points a finger to an alcove off the reception area. "Here are tables. And coffee all day."

The four walls are lined with sofas and mismatched dining chairs. A television lights up four melamine breakfast tables. It smells of evaporated coffee.

"Is there a restaurant?" Steve asks.

He's hungry. They'll have to eat their tuna and bread. If they start up with restaurants, they'll run out of money.

"Restaurant no, but room delivery we have. If you want sandwiches with salad on one side of the plate, yes we have. Please dial zero and I will bring it to you. I am faster than pizza delivery." He laughs. "Any time. Eighteen hours a day we have sandwiches. And if you want to try something delicious, we make the Egyptian national dish." He hands them each a paper menu. "Please see item ten. Very nutritious. Also very reasonable." He rubs his hands. "You will have room number two and please park in any convenient space number. Anything else I can do for you?"

"How about the key?"

Khalif bursts into laughter and insists on carrying their duffle bags to a room just adjacent to the reception. "You will be happy to know we have here a brand-new security lock." He slides a plastic card into a slot and swings the door open. "See," he announces. "Very clean."

The room, equipped with two double beds, one bedside table and a dresser topped with a TV, is indeed clean. It is also unadorned by either wall hangings or lamps and chairs, and entirely run down. They sit on their respective beds staring at the dark television.

"Are you hungry?"

Steve shrugs.

"I'm going to need a nap before we eat."

Paula slides between sheets so thin, they feel like Kleenex. One grunt and they'll rip. She tries to sleep but can't. Her legs twitch involuntarily. Cartoons squawk from the TV. She presses her legs together, keeps feeling the nerves ripple under the skin of her calves and finally sits up to face the television.

"We have peanut butter," she tells Steve. "I don't think I can handle the Egyptian national dish tonight."

He makes a face. "Last chance. We're leaving tomorrow."

They sleep until noon on Khalif's very-best-brand-new mattresses, order pita sandwiches, and watch TV. All afternoon it rains, a grey, soundless drizzle. Early in the evening they wander into the used furniture room. Games are set up on some of the tables– checkers, chess, a Monopoly board dotted with green hotels, an elaborate backgammon board inlaid with ivory.

Paula lifts the pot of free coffee and sniffs.

"I will make one fresh." A woman's teased black hair rises above a sofa. Bright red lipstick curves upward between a dimple and an ear. "My name is A-mi-ra." She sounds as if she studied English from British tapes.

Khalif sweeps in from the reception area. "She is our cook," he tells them. "Also my mother."

"Milk? Sugar?" Amira settles Paula into an armchair and pats the pile of magazines beside the chair. Mug in hand, Steve tours the room examining the games. He fingers the wooden pieces arranged on the backgammon board.

"Do you want a game?" Khalif says. "I need to break my studies."

"I don't know how to play."

"This tawla game is simple. I will teach you."

"Is it the Egyptian national game?"

Khalif shouts with laughter.

Amira keeps nodding and smiling. "It is raining, raining," she fusses. "In this country it is snowing or raining. Have a pillow for your head."

Paula feels obliged to order the national brown beans for dinner. Their plates arrive at one of the melamine tables, surrounded with chopped salads and pita and boiled eggs. She pokes her plastic fork at the puddle of oil topping the beans. Another night at the motel will be alright but really, they'd better get moving soon. Things are adding up. Beans in the can cost a dollar, even less when they're on special. But these, Steve gulps down.

They finish eating and tour the room as if sightseeing, as if the poster of the parliament buildings that decorates the wall is a museum piece. Steve gazes at the flickering images of a silent television– a basketball hoop, the bouncing figure of an athlete dribbling a ball across a gym floor, the plunge of an arm into a hoop.

"I play basketball sometimes," Khalif says. "In the summer we can play. And maybe I will not lose even if you are a giant." He throws back his head and laughs. "I play everything. And you?"

"I don't know."

"What would you like to play? Chess? Checkers?"

Steve glances at the board games.

"We will play whatever you want. Tawla you are interested, I see that. Yes?" He peers into Steve's downcast face. "So so easy. First you make up the board." Khalif picks out the tokens and lays them along the rows of narrow triangles that pattern the wood board. "See? Then you roll one dice and the biggest number goes first. Sit sit sit." He hands Steve a die. "Go. Roll. Okay never mind. You go first. What colour you want?"

"I don't know."

"Take white. Your side is on white. Okay, never mind." He rearranges the board. "There. Now you have black." He indicates the five black tokens that lie in a straight line on one of the triangles, picks up Steve's left hand and lays it beside the tokens. "This side is yours." Khalif pours the dice into Steve's hand and motions for him to roll. "Go go."

Steve glances at Paula standing behind him, then scatters the dice across the two extremities of the board.

"Two, three. See." Khalif slides some of the black tokens from one triangle to the next. He cups the dice between his palms, blows on them, and tosses. "Look. You count each one separately and you move out your pieces all the way around back to your side and then off."

So much bigger is Steve than Khalif, that he appears to be the man to Khalif's toddler. The chair under him seems dwarf like. On second glance, Steve's shiny cheeks and oversized clothing, his habit of leaning on his elbow, mouth in the cup of his hand as he speaks, give away his age. But never mind their differences, they're both school boys with nothing much to do than have fun.

Paula stands by the phone, her feet planted on the thin carpet. The utter hush in the room feels visible. Sharon will have called at least once. And her voice on the answering machine will be demanding, a little hysterical.

She dials.

As if she'd been waiting, Sharon answers on the first ring. "Mom?"

"Hi."

"Where are you? That was a long-distance ring."

"On a trip."

"What trip? You didn't tell me you were going anywhere. I've been calling you forever."

"Ontario."

"Ontario? What's in Ontario for God's sake?"

"University. For Steve."

"What are you talking about? He's fifteen. He didn't even finish high school."

"He wanted to visit the universities. We like to plan ahead."

There's no answer.

"Sharon?"

"That doesn't make sense. Who did you go with?"

"Steve."

"Yeah but– who drove?"

"There are about a million ways to get to Rome."

"You took the bus? To where? Toronto?"

All this time Paula's been standing by the telephone. She sits on the bed, resentful of her aching back. "I'm really tired, Sharon. I'll call you tomorrow."

"Don't hang up. Are you in Toronto or not?"

Paula fingers a magazine. She could look at a couple of recipes and let Sharon prattle on.

But the girl won't let go until Paula gives her the answer she wants. "I'm in Cornwall."

"There's no university there."

"Right. Well. Tomorrow we're going to Kingston."

"By bus?"

She doesn't want to hang up on Sharon.

"Mom? Don't tell me you let that little kid drive. Oh my God, how could you do that? He's just a kid."

"For God's sake. We took the bus. I'm not a total moron."

"You sure?"

"Of course I'm sure."

"What about school?"

"It's a holiday."

"What holiday?"

"A professional day and then we're taking a couple of extra days. I'll call you when I get home. Goodbye."

Chapter 22

Why anybody stays at the pink Excelsior Motel is a real good question. The old owners used to treat their clients to a complimentary trucker's breakfast of eggs and bacon with hash browns and gravy. For the copious breakfast alone, people in the transport business knew where to bunk when they roared west on the 401, just past Montreal. So as soon as the Roumys threw out breakfast along with the unbreakable beige crockery it was served on, the regulars went elsewhere. Renovations on the fifteen rooms and its aquamarine receptacle of a pool creaked forward and prices rose. Obliged by snow storms or sheer exhaustion, a few customers stay overnight and leave early the next day. Sometimes the Excelsior receives the overflow from the Journey's End. These guests also drive away after a night. Not one of them realizes that the motel is luxurious in its heart, if not in its appearance.

Every morning Khalif sets out the continental, basically coffee and grocery store muffins. He cheers the morning with his smile and makes sure everybody gets his, welcome-welcome greeting. It's his job to check people in and out but is primarily expected to study for the engineering school that he does not yet attend. His father, an unsmiling imprint of Khalif, runs the intricacies of the motel from a cellular telephone looped to his belt. Khalif's mother does not show her powdered cheeks until late morning, her sandwiches prepared and wrapped tightly in cellophane. Badri and Amira bought the motel expressly to ensure the prosperity of their only child.

Paula and Steve don't consciously decide to stay. They just don't leave. Three days of intermittent rain justifies their interlude. And while it should be dull at the Excelsior, dull enclosed by the claustrophobic furniture and the hush of the all-weather carpet, Khalif's peppery laugh won't allow it.

After his a.m. checkouts he pulls out a chair for Steve at the backgammon board. Though the wooden box is painted up with isosceles triangles along two sides, Steve feels like he's being subjected to an algebra lesson rather than geometry. Meaningless equations everywhere– tokens that go left and right, or are held in limbo on the centre of the board then returned to circulation on some whim– others that are removed due to scores that don't add up.

Khalif slaps the white pieces from one side of the board to the other. "Your turn."

"Yeah– I don't really feel like playing."

"Don't worry, you will learn. There's no money here. Go on, roll."

Steve looks at his feet. Giant shufflers that aren't doing their job. He admittedly became an expert at slamming the pieces on the board. But the algebra or geometry or whatever the heck it is, isn't any clearer after a night to dream on the game's meaning.

"Okay. We play a serious game?" Khalif's little mustache stretches across his face. "With toothpicks. We have a thousand ones to lose." He barks out a laugh. "Or win."

Steve lets Khalif shout out the numbers on his dice in some language he never heard before and within the hour can associate the words with the numbers, a feat Khalif calls genius. By dinner time he has learned how to line up his black tokens on the correct triangles. The heap of toothpicks on his side looks about equal to Khalif's.

Arms curved around the wooden board as if at the arcade, Steve chews on a toothpick. Most of his pieces are discarded on one side of the board. He's about to win. He feels it in his blood. He rolls a double three.

"Ah," Khalif shouts. "Three and three and three and three. You are a lucky man."

Steve clears his tokens so quickly, so instinctively, he's amazed at his own understanding of the moves. "Yesss– You owe me a few toothpicks."

Khalif bursts out laughing.

After swallowing two bran muffins and three coffees, Paula buys the paper with the intention of strengthening her eye muscles on the daily news. She lies on the bed much of the day snacking on bread and peanut butter and gets up only to use the toilet and to check on Steve in the games room. When the bread runs out she'll have to find a different alternative to the food problem but meanwhile, Steve is well fed on pita sandwiches. And she has all day to work on her eyesight as long as she doesn't snooze. She leans over the headlines, focuses and widens her eyes, closes them and widens them again. She makes the aerobic effort seven more times, tires, and turns on the TV.

Steve has five dollars in change that he hands over to Khalif almost immediately in a bad streak. Then he runs up a debt on scrap paper. At the end of the day Khalif annuls the debt with the crisscross of a pen. Steve charges soft drinks to room 2, passes one to Khalif, and challenges him to another game. A real one this time. They're having a great time. It's so practical to charge everything to the room.

Twice he wins. Most of the time Steve hunches over the backgammon board and doesn't know what to do next. The black checkers are useless. But when he trades for the lucky white ones, things get worse. Khalif only has to kiss the dice to win. And the guy's full of advice that doesn't work.

"You must roll freely and not think when you roll," he says. "And you must take a deep, deep breath and a deep, deep thought where to move those pieces."

Yeah, yeah. Deep, deep. But Steve doesn't know what to think about. No matter how deeply he considers his strategy, breathing till he feels dizzy, he always makes the wrong move.

"You know, If you are too tired, you will not to think." For the past six plus two hours, Khalif's been reiterating that for sure, Steve is too hungry or thirsty or too tired to concentrate. "Take your time, no need to go on. Really we can stop right now."

Steve needs to pee but is neither hungry nor thirsty though his mouth is dry.

Khalif raises his arms as if to surrender. "Let us fold the board and forget the whole thing. It's bedtime, yes?"

"No way. I just need a little break."

"Tomorrow is another day. We will start again."

"Give me five minutes. I'll be back."

Steve lets himself into the room. The television blares at Paula's open mouth as she sleeps. The back of his neck is wet. That morning he held one hundred even dollars, every cent gathered more slowly than a snail crawls. And now in the washroom he pulls out three fives and less than a dollar in change. He squeezes his pittance till his fingers cramp. By nature he's unlucky, by birth handicapped. But he has no intention of losing. He will not. He puts the cash back in his pocket, sits on the toilet, slips off his shoes and peels away the inner soles. A plush layer of money cushions his feet. That part is sacred. The green face of some old prime minister tells him not to exchange the money till there's nothing to eat but grass. And even then, eat the grass. He passes his hands under the cold water and wipes his face. There's a technique to the game that he hasn't yet mastered. Maybe he doesn't snap his wrist sharply enough as he rolls the dice. Or his concentration is poor. It will all straighten itself out in the next round. He knows it from the arcade. Practice practice. He lifts his head, opens the bathroom door, and peers at Paula's outstretched legs. She'll be thrilled when he doubles her money. She'll dance around the beds making loony faces. They'll rent a limo to get them out of here.

Steve creeps to the clothes rack, slips his hand under a pile of blankets, lowers the purse into his arms and carries it back to the toilet. Before he can close the door– less than a meter away, her arm shoots up and flaps down on the bed. He's been sleeping in the same room as Paula for three days but never knew how she slept. It'll be okay. Even if she wakes and stares right at him, she wouldn't have a clue. Silently, he closes the bathroom door.

He unclips the stiff black leather that Paula repeatedly threatens to trash. The smell of feet emanates from the bag. He reaches in. A bunch of receipts thicken the wallet. Except for a few cards it seems empty. But when he slides his fingers over every slot, he finds a wrinkled envelope so thin it's almost see-through and in it, a few twenties. He peers into the bottom of the purse. Scattered among the fluff of used tissues are five-dollar bills. He unzips the side pocket. Steve has never seen those before. The bills in his hand feel strange. Like the paper they're made of is young. He's tempted to take the entire stack of red fifties, takes only two and puts back the rest. He helps himself to a few fives and twenties, buckles the silver fastener and stashes the purse in its hideaway. Beside Paula's bed, he waits. His breath is quieter than hers. She sounds like a paper bag filling and collapsing. She curls into a question mark. If she had not moved, he would have kissed her on the cheek. He waits till she opens her eyes.

"Steve?"

"I'm here."

She smiles. "You want something to eat?"

"No thank you."

"Are you all right? Do you want to watch TV?" She's always offering something.

"I just came in for a second. I'm hanging out with Khalif."

"Oh yes. Are you having fun?"

He shrugs. "I guess so. He's teaching me all kinds of things."

Chapter 23

Once in a while Paula suggests that they leave though not yet, as long as they're comfortable and safe and as long as Steve also, says not yet. He's more energetic than he was at home, getting up before Paula to watch the early morning news. Over their breakfast muffins he appraises the world events with the stern judgment of an officer. In a few days he's gained years of maturity. He cleans up their paper plates and styrofoam cups and with business-like punctuality, goes straight to the backgammon board. He must reign like a king over that game.

Steve is not about to close the backgammon case. He keeps his nose lowered, sliding his tokens from one side to the next with Khalif-like agility. He isn't yet as tactical a player but will, like the turtle to the hare, surpass his buddy.

"I don't want to rob you anymore." Khalif pockets the dice in a motion of finality, watches Steve through his smiling eyelashes, then throws the dice back on the board with a grin that spreads his mustache into a thread. "Alright, alright, we play one more game and this time you be top winner."

"I was letting you win just to be nice."

"Another coke, yes?"

"I'll take a glass of water."

Khalif keeps standing him up to chips and drinks from the reception desk, and to his mother's sandwiches. Badri complains loudly that Khalif's studies are not progressing. While they're deep into their game, Badri strides in, clicking his keys.

"Khalif– why does the cash not balance?" The creases in his forehead eat up his face.

Khalif nods at the telephone. "We have a reservation for tomorrow."

Badri locks the till and leaves. They go on playing. After most of the lights are out, his aunt goes around the used furniture room sipping coffee. Now part of the household, she too, wears slippers. It's good for her to rest. She's told him that she's menopausal, whatever that is, and always tired. Between rounds at the backgammon board, Steve checks in. There are twenty- four channels for her to choose from and a pile of magazines by her bed. Sometimes as he opens the door he finds her face tipped close to the page of a magazine. He doesn't know what she stares at, probably not the clothing that was fashionable three years earlier. Once she asked him to read the recipes: some kind of grilled chicken thing with tarragon, layer cakes they both slurped over, vegetable casseroles that he made her promise never to cook. She's especially interested in children, how to feed them and solve their behavioural problems. He sits beside the bed and reads a whole lot of articles about how to give them self-esteem. She calls his reading voice distinguished. She loves when he reads and always asks what she can get him when really– he's getting stuff for her– a coffee, a sandwich, a fresh magazine, anything.

And when the blanket is tucked under Paula's chin and small rumbles escape from her mouth, Steve searches for bills and change in every compartment of her purse, in Paula's coat pockets and in the pants that hang like water-logged spaghetti over a wire hanger.

Paula doesn't care about money. If she did, she'd line the bills up neatly in her wallet. He tries to avoid the wallet out of respect for wallets in general. Her's is made of some kind of weepy leather that needs ironing just to keep it straight. It doesn't really matter. He'll buy her a new one. In a couple of days or maybe even in an hour, he'll bring her such a fortune, she'll be jumping around like crazy. All he needs is a little confidence. And maybe more self-esteem. And definitely luck. He finds one lone copper on the closet floor. Rubbing it between his palms, he mutters, Luck, luck, luck, luck– waits for the noise in his head to stop, and takes the last remaining bills out of the wallet.

Before Paula understands what has jarred her awake, she scrambles to the door, then to the ringing telephone. It's too late, almost midnight, for any kind of phone call except the emergency kind. Something happened to Sharon or to Steve or it's the police coming to take her away. She knocks the receiver off its cradle and answers to some guy–

Are you out of your mind?– you took that car– they could put you in jail for this– you could have killed him– the Dumonts are–

Shelly, who else, screaming louder than a bomb on a skyscraper. She drops the receiver on the carpet and steps on it.

"Paula? Paula, answer me!" He sounds like his own howling dog.

She finally takes her heel off the receiver and interrupts. "What are you screaming for?"

"Do you know what I've been doing for the past three days? What do you think I've been doing?"

"How should I know."

"I called every single hole-in-the-wall hotel from here to Cornwall. You're lucky Paula. You're the luckiest woman on the face of the earth, is all I can say. In the next hour if I didn't find you, I'd have been on the phone with the police. And then where would you be?" He pauses for the non-answer. "You want to know where? I'll tell you where."

"Don't bother."

"In jail. That's where. Or in a psychiatric hospital. Paula, I'm not joking."

"Who's laughing?"

"You don't deserve it but I'm going to save your ass. Sharon and I are coming to get you. Tomorrow morning. Early. Save us some breakfast." The telephone clicks.

As ordered, she doesn't move. Not at first. A headache is pulling her right eye down to her shoulder. The distant clink-clink of Badri's keys will soon announce midnight. She lies down, her head angled on the pillow. Midnight and bedtime and the tick of her watch by her ear, she watches the blank ceiling and waits for Steve.

Steve eventually bustles in announcing that he won.

"Steve?"

"What?" He goes to the bathroom and closes the door.

"We have to go."

The toilet flushes. Water spurts from the faucet. He's brushing his teeth, ignoring her, she's sure. She leans against the door till he opens it, his hands dripping, his face moist.

"Did you hear me?"

"What?"

"Tomorrow we're leaving."

"I'm not ready."

"I thought you wanted to go west."

"Yeah. As soon as I'm ready." He kicks off his shoes, gets into bed fully dressed, and covers his dewy face with the blanket.

"We can find a school for you in Cornwall."

"I'm not living in Cornwall."

"Khalif can visit."

"And I'm not going to school."

Paula wrings her hands. She'd have smacked him if she wasn't clinging to her fingers. He's like his father. Rock-headed. Intractable. Alright, not always. No child should suffer the way he has. And he's been sweet these last few days of gathering up one's strength. But he's insatiable. For five days he's done nothing but play silly games. He's a fifteen-year-old-two-year-old and it has to stop.

Paula hits the bell. After an hour or hours or at least a very long minute, Badri reaches the reception desk in his bedroom slippers.

"You will be leaving us. I'm so sorry. You have become part of the family. If you would like to go back to your room, very comfortable, I will deliver the bill under your door. You did not have to come all the way here for a little bill."

"I'll wait."

He taps at the keyboard, his face scrunched. Tap. Tap tap. Tap. One finger at a time. Eventually he draws out an invoice from the printer. He folds it three times, slides it into an envelope and presents it to Paula.

What a huge flourish for such miniature lettering.

"What's the damage?"

Stretching his mouth, Badri indicates the bill.

"I can't see what it says. What's the total?" Paula hears a figure that makes her sorry to have asked. "Isn't it seventy-nine dollars a day?"

"Yes Madam. But here is a nice discount. Four dollars off every day. Seventy-five dollars instead of seventy-nine."

"Then you made a mistake. It should be three-hundred-and-seventy-five dollars plus a few sandwiches."

"Yes Madam. And tax. And one long distance telephone call. A grand total of six hundred five dollars. I will scratch away the cents." He scribbles on the bill and hands it back to her.

His curved mouth leaves her speechless.

The coffee pot is washed and empty. Paula would have taken a cup, the only free thing in that motel, and then would not be able to sleep. She's not going to sleep anyway. How many sandwiches could they have eaten?

"I'll pay in the morning."

"Of course, Madam. We will be happy to accept all the credit cards."

The hotel room smells of fake pine. Her problem is that she never complains about anything. Steve lifts his torso from his nest of blankets, aims the remote control at the television and turns it on. He'll flip from channel to channel till he drops.

Paula tugs her purse from the luggage rack, sits on the toilet and rifles through the purse. She has enough cash for the room bill but not much more. On the fifteenth of every month, Shelly deposits money into her account. If they're careful, they'll manage till then.

The money is in there somewhere. Paula has a system. The fives she leaves loose in the bottom of the purse. Ten dollar bills she keeps in the front of the wallet and in the back slot, the twenties. The zipper pocket of the purse holds the fifties. She's never had anything larger, never thought to need it.

The wallet feels limp. She pulls out the usual cards– her single credit card, her medicare, a most important card for collecting points from the pharmacy, all laid out exactly where they belong. She finds also a bunch of grocery bills, stamps, bus tickets, bits of paper. But there is no cash in the wallet or in her purse. Not even change. Not a cent. A shutout panic rises in her chest. She dumps the contents of the purse onto the tiles. Plenty of dirty Kleenex litter the floor, plenty more paper, none of it money. A slice of hardened bread wrapped in a napkin drops out. At least they won't starve to death.

She gulps back a stinging glob of acid, takes down her pants and sits on the toilet to think. Paula has the propensity to hide things then forgets where she put them. Another fault of menopause. The money is somewhere. In one of her deep pockets, probably. Of course. Foolish to leave money in a purse. In the alcove where the clothes hang she examines the pockets of her jacket, her pants. Steve turns off the TV, lays a pillow over his head and goes to sleep. Not bothering to wait for the silence of his sleep, Paula passes her hand between her mattress and box spring, then his. She shakes out her shoes and sweaters, unrolls her socks, her underpants.

Maybe the money never really existed. She remembers wanting to go to the bank but doesn't remember standing in front of a teller. Yes, she distributed cash throughout the purse but can't say for sure which week she did that. But– there was a pack of bills in there when she bought breakfast at the Tim Hortons. Wasn't there? Leaning against the wall she circles the room till she's back at the bathroom. She looks around. Somebody was here. The cleaning lady with her cart of white sheets and towels has the key. They all have the key. There's nowhere to hide anything. There's nowhere to hide yourself. She shivers and crawls into bed and for a while, rolls around in it. And to pay by credit card? So they could send the bill to an empty house for who else but Shelly to find? No. There are other solutions.

Sometime in the night, Steve goes to the toilet and when she hears, she sits up. "Steve?"

"What?"

"I need your help."

"What?"

"I want to write a note to the hotel. I don't want them to think that I'm the thief around here." She hears him breathe and regrets opening her mouth. "Never mind. Go back to bed."

He doesn't need to know. In the morning she'll write her own note.

Paula races through her sleep with her teeth clenched over incoherent phrases of outrage. She should have called the police the minute she knew she was robbed. It would have calmed her to report the crime. But if she did that, she would have to read and sign papers. She would have to drive to the precinct behind the police car. And then they'd want to know why in the world she'd been staying at the Excelsior Motel with a schoolboy.

Day glints behind the curtains. Time to go.

"Steve, wake up." She turns the TV on just for the noise, dresses in the bathroom and loads her suitcase. "Steve– we have to leave before Shelly gets here."

She sits on her bed with a pen poised over a dismantled envelope, a stiff pad of folded newspaper under it. In this motel, they don't even give you note paper, much less a table to sit at. She applies the point of her pen to the envelope. What to write? She settles on her brain's number one refrain: *We owe you nothing*! *You have robbed us!*

"Steve–"

He doesn't stir.

On a full sheet of paper, she'd have explained how she left her purse in their lousy room in all trust and innocence and was taken advantage of. She considers listing a lawyerly timekeeping of the minutes she spent in and out of the room but can't remember the actual record. She holds the paper to her face. The writing looks slanted and squishy and huge all at once. She isn't even sure her writing is actually on the envelope. And if parts of her dishevelled words landed dismembered on the newspaper, her message would not be understood.

"Steve, wake up. I need your help. Hey–" She crushes the envelope and tosses it at him. "Steve," she shouts.

She goes to the bathroom and pees. They could leave and nobody would know. No need to hand over a note. That Badri isn't stupid. He knows perfectly well what's happening in his hotel. And if Steve wants to, he could even fetch the coffee and muffins and smile and be friendly and she'll wait for him in the car ready to take off. It'll take the hotel people hours to figure it out.

"Steve?" Paula stands at the side of his bed. Only then does she realize how completely still it is. She hears the drip of the faucet and nothing else. A voice in her head begins to scream– he's not breathing he's not– she pulls off the blanket and shakes it like a spray can. He isn't there. They've taken him, they– she drops the blanket. Shush. Don't be ridiculous. She counts downwards till the stupid voice in her head shuts off and her breath is even. A big boy like that wouldn't be kidnapped. He's at the backgammon board, obsessed with it. It's the only thing that gets him up in the morning. Paula turns out of the room and comes right back in. She'll load up the car first. She grabs her suitcase and heads out the side door at the end of the hall.

On the outer limits of the lot, the Malibu is not so much parked, as abandoned. Paula crisscrosses from one car to the other looking into every window. None of the four vehicles look like the Malibu even though the upholstery of all of them is as ineffably beige. Probably she passed it without knowing. Five solid days indoors and a variance of light could easily alter what something looks like. In the close sunlight every car is black until she gets right up to it. The vehicles seem smaller than the Malibu. Or much bigger and either too square or too oval. Oh– she's been so stupid. All she has to do is try the key. She reaches for it and remembers that the lucky horseshoe key is beside Steve at the backgammon board, with him wherever he goes.

She stands at the edge of the concrete and stares at the flat rectangle that is the Excelsior, its rusted marquee thrust over the door that dares her to enter. She cups her hands around her mouth. "Steve, Steve–"

The sound of her voice ricochets into the wind. She closes her eyes, pictures him bent over the triangles and tokens and wills him to jump away from the table and swing through the double glass doors, his red jacket snug over his shoulders– *Here I am, Aunt Paula, I'm ready. Let's go.*

Spotlights glow at her feet. Nobody's in sight. Straight ahead, the pink mortar of the Excelsior Motel beckons. The evergreen shrubs on either side of the doors seem to puff out like blowup beach balls as she bursts past them into the breakfast room. "Steve?" She peers at the tables.

"He was asking where is Walmart. I think he is there."

Paula hears Khalif before realizing that he's facing her.

"I keep telling him to take a walk, take a break. Too much sitting. Even when you are having fun it could be boring at the motel."

"Where is Walmart?"

"At the next exit. Not so far."

"He took the car?"

"He did not tell you? There is only one way to go." He takes her hand and shakes it. "Take a coffee. Sit down. I will get it for you. Milk and sugar? And a bran muffin?"

He's a nice boy even if he's the thief.

"When did he leave?"

"Five minutes, maybe." Khalif hands her a Styrofoam cup.

Paula gulps down the lukewarm coffee, stuffs the empty cup in her pocket and runs across the parking lot.

A gardener lifts a rake of tangled grass toward the highway. "It's a skinny boy you're looking for? Tree tall, brain still small? I told him," He pulls down the brim of his white cap, "Get off the road, boy. You're about to get yourself killed. Didn't hear me. Didn't even try."

Chapter 24

Guided by a curb that leads to the black tarmac, she runs. Her purse flaps at her side. Her knees ache. With every step, she grunts his name. Can't be too far. She runs. And soon, a few meters down the service road, she's on the Malibu's bumper. Yes, yes, he hears her. He's waiting for her.

"Steve, I'm coming."

She flings open the passenger door, apologizes. Wrong car. Except that she recognizes the smell. She pats the drooping upholstery and carefully, clambers in. Under her butt, she feels Oscar's lucky keys.

"Steve?"

Paula knows he isn't there but she continues to palpate the dry surfaces of the car. When his presence refuses to take shape, she grabs the only thing she finds, Sharon's folded eyeglasses from the dashboard, ready to illuminate the way. She slides over the centre hump into the driver's seat, perches the glasses on her nose and gazes through the windshield at the long grey dunes that lie between the sky and the ground.

The Excelsior is an isolated planet. Not too many cars pass the motel. But if the Walmart is close by, so is the traffic. She rolls down the windows. Better to see you with my dear. Better to hear you with. In one abrupt twist of her wrist, she turns on the ignition and rams the gear shift back and forth till it locks. The car jerks backwards. She hits the brakes, her heart slamming louder than the screech of the car. Yes– but she knows what to do next. She adjusts the gear and feels the car lurch. One at a time she takes her hands off the steering wheel and lets them cool. She lifts her foot gradually off the brake and the Malibu advances.

Alright.

Go.

She's not afraid to drive. As long as she keeps an eye on the grass strip beside the highway and her hands don't tremble too much, the car remains straight except for when it tilts briefly into the slope of the ditch. Steve will be trudging beyond the ditch, not as fast as a car, even with his long legs. Every few meters she squeezes on the brakes and thrusts her head out the window to call. When his name elicits nothing more than offended honks and chilli on her face, she toes the gas pedal and bumps onward. Mostly she doesn't lean into the ditch. On her right, the green strip of lawn guides her. She sees it well and along with that, a pencil line of white that is likely the sky above or beyond the green path, a river or maybe a field. Or if not that, the sea itself.

The Malibu shakes as vehicles speed by. Amidst the horns and her drumming heart, she listens for Steve's tramping feet. Her vision refuses to cooperate and she worries that in one split second, she'll miss him. There's too much to do, all the seeing and listening and pressing of pedals and jiggling of the steering wheel to really be afraid. She keeps calling, sees his long torso flit on the tarmac then disappears. It's either him or a tree or the limb of a tree or maybe a cardboard car carried by the wind. Sweat drips down her sides. Her face is tight with the effort of seeing.

At a clip, Steve walks faster than she drives. He glances backwards and sees her bounce onto the strip that separates her from the ditch. She knows what he's done, wants to get him. He runs faster but soon, feels the heat of the car against his legs. The Malibu is like Paula herself, warm and far too close. Its toothy front fenders are bared. She loves him. She loves him. Horvaths don't call the police even if they can. She'll chase him till the black tires pin him to the ground, till he's pinched between rubber and concrete. Till he howls. She loves him. She won't let anybody know he's a thief. She'll kill him first.

She's driving on three wheels. Each time he looks, she's about to tumble. He doesn't want her to die but doesn't know how to stop her. She'll be alright. For her, things always work out. She has Sharon and Shelly to fix things. He doesn't have her kind of luck. His only hope is to run.

Paula leans out the window calling his name.

"Hey, stop that," he tells her.

He dashes into the culvert, trips, picks himself up and climbs into the pine woods on the other side. He looks back though he knows he should not.

Here and there, here and there like a firefly on a green passage, a sliver of red glints. It grows larger, billowing in the wind.

"Steve," Paula shouts. She sticks her arm out the window. "Steve!"

The steering wheel swings toward the red jacket. The Malibu swings with the steering wheel. Its nose dips into the ravine. The car shivers. Like a fish on a hook, it flips. The crash reverberates through the valley.

*

He should have run till his stomach hurt, till he could not breathe. But he looked back and just as he did, the Malibu sprang into the ditch. Over and over it turned. The upended turtle crashed against the walls of the culvert and shuddered. Creaking, the door swung open.

She hangs by her seat belt, her arms and legs dangling. She's silent, looks as gone as the others. Death arrives too fast to let you think. He opens his mouth but is not free to scream. The silence that was placed in his heart since the death of his parents seals his mouth. He feels arms around him and doesn't know that they are his.

Chapter 25

Paula lies in room 2's familiar bed, a warm compress on her forehead. The skin between her breastbone and her right shoulder is purple. She can move her left fingers and most of her right. There's no need to move. Her home is in this bed.

Badri wants her in a hospital, but neither she nor the man who drove up to join her would hear about it. The man brought Mrs. Horvath's daughter and she's the one who clucks and worries and applies the compresses. She feeds her mother chicken broth that Amira cooks specially for them and covers her in extra blankets that Badri is expected to supply.

What part of Mrs. Horvath's family these people are, is not too clear. It looks like Mrs. Horvath ran away with her boy, leaving behind the other two. Even though he doesn't look mean, there surely is a very good reason to run away from that man. His hands are girlie soft maybe from all the time spent clinging to his telephone. And he has some kind of a girl's name. There's a worrisome tolerance of homosexuals among Canadians. But why on earth would a mother leave behind this silken-haired daughter? The only semblance of a loving family comes from the wide grey eyes of this girl.

Badri wrings his hands. He wants Paula to get better very fast. He wants them all out. Without asking permission, that man Shelly had the car pulled out of the ditch with a hook and a chain and towed back to the Excelsior. In the fall Badri had the parking lot repaved. And with her own hands, Amira planted at the front entrance of the motel the kind of shrub that stays green all winter long. She made the Excelsior look even better than its name, especially when the green bushes flicker like flags against the pink stucco. Now that the wrecked car's dislocated fenders litter the parking, their motel looks like a garbage depot.

Badri beckons to Khalif. "You go get a small bouquet for room 2. Then I will tell you what to say."

Paula's face on the pillow is pale blue and broader than before the accident.

Khalif holds up the daisies. "Mrs. Horvath. You are feeling alright?"

Under the shag of grey hair, her eyes blink. "Okay."

"My parents send you flowers and a little bit of our national brown beans for dinner, compliments of the house." He sloshes a microwave container in front of her face. "Very lemony."

"Thank you." Her face creases. "It hurts to smile."

"If you need to go to the hospital, I would be happy to drive you. Maybe you have broken bones?"

She lifts one arm, drops it on the bed, and does the same with the other. "No. Just bruised."

"That is wonderful."

Steve watches TV from the other bed. He does not once turn to look at Khalif. Just to be nice, Khalif would have offered to play a game with Steve and not a betting game. But he's been accepted to Engineering and needs to study.

Khalif lets his smile pause on Mrs. Horvath's daughter and at every corner of the room before stopping on Paula's husband. "Mr. Horvath–"

"Sheldon Shapiro." The man holds out his hand.

"Mr. Shapiro–" So. They are not married.

"Everybody calls me Shelly."

"Mr. Shelly, I am happy to meet you."

The man laughs.

"Mr. Shelly, my father has a membership with the CAA, Canadian Automobile Association. You know them?"

For some reason, Mr. Shelly Shapiro laughs.

"He would be happy to ask them to tow Mrs. Horvath's car to a good repair station."

"You think it's worth repairing?"

Khalif does not know if the question is for him.

"It would probably cost a zillion dollars to repair that carcass. Stevie, what do you think?"

Steve hunches closer to the television.

"Dad, we can discuss that later," the girl says.

"I am sure," Khalif says, "that it would not cost too much at a reputable station. And if the repairs are made very soon, it would be better for the bodywork and cheaper too. A little scratching you can paint and no one will know."

"We need some time to think about it," the daughter says.

"When the car is fixed, you can sell it. The way it is now, nobody will take it."

Again Shelly laughs. Everything is funny to him. "Now there's a good idea."

"We're not ready to take any decisions," the daughter says.

Khalif nods and bows his head. "Good health," he tells them.

His father is waiting in the kitchen. "Well?"

"He is not her husband. And he is a Jew."

"How do you know?"

"I know that name, Shapiro."

"They are everywhere."

They are even at the university in the Department of Engineering.

Amira clucks her tongue. Wearing surgical gloves to protect her red nail lacquer, she leans against the counter stuffing pita breads with cheese and olives.

"Maybe she ran away without paying," Khalif says.

"They are Jews, what do you expect," Badri says.

"No," Amira says. "She had to find the boy. He's the one who ran away."

"There is no order in that house. Even if they pay the final bill, they can still leave with all the blankets."

"They are guests with us. They will pay," Amira says.

The Roumys have no choice but to keep an eye on their tenants. Amira fills the sandwiches generously and offers Paula's people a plate of pastries from her own kitchen. She prays for them often. They have a home in Montreal to go to but for some reason, are troubled by it. To ward away the evil eye, she lights a bowl of incense and lifting it above her head, circles the tight enclosures of the living room and kitchen while the smoke wafts to the ceiling.

"What a stink," Badri complains.

"This stink will protect us." Amira waves the fumes in the direction of room 2. "And them too."

Amira prays harder for Steve than for the others. The boy slips in and out of the reception area buying chips and gum. He wants to play backgammon but Badri took away all the games.

He took away Khalif too. There is a library in Cornwall for students to go to. Steve keeps a sullen eye on the breakfast room TV no matter what's on. Whenever she has a moment, Amira sits beside him and during the commercials, asks a few questions. Steve says that they will be leaving soon and that his grandparents are waiting for him.

That the family in unison is anxious about him is a very good sign. On the journey home, his lemon face will turn sweet knowing that soon his grandparents will throw all their kisses at him.

Two days later the wrecked car is towed out of the parking without their intervention. Shapiro pays the bill and the family drives off in Shapiro's BMW.

"Didn't I tell you?" Amira says. "And I will tell you something else. Such a nice car, and such a big tip, goes with a very nice home."

Part 4
The Second Sight

Chapter 26

A new bedspread lies on the mattress. From the top of a metal desk, the vacant face of a computer stares at the giant race cars printed horizontally on the fabric. His grandmother fixed the room up for him though really, it's for a three-year-old and for storage. Along the perimeter of the room are bookshelves crammed with household cleansers and light bulbs toilet paper, batteries and canned goods, curtain hooks, lamp ballasts, jars of pickles and jam, empty jars and plastic containers, cardboard boxes filled with stuff of no apparent purpose. The windows are partially blocked by a folded card table. In front of the table, two mismatched chairs wait for an upholstery hammer. From the apertures in the window, Steve can see the domineering arms of a maple tree and nothing else.

He stands between the desk and the bed on a spot just large enough for his feet and takes a breath. There's no choice but to breathe.

The room that houses nothing but miscellany had been his mother's. Still is. Her scent clings to the walls. He gulps, hoping that the neutral odour of absolutely nothing will enter his nostrils. But her nearly palpable essence remains. He presses his nose to a spot of wallpaper above the computer and sniffs. There it is, lanolin, vaguely musky. Louise must have smoothed her cream-soft hands on the wallpaper, on everything. No way to mask it. He flops on the short bed, his feet hanging over the edge. The minute he moves out he'll get himself a king-sized bed. His own place will smell of laundry detergent.

Within a day of Steve's arrival in Brossard, the entire family celebrates with white cake and welcome-home speeches. They act as if he'd been in Timbuktu. Julie tucks a knitted pot holder around his neck and tells him that she made the scarf specially for him. Between bites of cake, she offers him stilted English words that come from the same arcane trunk as her knitting.

While they sip chamomile in the dining room, Luc Richard knocks and walks in.

Everybody applauds. Steve's Aunt Celine stands with her arms raised. His grandmother shouts, Bravo, and immediately slices up more cake. They're all smiling. Luc shades his eyes laughs and says that he only wrote a letter. He shakes Steve's hand. *"Bienvenue, mon cher."* Then proceeds to tell him that good luck will from then on, always follow him.

Réal taps the space on the couch beside him. *"Assis toi."* He blows his nose, tucks the tissue into his pocket and reverses the cheerful arch of his mouth into mournfulness. If Steve wants to start in a new school, he'll have to pass the exams from the old one. Luc has been in touch with the last principal. What's his name? Rickie? Summer school exams are available for a second chance. Otherwise, Steve will have to spend another year in the tenth grade.

"I'm not doing any of it." He speaks in English fast enough for his grandfather not to understand, not that he cares. "The minute I'm sixteen I'm outa there."

Réal holds up his hands. "Slow I understan' everyting. *Qu'est-ta-dit?*"

"I-do-not-like-school."

Réal grins. His oversized teeth jut over his lip. "Okay. Maybe it is you don' like de school but *si tu* learn good, you go *à l'université*. You go get you good job."

Steve rolls his eyes.

"*Mon gars, t'as pas l'choix.*" He waits for his grandson to speak. He knows about those kids. His church group works with troubled youth. The kids either talk too much or don't say a word. You have to tell them what to do, make them do it and let them think it's their idea. He begins to sing. His mother's folk songs often creep into his head and repeat themselves as if he's a baby still needing to be soothed. He sings the refrain of a hunting song twice and is about to begin again when Steve covers his ears. Réal blows out a whistle to stop the song. "Steve, *que veux-tu faire dans ta vie?*"

Steve shrugs.

Those kids all think they can make a living without learning anything. "You tink de money dey grow on tree?"

"I have money."

"Yeah? One million maybe? What you gonna be? Taxi driver?"

"No."

"Den you better finish de school. You noting widout de school. Look you mudder. She learn noting. She go pick dat Horvat." He spits the name and falls quiet. He places his hand on the taut nape of his grandson's neck. "Steve. *Ecoutes moi. Tu va etudier avec ton Oncle Marc. Il va-t'faire passer tes examins.*"

Exams. That's all they care about.

In a room of no privacy, there isn't a safe place to keep your money. His mother's voice tells him, *écoute-mot, écoute-moi.* The call is so loud and silent, it could only have come from her final note, the one that doesn't exist for him to hear. The demand that he listen up, seeps hoarsely from the tightly stacked books of his mother's childhood or maybe from the leaking batting of the two sobbing chairs. The chairs watch him unrelentingly. When he just can't stand it, he turns up his radio and blasts them.

Shut up, damn it.

He sound-blasts the insistent voice and can again breathe. The money crammed in his pocket is grimy and damp. Where to hide it gives him a headache. His grandparents invade the room at every opportunity– his grandmother with piles of clean socks and underwear, shirts and pants sized just for Steve. And with her weekly bucket and mop, her daily dust cloths, her usual demand for some jar or container. And now his grandfather who without knocking, ambles in for part two of the philosophical discourse that will lead to Steve's betterment.

Réal sits on the bed and pats the space beside him. Above Réal's jutting teeth is a lip that curves in all-encompassing optimism. Because his mother's *ecoute-moi* reverberates in this room, Steve sits close and listens. When Réal is through telling him how well he will succeed in school and ruffles his hair and leaves, Steve picks through a couple of volumes of his mother's old books. Most are faded by the sun, their spines barely touched. Only one has been read and if not read, coloured in and torn. He separates his money into two equal parts, opens the red spine of *Les Malheurs de Sophie,* and places one part for himself on page fifty, and the other for Paula on page one hundred. He closes the book, tucks it into the shelf and lies back on his bed. He promised his grandfather that he would concentrate. He's to learn a whole bunch of things. The peeling upholstery of the bedraggled chairs wink at him. Furniture's not cheap. He rolls off the bed, goes back to the desiccated volume of *Malheurs de Sophie* and redistributes the bills. Five dollars for Paula, the rest for him. He'll make a few more dollars and pay her back with interest.

To help with his summer school exams, Steve's Oncle Marc comes over with Julie twice a week and as the teens sit in front of their open books making faces at one another, Réal and Marc read. Every so often one of the adults raises his eyes till they lower theirs. Julie's English improves and Steve fails his first practice exam in French grammar, not that it matters in Ontario or British Columbia or another part of the world.

Julie stops coming and Oncle Marc stops reading. He presents his nephew with a series of exercise books that Steve is expected to fill up line by line, answering every question correctly. Sure enough, Steve's brain becomes more nimble. As his uncle explains the intricacies of grammar, Steve fills his mind with images of backgammon boards. He rolls the dice and slams the pieces from left to right winning every game. Pockets bulging, he drives himself to the edge of the ocean. Water licks the tires of a super-fast convertible– his car, a car that gleams red in the sun.

His uncle knocks on his head. "*Es-tu la*?"

He's right here, stuck at this dining table.

"You're almost sixteen. Do you want to learn to drive? *Parce que ça-t'prendra des leçons*." Apart from the accent, his uncle speaks English almost perfectly. He graduated from university and keeps taking courses on bicycle mechanics and other stuff. He studies all the time, with teachers and without. "Even if you think you know how to drive, they will not give you a license without the lessons. *Hein Père*?"

Réal nods.

"If you do not know how to study mathematics you will not know how to study to drive.

So you will not take driving lessons until you pass your exams. *Comprends-tu?*"

Ya. He gets it. He turns to the broad wood surface of the table and crams his head with useless information.

Whenever he thinks nobody will notice, Steve unlatches the wood doors of an old brick hangar behind the house where the crippled Malibu waits. He gets into the car and turns it on. Battered ugly by Paula, it still functions. He takes deep breaths of gas wondering how long it takes for carbon monoxide to put you to sleep. He switches the key on and off. They say you don't need too much of that stuff.

Carbon monoxide death is apparently not painful though it isn't pain that bothers him. It's the question of what happens when it's over. He believes in death after death– no heaven no hell, no angels or fire. But if you believe in nothing, where do you end up? He can't see himself disappearing. If the car and garage and the tree in the front yard are still here and he is not, then he might still be around, maybe floating in some white blankness. Or in a black one. Something that feels like an ocean or maybe cotton balls. Not that it would matter to anybody but him. To shake the thought of his deadness away, he imagines himself swimming in a gluey kind of space. Maybe naked, but not invisible. Safer to be suspended in glue than to be nowhere.

Gasping from his struggle with glue, he jumps out of the car and slams the door.

License or no license, he'd drive away from that cavern of a garage if not for his mother's voice. She makes him lose his confidence. Her murmuring chases him to every corner of the house. For some unfathomable reason, her lanolin scent pursues him into the car too. Her voice, resonating like from the bottom of a plastic container sounds thunderous even when he plugs up his ears. He's obliged to answer every one of her absurd questions.

–I see you at the wheel but the axle of the car is broken. You– something– is broken.

–You're wrong. I'm not going anywhere.

Too deep in the Tupperware, she never hears.

–You'd better not get any ideas. Your *grandmaman* and *grandpapa* are devoting their lives to you. In their old age! You better work hard.

–I am.

–All you do is hide under your bed.

–What are you talking about? I never go under the bed.

–What a lie.

The hot breath of her incredulous laughter makes him snatch at his face.

–I don't care what you think. I'm leaving this place. As soon as I get my license I'm getting a job.

–You think you can sell plastic boxes better than me?

Fuck, fuck, fuck, he screams from his cramped gut.

She doesn't let him think. A month earlier he'd have made some kind of move. But now, she's got him harnessed so tightly he can't budge. If the little government paper giving him permission to drive shuts her up, then fine. He'll get his permit, then get out. One huge jump out.

Five days a week it's the same morning bustle– the minty flavour of toothpaste– a breakfast of oatmeal and raisins– dishes cleared promptly at eight– books and notebooks held in his grandmother's freckled arms– pens and pencils on the table in front of his chair– the look on his grandfather's face that says, get to it. Steve sits behind his fortress of books more prepared to hide than do battle. His mother knows him well.

On the first day of the exams, too early for anyone in their right mind to wake up, his grandmother steps up to his bedside and hands him an ironed t-shirt.

"*Vites. Laves toi et habilles toi.*"

He doesn't remember washing and dressing. As his grandfather drives him to some school he never heard of, he keeps swallowing back oatmeal.

At the door of a gym, a woman crosses his name off a list, hands him pencils and a notebook and points her sagging chin at a desk. Réal claps him on the back and leaves. The other failures, a crew of baggy shirts and flip-flops, fill up row on row of desks. He stares at the sleeve crease of his white t-shirt till a bell rings and the hand of one of the invigilators stiffens into a stop sign. The lady with the sagging chin clicks through the aisles placing the exams face down on each desk. At the next ding-dong, the students turn over their exams.

Steve grips his sharpened pencil. Saggy chin walks by twice and stops at the desk one over from his. The arms of the boy at the desk are crossed, his exam untouched. So– that's another choice. Saggy chin looks at her watch and goes to the door. Two men march in, go straight to the boy who's not writing and taking him by the elbows, escort him out. The boy's Fuck You t-shirt passes through the door. His heart thrumming, Steve faces the questions that dare him to choose correctly. His pencil on the page, he answers them all.

The rest of the summer Steve scrounges a few bucks cutting grass and washing cars. He gets to the mail before his grandparents and when the envelope from the department of education drops through the slot, he files it beside his mother's baby books. As the days pass, he takes the mail– mostly junk– off the floor and puts it on the small table by the door. His grandparents talk about the important letter without letting up. He helps Réal empty the pool and rakes up crumpled yellow leaves into heaps. He counts his money. His grandparents talk about calling the Ministry of Education but who exactly should you address? They look at each other. His grandfather picks up the phone book. Mariette says, "No, something's wrong. Let's call Luc."

Steve plucks the envelope from the bookshelf and mixes it with the pile of mail. "Here it is. You just didn't see it."

The three of them sit on the porch. His grandfather unfolds the letter and hands it to him without looking.

"*Alors*?" Mariette says.

The blue and white flag of Quebec is at the top of the page. Steve is afraid to look at the list of marks. A gust of wind blows at the paper. He glances at the block of red on one side of the page and thrusts the official letter at his grandfather. Mostly he failed. It's what he wanted. But he doesn't know what he wanted.

His grandfather's teeth seem huge. "*Bonne nouvelle, ma chere.*"

Mariette beams.

No way. They don't know how to read. He couldn't have passed.

"The only test you failed," his grandfather says, "is *l'Histoire du Québec.*"

Doesn't make sense that his grandfather is smiling. He tries to remember what he learned about History– nothing that he could write on the exam.

"Don't worry too much about every little thing," *Oncle* Marc told him. "Some things you must remember all your life. Some things you remember only till you write your exam. Then you can forget them. There is no room in your brain for everything."

Well there isn't. He flicks the sheet of marks in the air and watches it land in the middle of the lawn.

Mariette makes a pie, dusts the furniture, and tells Steve to dress decently. Decent means shoes and socks and a button-down shirt well tucked into his pants. He and his grandparents sit in the living room and wait. The package that's about to come through the front door will be gift-wrapped and rare.

Réal stares at Steve's shoes and silently tabulates what he has to say. Thankfully, he has always been generous with the church, in particular, the Catholic girls' school Louise had attended. She was a difficult student, stubborn about mathematics and stupid about reading. Still, a donation is a donation and the nuns were kind.

Le Père Jean-Marie hugs Réal. He has a way of lowering his head as he speaks, ducking his voice into an incomprehensible tunnel. While Mariette boils water for tea, the men discuss education– something about refreshments, something about the pews of the chapel, something else about paint.

"I remember how quiet the chapel was, how very holy," Réal says. "Do the boys still pray on their knees?"

The Father laughs.

Réal presses his hands together and holds them to his lips. "Mariette and I pray for the success of these young scholars."

The Father raises his head. "All we need," he warbles to the ceiling, "is to get them into the chapel. If we do that– all that mess, their clothes, their hair, their foul language– disappears. And then they become, in spite of themselves, *croyez-moi*, men of fine standing."

Réal reaches into his pocket and withdraws an envelope. "To help you make men of them."

Whispering something, the priest bows.

They eat blueberry pie forever while the adults talk. Rules and more rules at that school. Steve swirls the tea in the cup betting himself that it won't spill. You have to wear black shoes and a tie. You can't even be one second late after the first bell. There must be over a hundred you can't's. No wonder his mother hated school.

"Steve–"

He glances from the priest's crooked finger to his grandfather.

"*Tu sais*, Steve," Réal says. "I've known le Père Jean-Marie since we were– five, six." He holds his hand as high as his waist. "*Imagine-toi*, Steve, in the same school as you, we were.

There were too many boys in the classes and we had to share a bench. Well, one day, so hot it was," He smiles at the priest, "we both wriggled outside – little worms we were– and hid in the bushes while the catechism was being read. And now, this same little fellow is a man of the cloth."

Le Père Jean-Marie laughs. "My mother promised me to the church. I had no choice. *Et toi*, Steve, do you read your catechism?"

"Steve is a good boy," Mariette breaks in. She pulls him up by the hand to stand him in front of the priest.

"Steve," he whispers, "*tu es un bon garçon.*" As if his muffled throat is waded up with syrupy blueberries, his voice has become as grave as it is high-pitched. Steve waits for him to swallow. The priest crooks his finger again. "You do not understand, eh?" he whispers in a British accent. "I said that you are a good boy." He mutters a few things that sound like, 'respect' and 'honesty' and maybe, 'tea too hot'. The other words, Steve can't fathom. He keeps nodding. His grandparents seem happy with that. They drink a gallon of tea. Le Père stops talking.

Steve's grandparents stand on either side of him and bow their heads. "*Baisses ta tête,*" his grandfather tells him.

Steve bows his head.

Jean-Marie makes the sign of the cross, places his palm on Steve's head, and murmurs a prayer. "*Je vous salue Marie...*"

This, the Hail Mary, Steve well understands. He doesn't have to hear to know. His mother who rarely set foot in the church often muttered it. She must have known how soon she would have to go. Those calls to the Holy Virgin were for the sake of her life and for the hour of her death. And in that hour she must have called God and Jesus and Mary. And Steve.

Steve shakes off the priest's hand.

"*Mon petit gas*," the priest murmurs. And when Steve does not answer, he whispers, "Steve, your mother is with God." And then, as loud as his warble allows, he calls, "Steve Dumont, *sois béni.*"

And so, whether he wants it or not– he is blessed.

His mother, or the priest, tells him to study the catechism. Her caterwauling rolls into bed with him. And now that she can only speak to him from inside his ears, the voice that comes from having her larynx cut till her neck lolled, etches out a tune as sharp as it is hoarse. He lies in his bed, his damp hands cupped over his aching ears. She tells him, Be polite and do what they want and please remember to be polite and do what they say and don't argue. And keep your clothes clean and neat and also your room. And if you stay quiet and polite, you will find a small piece of happiness all the days of your life. All of them.

He waits for Paula to call, not that he wants her to, but if she does, there are things he has to tell her. Except that he can only think of these things in French so she won't understand. Maybe if the language in his ears is not French, his mother's natter will stop. But he doesn't want to tell his *maman* to stop. She is, was, his real mother. And he's trying to be polite.

He brings a portable phone to his room and presses the dial tone to his ear. There she is, making her demands from the other end of the line. And he has no choice but to answer.

—Drive carefully.

—I don't have a license.

—Apologize.

—I'm sorry. I'm so sorry. I didn't know what to do. I didn't know what he was doing to you.

—I said, *excuse-toi* right now.

—I do, I'm so sorry.

—No— not like that.

—I don't understand.

—To your aunt, you apologize.

—For what? I didn't do anything.

—*Dis la verité*.

—I am, I am. I'm telling you the truth. I only borrowed it. I'm saving up. As soon as I have enough, plus interest I mean, I'll call her.

—Hah.

—You're not so smart. If you were smart, you'd have left him. You wouldn't even marry him.

—*Et toi*? Where would you be? There would not be a Steve Horvath.

—You have it wrong. I'm Steve Dumont. Even the priest said.

He scratches his forearms and keeps scratching. The pale skin along his veins peels from his elbows to the folds of his wrists. A smear of blood dirties the inside of his elbow but not nearly enough. He means to get rid of the Horvath genes even though he is not a

Horvath. Not really, not anymore. He scratches his belly. He is Steve Dumont. He is a good boy.

Welts appear on his belly. Steve puts his nose to the wall. The smell of soup permeates even the clothes in his bedroom. There is no English in the Dumont house and hardly any conversation these days. The only live person who talks anymore is Mariette. The others are gone. Julie has already started school. Oncle Marc is too busy studying some accounting thing to show up. Steve's grandfather works all day finishing somebody's basement. Before Louise died, he was retired from his job doing the cost estimates for a construction company. Everything in construction he knows.

Dabbing at the scratches on his wrist, he creeps to the edge of the kitchen and watches his grandmother cut up piles of vegetables. All week Mariette has been pulling stuff from the soil, cooking and freezing. The minute she sees him she invites him for a taste– a spoonful of ketchup, some green tomato relish. She makes him pass the utensils, and talks without cease about politics, how if they all vote the right way, Quebec will separate itself from Canada and become a free-standing nation. "*Une nation avec son drapeau*," she tells Steve.

He escapes to his room. How come they rarely ate zucchini at his father's house? Garden zucchini and tomatoes and stuff he can't even recognize grow free at the far end of the yard even before his birth. Oscar would not take from others– No, take back those tomatoes, we have no room for them. Next thing you know, your daughter will want a bigger fridge. But– did he say those actual words? He must have said something. Even Aunt Paula's bags of socks and underwear stopped coming.

Outside the closed door of his room tomato sauce bubbles. He hears Mariette's radio and nothing else. Okay. Now he knows what to say. The moment she answers the phone with her first English Hello, his brain will switch automatically to his other language. Aunt Paula, the minute I turn sixteen I'll quit school and get a job. And then–

He aims a trembling finger at the numbers on the keypad and dials.

Chapter 27

Shelly started in on her back at the Cornwall garage the moment Steve and Sharon climbed into the speedily regenerated cab and shot off to Montreal.

"You could have killed him. You just about did. You weren't a sane mother either. Like idiots, we blamed your moods on the pill. Poor little hormones had nothing to do with anything. You're nuts all by yourself. You can't take care of kids. You shouldn't be near them."

Nonstop from Cornwall to Montreal, Shelly reiterated his arguments with all its variants. Immediately over the threshold of Paula's apartment, Steve took himself to his room and his own face-eating thoughts. Shelly parked Paula in the straight-backed chair at the far corner of the living room and whispering, continued on with parenting 101.

"Think for a change. At least think of the boy. If you can, if there's a brain in that head of yours you'll know you can't keep him."

Shelly got comfortable. He and Sharon each took a couch while Paula's bruises throbbed on the chair. She heard little of his blather. Paula already knew. If the boy stayed, she might be his destruction. But not out of stupidity. Out of too much love. Not a feeling she should ever lose. Not to lose her also, she kept her eye on her daughter's slumped outline. Among a group of girls smiling, it was impossible for Paula to know which of them was Sharon. She had the same orthodontically correct teeth as her friends, the same length of hair. What kind of mother could not pick out her own daughter's waving hand from among a mass of anonymous teeth and hair?

Deep in the couch surrounded by pillows, Sharon pushes back her cuticles with her finger. Her hair hung over her eyes. According to Shelly, Paula could have destroyed Sharon too if the girl hadn't run to his sane embrace. Not likely. But in truth, Paula became a mother by accident. Pure love might not enough to raise a child. Better to study motherhood, than algebra.

She let Shelly go on till his insults actually bored her then said, "For your uneducated information, I was just about to write a letter to that lawyer. If Steve's grandparents put him in a private school that treats him better than the last one, he should go there."

The moment she spoke up she felt noble. She limped to the kitchen and pulled Luc Richard's crumpled letter from the jar in the back of the cupboard. She'd never thought to return to this house and yet found herself relieved to rediscover her belongings, even this wet scrap of paper. The certified letter, like her socks and sweaters, her cups and dishes, unable to follow her down the highway west, had demanded her return. Her clamouring bric-a-brac, knowing every one of her limits, begged her to give Steve up to a better future.

"He'll be happy to go," Shelly said.

Happy? Nobody knows what's in that boy's head.

So what is she to do now but slink toward the stiff upholstery of that chair whenever a thought flips her stomach. Because basically, she has to keep the thoughts from splitting her brain apart. If she has a brain.

It's too late for new ideas, too late even to think. She's already given Steve up. While Shelly's volcano was blowing so-called common sense in her direction, it seemed like the only choice she had. Ultimately, it was she who'd spun her little boy toward the edge of a cliff. And while he stood on the precipice, pushed at him till only his fingernails kept him from falling. The only thing left for her now, is to huddle into the corner and reap her punishment.

Steve spent one more night in the pink room. Mumbling from some part of that cell, he agreed to crack the door and accept half a box of sweet and sour chicken. The next day it took about five minutes for him to bundle his used sheets on the foot of the bed, stride out and close the door. Everything he owned was in his bag. Luc Richard was waiting outside. Barely mentioning it to the boy, Shelly had arranged the transfer as though Steve lived in two interchangeable houses, one heap of bricks and mortar no different from the other. Before leaving, Steve paused long enough for Paula to brush his cheek with hers. "Goodbye," he muttered, eyes to the floor.

Late in the afternoon the lawyer showed up again. That pain in the ass wanted Paula to sign papers. Like a vulture he was, the back of his suit jacket up against his ears, his grey head perched above his shield of papers.

"All custody to the grandparents."

"Okay."

"No visiting rights for now. This can be arranged later when things calm down."

"Okay."

"Think of the child. He failed his school year. A boy like that is at risk in this neighbourhood."

"I said, Okay."

"Please sign. One signature here, one here, another one right here. Thank you *Madame* Horvath. All copies you will receive by mail."

Maybe he held out his hand. Paula didn't see and didn't care.

It is all fine. She couldn't in any case have moved away from her practical neighbourhood. In a city without bus service she'd be blinder than she already is. If she had to live without a grocery store in walking distance, she'd be a prisoner. Forced to rely on the occasional cab and her disgruntled feet, she'd pass unending days inside the four walls of a room chosen by income alone.

Yes, perfectly fine except that all manner of housekeeping has become unimportant. Dust and clutter accumulate on the counters and floors, on tables, on top of the television set. The white scum of soap lies grimy on the bathroom sink. Dirty dishes litter the couches.

Paula reuses the dishes, wiping the crumbs to the floor with her fingers if absolutely necessary. In any case the food is never wet. Three times a day she eats toast and peanut butter. Or five times a day. Or once a day. The radio stays on but what in the world those people are talking about, Paula has no clue. Songs and laughter filter dimly through the speaker along with news that is better left unheard. Her door is closed to the neighbours. With the radio for company, Paula's only other requirement for sound is the ring of the telephone as long as it's Sharon or hopefully Steve. She wills and waits for her daughter's voice to spring from the answering machine before lifting the receiver. But Sharon does not often call and doesn't come to the door. She's busy with some vaguely mentioned project and unnecessary visits to Toronto. That's how it is with children. When they don't need you, they leave. A few times the telephone rings but stops the moment the answering machine picks up. If those callers don't want to leave a message, to hell with them. To hell with them all.

Chapter 28

Sharon's cry is so shrill that Paula jerks away from the dim screen of the television, her mouth hanging as wide open as her daughter's.

"Ma– what's going on?"

"What?"

"It stinks in here." She strides past her mother to open the windows. "You stink." She starts to grab at the pile of dishes on the couch.

"Yeah, I've been busy."

There's a clatter in the sink. Sharon interrupts her TV show with four letter words, the barrage of water, the slap of a towel. Worn out by Sharon's energy, Paula lies on the couch and closes her eyes. In a little while she'll make Sharon a sardine sandwich. And a cup of tea. When she opens her eyes in the unusual quiet of the room, it's already late afternoon and there's Sharon, hovering over her.

"Mother, you need to take a shower."

"I'm tired."

"You don't get it. You smell really bad. Looks like salad dressing on your hair."

Involuntarily, Paula reaches back to feel a slick of oil on her scalp. She lifts her head away from the couch. In her mother's house, there had always been a patch of cloth on the headrests to protect the upholstery.

"Go on, go take your shower. We're going out."

Paula's damp legs hang off the edge of the bed. She used to indulge in the occasional pedicure, each time feeling as polished as her nails. She lifts her foot and sniffs.

"What's your problem? You washed them didn't you?"

Paula has more or less, done just that, though she doesn't remember scrubbing off her putrid odour.

"Happy Mother's Day," Sharon says.

An awful, flimsy dress is stretched out on the sheet.

Paula opens her mouth.

"Stop. I want you to look good for a change."

"But it's pink."

"Yellow for god's sake. Try it on."

It fits too tightly around her torso.

"Looks great, Mom."

"I don't think I can breathe."

Her stubby toes are too shabby for the dress. The nails are ragged. She covers them with nylon knee highs and clunky black shoes, as tight as the dress. To cheer Sharon up she puts on lipstick and feels herself propelled toward Shelly's car. And when they arrive wherever they're going, she takes Shelly's elbow and clumps through the door of a pitch-dark restaurant. Better not to see you, my dear.

She eats curry and fried appetizers and papadums till the food turns sour in her mouth. The whole time, Sharon and Shelly talk about the province– how if it separates, they'll separate from it too. They stop yabbing and glance at one another while Paula burps.

"That was very good. Thank you," Paula says.

"I'm glad you enjoyed it. You must have been starved."

Not starved. Just too indifferent to listen politely. But who cares if she ate too much. Nobody's looking at her. "Why didn't Eli join us?"

"He's with his mother."

"Well. That makes sense."

"Mom?"

Paula waits.

"He's moving to Toronto. He found a job there."

Paula fills her mouth with the last of the chicken. Her stomach burns.

"His French is lousy. He has no choice."

So what– She's about to start a lecture on if the guy actually cared about more than himself–.

"In a year you'll be dancing at your daughter's wedding," Shelly says. "In less than a year."

"Dad–"

"Don't Dad me. I want grandchildren."

"Don't tell me you're going to Toronto." She is of course. It's been plain on her nose ever since the Parti Quebecois and their separatist platform stepped into power and ever since she met that boy. "And when were you planning to tell me?"

"I'm telling you now."

"They have no choice. This province will never leave us in peace. Every time you turn your head they're talking about separation. The sooner the kids get out, the better."

Her voice low, as if only she and Sharon are at the table, she says, "What are you going to do? Just quit your job?"

"I can't work at that place anymore. People are being really weird. It's like, all the English people are on one side. Then there's the militant French who want everybody to vote like them. You're afraid to speak English if you're anywhere near them. Then there's the non-militants who pretend like there's no vote at all. Except you don't always know which one's militant and which one's not."

"Who cares? This is temporary. It'll all pass."

"I'm sick of it. I don't want to live where people argue over stupidities. I don't feel welcome here."

"What about your father? You're just going to leave him?"

"We'll all go," Sharon says. "Dad, you can open an office in T.O."

So it's decided. And signed and sealed.

"The big thing is to get your money out. Sharon, I want you to open an account in Ontario. I'm not even leaving a safety deposit box in this province."

"But if your address is here, they can freeze your assets and then change it to their own currency, whatever that is. And then we're really screwed."

"It's a good thing you don't own a home, Paula. The worst thing that can happen to you, is your rent won't go down." Shelly laughs.

Yeah. He's the one who brought them back to where they shouldn't stay.

Sharon tells them about job opportunities in other provinces and how much higher the pay is. Shelly's about to buy an over priced condominium in Toronto. According to him, the future is there. They'll take off arm-in-arm and she'll be left alone in her low rent district. Paula pours four teaspoons of sugar into her tea and clanks the spoon in the cup.

They get up to leave. The yellow dress clings to her plush stomach. She's gotten used to the feel of the stretchy fabric. As long as she can't see herself in the mirror it doesn't matter that her clothes are too tight. Or that most of them are stained and lopsided, hems frayed or undone. She doesn't know that after separating from Shelly she gained forty pounds and that the excess weight makes her gait uneven. She doesn't notice how people perceive her in the street, that her droopy eyes make her seem dimwitted. She's a massive wad on Shelly's arm. And the only one without a plan.

Even little Steve has a plan.

Chapter 29

The days of July and August are painfully bright. Behind the closed windows, Paula lies on her damp sheets smothered by the heat. Swaying the drawn curtains, a fan buzzes at her face.

In the consoling day-long dusk, she's able to decipher passing street shadows on the wall. Voices from the radio rumble to the tune of her thoughts. She tries to work out a plan for herself and for Steve except that her thoughts are as sticky as the cotton T-shirt she calls a night gown. So many words cross her eyes and ears that she can neither phrase nor differentiate her ideas from the radio's. Among a jumble of sounds and images, Sharon's shoes define themselves and run out of the apartment. Steve materializes beside his cousin. They climb into the black cab and side by side behind the steering wheel, they negotiate a blue highway bordered by evergreen cones. Paula's white calves are flexed for the sprint. And when she catches up at last, she jerks Steve out the window and onto the dotted lines of the highway, straight to the slam of brakes and rubber. No better than her brother, Paula Horvath flattens her bitter pillow and covers her face.

Paula only has to obliterate her dreams to sleep. But the phone keeps ringing with offers of insurance or alarm services or credit cards. Old, barely remembered friends wrench her out of her somnolence to say nothing important. All they care about is the weather and politics. Stonily, she nods to the receiver till the phone goes dead. Only to Sharon will she speak. But Sharon's busy– a two-week vacation on the edge of the ocean in July and in August, she treks out to Toronto three weekends in a row to search for an apartment. She's placed her hand in someone else's, is making a home where she feels welcome. She'll leave her box of shoes in the empty pink room.

Chapter 30

Finger-by-finger, ivy creeps up the century-old facade of the Ecole Notre Dame. Some of the red bricks have been haphazardly repaired with sand and cement leaving the structure miserably bandaged. In the rooms that are too huge to use, old army blankets coat the windows. Doors are kept locked. The Sulpicians of the 1950s educated five hundred and forty boys a year. In 1995 just over two hundred will sit in the year's opening assembly.

Steve and his grandfather make their way up the sprawling stone steps that lead into the school's resounding corridors. Ever since the priest's benediction, Steve thinks of himself unhesitatingly as a Dumont. He whispers his new name to the wallpaper in his bedroom and without a qualm, takes a seat in the director's office and registers as Steve Dumont. A new school, a new name, a new person. He feels clean.

The boys arrive at Ecole Notre Dame identically dressed in blue jackets and grey slacks. They're ushered into a clattering assembly that becomes utterly silent with the first words of the Lord's prayer. With the final Amen, the director taps a wand first at the podium, then to the front of his collar. The students tighten their ties. Kissing the microphone, he proceeds with a speech about hard work and welcoming newcomers and how friendships formed in school will lead to lifelong associations and that faith in the Father, the Son, and the Holy Ghost, will follow them all the days of their lives. The boys poke one another. With faith, they will find salvation. The director's upper lip arches like a bird's: Faith and faith and faith and faith–. If the benches were less hard, Steve would doze a little.

Steve is assigned to a monitor, a boy in round glasses who nods at him as if to say, Yes, you've got it right. This is me.

He holds out his hand for a shake, says, "Benoit," and turns on his heel. Pointing from one direction to the next, he strides down the corridor showing Steve the toilets, a lunch room of wood benches and tables, the cathedral walls of the library and in the science room, the skeletons of a frog and a bird. A few dishevelled bones litter a white table.

"Cute isn't it? Used to be Le Père Jean-Marie's puppy." Benoit laughs. "*Oui monsieur,* that was a joke. You are permitted to smile. Eh," Benoit tugs at his sleeve. "*Viens avec moi,*" and Steve has no choice but to follow him. At the end of the hall Benoit shoves a steel door open and bursts outside.

"*Aie, j'ai donc besoin d'une clope.*" He takes a cigarette from a package and hands another to Steve.

His complexion growing visibly pinker in the sun, Benoit blows smoke rings above their heads."You planning to smoke that, or eat it? Cause if you don't want it–"

"*Mais non*." Steve takes a rapid puff off his smoke.

"Did I forget to tell you? I'm your history tutor."

"Whatever. I don't need a tutor."

"You're a genius all of a sudden?"

"I don't need to pass that stupid course. The minute I'm sixteen I'm getting out of this hole."

"Why? Where are you going?"

"I'm quitting school."

"*T'as une job?*"

"*Non.*"

Benoit smirks, the goggly glasses balanced on the edge of his nose. "So, what are you going to do for money?"

"I have money."

"Yeah sure, your father's rich."

That Benoit might know something about his father, even the wrong thing, shakes him. He glares at the weeds edging the building bricks.

"You've got an exam in three weeks. Every lunch we study. You get fifteen minutes to eat and a half hour to learn. It won't kill you."

"You get paid for that?"

"The priests don't pay."

"So what's in it for you?"

Benoit takes a long drag off his cigarette. "Nothing. Sometimes I just like to be nice."

A scattering of boys joins them outside. One of them jostles his way through the group handing out small Quebec flags. He points to each of the guys with the sprout of beard on the tip of his chin. "*T'es avec nous? Puis toi? Et toi?*"

To Steve, he asks the same question. "Eh, *toi*, are you with us?"

Steve scrutinizes the cobblestone floor of their hideaway. Locked in by a wrought iron gate, surrounded by plastic garbage bins, where else could he be but here with the cigarette smokers.

"Yeah," he says, though that too will cost money.

Benoit leads Steve to the cafeteria.

"Do you know why I get to be your history tutor? No? You don't care? Okay I'll tell you.

It so happens that I've been first in *Histoire* for the past three years. Do you know why that is? Let's see if you can guess." Benoit unwraps his ham and cheese and gulps down a mouthful.

Steve isn't sure if he should roll his eyes and eat his sandwich or answer the question.

"Ding ding ding, time's out. You lose. The reason I have the honour to teach you, is because I am a great observer. I watch, I observe, I remember. And here's what I noticed during our little break." He tips his head at Steve and smiles. "You don't have an earthly clue about what Eric was saying, right?"

"Who's Eric?"

Benoit pulls at his chin. "The little beardie."

"I don't know what you're talking about."

"He was referring to the referendum. Basically, if you're with us, you vote Yes for Quebec to become an independent nation. And if you're not, you're an asshole."

"You know perfectly well I'm not old enough to vote."

"I'm talking about the theoretical. If you were going to vote, how would you vote?"

Steve unwraps his sandwich. The very thought of peanut butter dries him up.

"You don't have to tell me. You can vote any way you want. I believe in democracy. But you can't ignore what's going on in this province– *bientôt* a country." Benoit chomps down the rest of his sandwich and balls up the wax paper. "Eh, eat you' lunch *mon p'tit gas.* You'll need to take notes. Wait till you learn what *les anglais* did to us."

And so Benoit begins his first lecture on the history of Canada and Quebec, a one-themed affair that will go on for weeks. The story starts with a battle that took place two centuries earlier on the plains of Abraham– a battle that put the English in control of New France– that subjugated the French to English rule– that Quebec and Quebec and more Quebec. On and on and on it went.

"It won't end," Benoit reiterates, "till we get rid of Canada. I don't mean go to war or anything. I mean come to a nice understanding." He watches Steve chew. "Did you understand a word I said?"

"The French lost *les plaines d'abraham*?"

"Yeah– but right now what's important is to win it back. See– here's what I'm telling you– that military offence on the *plaines d'abraham* in 1759 affected modern politics. History influences the modern world– the bolt and the screw. Get that? Whatever happened then, gives reason to what's happening now."

Steve's uncle drummed a different history into him than this one though some of the details sound hazily similar. He made Steve read the text and write down dates. Accuracy and order came in the form of numbers for Oncle Marc. He called out every date of historical importance and expected Steve to memorize them. Steve managed to remember the timing but rarely the events that went with them.

Benoit's version is all about who killed who and how they did it. Every other minute he jumps off his chair and flapping his arms, spits out an opinion along with bits of chocolate chip cookie. Steve slides into the next chair.

What it comes down to, is that the Indians and the French are in the same boat because of what the English did to them. Or that the French are in a hole because the English put them there. All this because of one stupid, unfair battle on the Plains of Abraham. The English won but not really because the English were boors and crooks way back in history and nothing has changed. Even now in 1995 the English are still the bosses and landlords. And you never get a decent job if you can't speak English. And when you walk into a store in Montreal they don't even know how to say, can I help you, in French.

"It's time to clean out the filth in Quebec," Benoit scowls. "For centuries it's been dripping on us. *C'est à nous de changer ça.*"

Change what? You can't very well change the outcome of the battle.

Benoit brushes the crumbs off his pants.

An awful lot of people take great offence to dirt. Especially Catholics. The whole group of them are always cleaning something. Steve wipes the surface of the table with the crushed wax paper that wrapped his sandwich. He too is Catholic though admittedly not so clean.

Benoit passes him a text book. "Read and memorize. It'll be on your exam in three weeks. If you don't pass, you'll be put back."

It's possible that part of Benoit's history lesson is in the textbook and on the exam that Steve is supposed to pass. But not one date that must be remembered came from Benoit's mouth. If Steve didn't already know better, the battle on the Plains of Abraham could have occurred just last week. It's not fair for him to remember dates. Seventeen-hundred, eighteen-hundred, nineteen-hundred– big dif. And what does history have to do with anything?

Chapter 31

Only Paula's need to relive herself gets her out of bed. Over days, maybe weeks, she gnaws through the dilapidated guts of the fridge and pantry till they are as barren as her appetite. She neither wants nor craves food. A Neanderthal, she needs it.

She opens the refrigerator, jiggles the empty vegetable drawers and passes her hand along the plastic shelving. On the top corner are the skimpy remains of jam and a jar of pickle brine. Caught between the brackets, is a sachet of instant coffee. She dissolves the coffee in tap water and licks up the remains of the jam. Not satisfied by jam and black water, she sips the pickle juice, retches and hangs her head over the sink, sobbing. Saliva and tears drip from her mouth. Her own baying obliges her to stop, hiccup her way to the bathroom and wash her face. Prodded by the persistent growing in her stomach or by the pure impulse for life, she shrugs on her clothes and takes the familiar path to the shopping centre.

The spindly flowers of the bordering Hostas point their violet tentacles at her passing shadow. In the dwindling September light the homes she once knew, the trees and the flowers, the black metal pegs of a fence, the sky itself, gleaming white above her, seem freshly painted. The threatening clock of winter clicks forward. Somehow she skipped a season, wasted it.

Paula lowers her head and trudges on, stepping down at each curb, crossing to the next. This is what ants angling for crumbs do, or mice, with their mindless instincts. It's one foot in front of the other for the bugs and rodents of the world.

If she had an occupation, a job, any kind, she'd be forced to take her place in society. She'd be a normal person, going in and out morning and night, giving thought to the flow of traffic and her to-do lists. Beyond her menial tasks, she'd have activities to fill her leisure hours. As it is, she has no purpose. The only thing that brings Paula-the-rodent out in the open, is her search for food.

Paula pulls at the weight of the glass door and walks into the air conditioning. She shivers, forgetting why she came. Her legs move her toward the sweet odour of baking at a muffin counter. She points to one of the muffins with a trembling finger and sits down to eat it. She can't be hungry. It's the cold that makes her mouth open and close so rapidly. In a moment the muffin is finished. Paula licks two of her fingers and curls them into her fist. She orders coffee and another muffin and for the first time since she entered the mall, notices the outlines of Marnie's stand across the aisle. A neon circle blinks gigantically above the booth. On either side of the blinker is something that looks like a billboard. Paula sticks her face inside the cup but before the steam could tickle her nose, she feels Marnie's hot smile. Paula almost lifts her face then stops. No reason to be polite. It's all her fault– her and her fake fortunes.

"It's me." Marnie thrusts her long fingers into Paula's fist.

"Great."

"I saw you gulp down the two muffins. You must have been starved. Go ahead, drink up while it's good and hot."

"I'll drink when I'm good and ready."

"I'm always ready to eat and drink." Marnie pulls up a seat. "That's the problem."

Marnie's client grimaces. The woman's been staring off into the universe ever since she sat down, making a big pretence of not seeing her.

Lugging her from one table to the next isn't a big deal. The real problem is getting her sedated enough to speak.

"I'm less expensive than a psychologist," Marnie says.

"What are you talking about? I didn't come to see you or a psychologist."

"People don't know why they come. They think they're here to pick up some milk or moth balls or something. And they end up, guess where?"

"I haven't the faintest."

"At my booth. And then they feel better. Did you notice my new sign?"

"I did not. My eyes aren't any better than they were when you made me those empty promises. They're worse in fact."

"What did I promise?"

"That my eyes would improve."

"Why? Can't you see?" Marnie waves at Paula's sunglasses and sees her eyes flicker. "They're working all right."

"They're not. I can't even think straight when I can't see." No sense explaining. People are dumb.

"So what are you here for?"

"I'm here to eat two muffins and drink a coffee in peace, if you don't mind."

"I've got a two for one special on today."

"We did that already."

"I've got a clairvoyance special. Seven bucks for five minutes. But for you I'll make it five. Five for five. How about it?"

Paula swallows the rest of her coffee and begins to gather up her belongings.

"Excellent. And because you're such a faithful client, I'll even make it–"

"I don't have time for that. I'm busy."

"Ten for five. Minutes, that is. Ten whole minutes for five bucks. You won't get a bargain like that anywhere."

Paula's jaw hurts. She turns her back to Marnie and walks.

Marnie joins her. "What are you so busy with? You're buying something?"

"Party decorations."

"What for?"

"My nephew's birthday."

"Good that you're so cheerful. Have a referendum party while you're at it."

"What are you talking about? We're going to lose."

"I wouldn't know. If I could look into my crystal ball and tell you who's the winner, I'd be a millionaire by now. I'm not a fortune teller, even though half the neighbourhood thinks I am. Hey– slow down."

Paula increases her pace.

"The truth is, in this country you don't need to know anything about the future. All you need is optimism. If you're optimistic, things work themselves out. People don't get that. They make all kinds of mistakes. Half my clients are leaving. And their money's going with them. The entire neighbourhood has bank accounts in Ontario."

"Get yourself an account and go with them."

"Me? I was born here. I speak French."

"Yeah right. I heard you."

"You only heard the accent. That counts for nothing. I speak well enough to give the tarot at least. If all my English clients disappear, so what? I'm still a clairvoyant. People come. They don't care about language. All they care about is themselves."

Paula snorts. "That's because the world is falling apart."

"Nah. It's only the country. So what if it does? You speak French, don't you?"

"I can barely say bon-jour."

"So you'll learn."

"Sure," Paula huffs. She's out of breath, doesn't know how to get away from that woman. Not without being downright rude. She halts at the grocery store. "I really do have some shopping to do, so if you'll excuse me–"

"There's nothing to buy here except food. You didn't come here for shopping. You came to see me." Marnie takes Paula's limp hand, shakes it up and down as if they just made a deal and tucks it under her elbow. "Come and sit with me. I'm tired of walking." She turns Paula back toward her booth. "Now, tell me how you're going to learn French."

"Everything's easy for you," Paula whines.

"For you too."

"I'm visually impaired."

"Excellent. If you don't see well enough to read and write, you just have to talk. Much easier."

Marnie places a chair under Paula's butt and pushes her into it. "Now, give me a twenty and we'll start."

"You said five. And anyway I'm not interested."

"Alright. It'll be five minutes for free and twenty for twenty. Starting now." She draws a paisley curtain around her booth. Setting her crystal ball between them, she rotates the fluorescent bulb till it lights up like a raised finger poking out of the glass ball. "I don't want to be a buttinsky or anything, but when all you do is procrastinate in your apartment, you're wasting your life. There's not much time, you know. There's things you must do. That much I can tell you."

Paula feels her heart in her ears. She averts her face and waits for more. She wants Marnie to tell her what to do next, what to do all day. The only thing she's sure of is having to brush her teeth. If she knew what to do after that, things would go so much better.

"This is costing you. You'd better pay attention." The clairvoyant's voice is more urgent than angry.

"I am." Paula barely breaths, so sure is she that Marnie's about to say something important enough to change her life.

"So." Marnie palpates the crystal ball. "You're sitting in your house doing nothing. What else do you want to tell me?"

"I'm not telling you anything."

"Alright. Give me twenty and we'll keep going."

Paula fishes out a green bill. She can't help it. She needs to know.

Chapter 32

Paula drags a chair around the living room and tapes blue and red streamers from one wall to another. There are balloons to blow up but no, first there's the matter of who to invite. Who?

Well, there's Sharon. There's Shelly. Except that Sharon will tap the chocolate fudge on the Happy Birthday Steve cake with her fingernail and immediately wrinkle her nose as if cement itself is more tasty. And Shelly will lead her to the stiff chair of reflection and punishment for a lesson on surprise birthday parties for boys who must never never place even the edge of their rubber soles in her apartment.

Never mind them. Lots of other people in the world. She sits by the phone. Tons. There's Nick. As soon as she remembers how to get hold of him, she'll invite him and all of Steve's other friends. If he has any apart from Nick. She has to fill the place. She has to– Yes, absolutely, the Dumonts. Paula claps. They must be invited. That's what Marnie would tell her.

She squints at the scrap of paper secured to the fridge by a banana magnet. The first three digits of their number she knows by heart. The next is either a five or a six. She picks up the phone. *Bon-jour*, she booms. She listens to the blank receiver and repeats her *Bonjour*, using the syrupy welcome welcome quality of the Excelsior Motel. Too loud. It didn't much work for the motel. She lowers her voice to a thoughtful, sophisticated, Bon-jour. Bon-jour, bon-jour bon-jour. That word, spoken in the right tone, will open the door. She dials.

An English answering machine responds. She apologizes to the stiff-necked phone. On the next dial, a potato chip company greets her. "Sorry, so sorry, so very sorry." She dials again.

By then her elbow aches.

"*Allo?*"

"Oh, hi– it's Paula Horvath." Already she's made a mistake. "I mean, Shapiro."

"*Qu'est-ce-que vous voulez?*"

Paula's amazed at her ability to understand. "Soon it'll be Steve's birthday." She curls her mouth around the next phrase. "Anni-ver-sary *de* Steve. I'm having a surprise party for him at my house. *Une* partay surprisay."

No answer on the other end.

"You're all invited. All of you, the whole gang, uncles, aunts, cousins. And for his birthday gift, I'll get the car fixed. I'll send a tow truck to pick it up." This last, Paula thinks of as she speaks. He'll be thrilled.

"*Quoi?*"

"La auto. Je fixay for Steve. Je payay for fixay." By not eating over the summer, she's already saved a few bucks. Too bad she gave twenty percent of her cash to the fortune teller, though face it, she might never have made this phone call if it wasn't for her. Never mind the shortage of money. Next month she won't eat.

"*Madame* Orvat,"

Paula hears the sniff of a nose pointed to the ceiling.

"*L'auto de votre frère est dan-ge-reuse.*"

Dangerous. Yeah no kidding. That's why she's getting it fixed. "*Je payay,*" Paula repeats, "*pour* fixay. *Et–* the party for Steve is on Saturday the 24th. Promptly at noon. Lunch. I'll see you all then."

Chapter 33

Wings in Mariette's heart are flapping like those of a bird caught in a brush fire. She lifts the telephone, edges it to her ear and immediately snaps it back in its cradle in case that Horvat' woman is still there.

Breathe deeply when you are upset. Or– she holds her breath and counts silently backwards from ten. Soon Steve will fling open the door, ready for a snack. And she will offer him a glass of milk and a bran muffin and yogourt and an apple. She has cleaned his clothes and his room and the floor he walks on.

She urinates and washes her hands. The main thing would be to clean him up completely– his blood stream, his brain, his genes. Get the rusted taxi out of Steve's mind. Piece by piece if necessary. She applies a coat of lipstick to her mouth and practices the motions of a smile in front of the mirror. A smiling red kiss on his cheek will prove how much he is loved. She and Réal have plans for his birthday– a gift of skis and a party with a layer cake. This crazy aunt of his is about to ruin everything. Mariette should call– no– forget about Réal. Better to deal with it herself. She leafs through the Yellow Pages and dials the first number on the list.

Tire tracks are outlined on the asphalt driveway that leads to the shed. And there's something weird about the hinge on the door. Only yesterday Steve tightened the clasp to keep dust off the Malibu and now– it looks as though the doors were opened and the car, in ghostly rebellion, backed out of its enclosure.

The after-school routine outlined by the grandparents is that Steve is supposed to proceed straight to the kitchen table, to a snack of fruit and milk and a whole grain muffin and to the open pages of a text book. After an obligatory two hours on the chair, he's free to bounce a basketball toward the backyard. He approaches the shed, the cockeyed hinge on the door appearing to blink. A drizzle begins to erase the dusky tracks on the paving. The double-sided door swings apart as he unhooks the metal bar. Feeling as if he's about to fall down a rabbit hole, he steps into the dim the shed.

A rubble of broken concrete lies on the ground where the car should have been. Swinging from the ceiling, his grandmother's shrunken herbs hang by their stems on metal hangers. A gust of air rustles the basil, letting off a hint of scent in the deserted shed.

It doesn't matter, really. That old wreck's a waste of time. The thing could barely budge, never mind be expected to go across the country. Useless machine. He raises his leg, aims at its old parking spot and kicks at the air. Old useless bin. Hearing himself pant, he kicks the walls till his ankles sting. Again, he pounds the black oxfords he was supposed to have changed, against the bricks. He dashes back and forth, slapping and slamming till he can't breathe, till he's forced to stand teeth clenched in the middle of the garage, his breath as hoarse as the Malibu's.

When he and his dad bought that Malibu, slightly used but new to them, Oscar took him on his lap. Together they sat behind the wheel. He took Steve's fingers and smoothed them over every single lever, every button, every control on the dashboard. In those days they were in control, his father and mother. In control by logic and order. Mathematics and philosophy. They only had to point and he knew where to go, how to get there, and what to do next.

He opens his mouth, about to wail and slobber over what he knows perfectly well is impossible to have. That old black car with his parents in the front seat. He slaps at a tear that rolls into the cavity of his left ear. One, two, three times. Baby thoughts, good riddance to them. He isn't a kid anymore. Good riddance to the old bin. He'll practice driving in cars that actually work. His face tightens. Oblivious to logic, tears drop out of his eyes.

Where is it? Why'd you take it away, what for, why?

A flag in the wind, the boy keeps waving his arms, screaming for the return of his tin box in spite of the crinkly one-hundred-dollar bill he received for its sale.

Sputter all you want. As far as Réal is concerned, a sixteen-year-old boy shouldn't have a car he didn't work for. Vehicles too easily had are open invitations to fast, late nights and liquor.

Still, the boy doesn't have a mother. They have to give him something.

Chapter 34

Steve leans into the wicket. Around here you have to pay for everything– first for the test then for the permit. Not even the real one. Just the permit to let you practice. As if he needs to practice.

"Today you're sixteen?" The guy at the wicket has shoulders like a vampire's. "*T'es ben pressé toi.*"

Steve shrugs.

"What's that you said?"

"Nothing."

"I said, in case you didn't hear me, don't be in such a big hurry. Sit down and wait for your name to be called."

He memorized the rules on his mother's driving manual before she did. She left the booklet lying around. If he had to sit on the couch with his parents, it was a good idea to look at arrows and squiggles and yellow triangles. It was a good idea to stare at anything.

The same vampire shoulders guy who sat at Wicket One now sits at Wicket Two.

"Thought you could get rid of me?"

"No."

"No what?"

"*Non monsieur.*"

"Now you listen to me. I don't want you to race down the road like you raced to this appointment. Got it?"

"Yes."

"Yes what?"

"*Oui monsieur.*"

Steve gets a list to obey, signs the permit and pays.

"You passed?" Réal doesn't say another word as he drives them back home. When they reach the quiet streets of their neighbourhood he pulls the car up to a curb, turns off the motor, gets out of the car and opens Steve's door.

"I'd like to relax for a change." Frowning, he holds out the keys. "Yeah, I'm tired. You drive."

Steve glances from the dangling keys to his grandfather's cheeks as they begin to crease irrepressibly into a grin that stretches from one side of his eyes to the other.

The whole gang of them is assembled in the driveway looking like a live version of a family portrait— a wriggling mass of arms and heads and knees pointing in all directions. Foot on the brake, Steve approaches the house. Oncle Marc and tante Celine straddle the middle of the driveway. An elderly aunt holds out her arms like one of the signs on his driving test. There's another one, looks like *ma tante* Mathilde, so old she can barely stand. A whole block of people. Even Arlette is there. Julie grabs her mother's hand and starts to hop.

Steve brakes.

"*Gares ici,*" Réal says.

Okay. He pulls the car beside the curb and turns off the motor. The line of people is separating, opening up gradually like an accordion door. He's about to insert the key back into the ignition. The car isn't straight. Réal pokes him on the shoulder. He looks up and there, smack in the middle of the driveway is a green hatchback crowned by a massive gold bow.

Cheering, the crowd applauds. "*Bravo, Steve. Bonne fête! Bravo—*"

He slides out of his grandfather's car. Arms limp at his side, he stands completely still, not sure what the freakish gift-box car is doing in the driveway. Nor why everybody's shouting.

Julie hands him a giant construction paper card in the shape of the original Ford. *Ta permière*, it raptures. Your first what? And while he blushes, fingering the surface of the card, Mariette hands him a cardboard shoe box decorated with birthday cake stickers.

"Shake it," Julie shouts. "Open it."

The windblown bow is gold on top of this fake car. It's some kind of green decoration, some kind of joke.

"*Ouvre la boîte, ouvre la boîte,*" they chorus.

He opens the box. Keys and a key ring with his name on it— Steve. Or not his name. Another Steve. His grandmother crushes him and the stupid box in her arms. Now he gets it. He's being rewarded for being one year older. For living. For nothing.

Be polite, his mother mutters in his ear.

He forces out a smile.

The family, the neighbours, all the bystanders on the street shout Hurrah while Réal kisses his grandson loudly on both cheeks. He pushes Steve into the driver's seat of the green car and shows him how to work the knobs. Every single person, even tante Mathilde, takes turns sitting beside Steve just so they can breathe in the smell of fresh shampoo and slide their admiring hands over the dashboard.

They must have dug into their savings for his birthday. And now he'll have to please them every day of the week, every minute. He'll be obliged to hand over high marks, be on time for dinner, keep his room clean. She'll sell her jam to make up the money. She'll put together Christmas cakes and sell them. She'll sew aprons and old lady pants with elastic waists and those too, she'll sell. Except that all the pennies she earns won't be enough to pay even the front fender. And when the payments are due, there won't be anything left but a coin jar in the fridge.

Just as the mob begins to file into the house, Luc Richard's grey head, visibly higher than everybody else's, joins the queue. Over chocolate cake they sing Happy Birthday followed by the Quebec birthday song that assures him that it's his turn to talk about love.

Love. The bungee cord around his neck. That ugly car with its camouflaged patches of rust, its old age coated in green paint.

Mariette pulls Luc into the kitchen and fills the sink with scalding water. "You'll have to do something about her. *Elle ne fait qu'appeler.*"

"I spoke to her. Everything is in order."

"Then, why does she still call? All day long she wants to say happy birthday, happy birthday."

"It is his birthday."

"And so? He is not eighteen. She signed to leave him in peace. Tell the judge what she does."

"You know what, *ma chère*? You listen to the answering machine and if you hear her voice, don't answer the phone."

Mariette squirts a noisy stream of dish soap into the sink.

"*Ma tante*, you're not using the dishwasher?"

"Do you think I don't know how to wash a dish?"

Benoit opens the history text and flattens the spine. "Did you study?"

"Nah. I didn't have time."

"What's time got to do with it?"

"I took my learner's permit."

"So?"

"It was my birthday."

"Yeah so? I thought you were going to quit school the minute you turned sixteen."

"I got a car."

Four words and ten minutes later, the entire student body learns that Steve's sixteenth birthday blessed him with a 1987 Toyota Tercel. Unbelievable. He's the luckiest guy on earth.

*

Because they're limited to one seat belt per man, Benoit invites the closest and dearest to chance their luck in a lottery. A group of them meet in the garbage bin alcove during the five minutes between Biology and Latin. Guimauve empties his paper lunch sack and he and Alexandre and the three unrelated Bertrand boys and about six other guys, write their names on strips of foolscap and throw them into the sack.

André takes a deep hit off his smoke. "Eh Benoit, *tu vas prendre ton drink avec ta carte d'ecole? Gang d'idiots.*"

Benoit shoves him. "You're the idiot. I'll get you a card."

"What card?"

"An André Lebeau card. Student at UQUAM. Eighteen years old. Or would you rather be nineteen? You're so fucking brilliant you could be thirty."

They give each other a friendly pummelling and André dips his ink-stained fingers into the sack and pulls out his own name. Alexandre Gervais brings his baby face so close to the bag, the others accuse him of cheating. He walks away shrugging his pinpointed shoulders.

"Who's driving, assholes? You need a real license to drive a car. I'll bet his so-called car doesn't even exist."

Steve watches Gervais's retreating back. He's only allowed to drive as long as his grandfather sits beside him. And only if his homework is finished and it's not too late and there's nothing to watch on TV.

"I have a license."

The voice is so quiet it sounds as if it's coming from another room. It could even be Steve talking in his new quiet voice except that ever since he arrived at this school, his mouth has been so tightly clamped, he only utters a few words if he absolutely must. So, who?

"Eh, Eric–"

"Got it in August." The guy with the wispy beard steps away from the dark entrance of the metal doorway. "Guess you'll need a driver."

I'm the driver, Steve almost says.

In the end, it's André and Eric and the acne scarred Guy, otherwise called Guimauve, or even *mash-mallow*, by those boys who truly love him, who get voted into the car. As the bell rings, they shake hands. Before Steve can hold out his hand, Benoit grabs his sleeve and runs him into the building.

The next day Benoit hustles them to the school's unlit basement and makes them stand one at a time in front of the utility room's beige door. To the light of a battery charged lantern, Benoit snaps their pictures. His brother knows a guy who produces genuine student ID cards in about ten seconds as long as you bring him a picture and twenty bucks. Guimauve holds his twenty between his teeth and flaps the bill at Benoit. Steve keeps his money clamped in his wallet between a coupon for a free ice cream cone and the folded picture of his mother. He grimaces for his photo and rubs the bill between his fingers before giving it up. He tries to forget that he ever had that twenty. Really, he tries.

For what feels like hours, Steve talks to the stern faces of his grandparents.

–One of the guys has a license– it's only a ten-block drive to the movie– I need to practice– you need to trust me– we'll be back the minute the film is over. You, me, us, we–

His throat is sore from begging and explaining and creating some story that sounds like it might almost be true.

On Friday night the guys arrive via Eric's mother's car. In a complicated show of his driving talent, Eric cruises past the house and backs in and out of the space in front of the house till the car is at a perfect two centimetres from the curb and the wheels are completely straight. At the open doorway, the grandparents watch the performance. The guys tumble out of the car and Eric steps forward with a handshake and two foil wrapped cupcakes that he made himself.

Amazing what cake will do. Or maybe it's the hypnotic effect of Poulin's tweed jacket on his teeny little carcass. The grandparents wave them off without another reference to careful driving.

Poulin buckles himself in beside him. "Buckle up boozers."

"*C'est toi l' boozer*, Eric. Looks like you're dressed for halloween," Benoit snorts.

"Maybe I'll get in and you won't."

"Yeah? You look like a three-year-old in his father's suit."

"Eh– I'm Eric Poulin, nineteen years old, student at UQAM."

Guy brays so hard, the car practically vibrates.

On the boulevard, they stop at three red lights on their way to the Gros Mouton, a flat, red brick structure with few windows. The guys let Steve know how smooth he is with the brakes.

They talk about Guy's girlfriend, if she really is his girlfriend, who refuses to kiss him on the mouth.

"*Guimauve, montre-lui pas ta langue quand tu l'approches,* my god."

Benoit approaches the entrance to the bar first and lines Steve up behind him. He has some experience with getting into places that are off limits to the underaged. His height alone permits him access. Grinning back at his buddies, he shows his ID card and the bouncer allows them through.

As long as those gangly boys carry proof of maturity, he doesn't care how fake their paperwork is.

Unfashionably early, they saunter in to join four other people in the hall. The drinking crowd will arrive in time for Steve's curfew. Cupcakes and tea well digested, his grandparents will be watching for his arrival not one minute later than eleven-fifteen in case he turns into a pumpkin. The boys start out with three beers apiece. That's three times three on the table three steps from the toilet, plus one for Eric the responsible. Steve gets a diet coke. They have a great laugh at the sight of the lone coke. Steve pretends to sob though the soft drink makes him feel safe. Guimauve raises his voice as loudly as conversation allows and asks them how they'll vote and where their ridings are. He goes on to complain about the courses at university. The philosophy of Voltaire is too deadly to speak about. And triple squared mathematics is too easy for brilliant guys like them. When they stop whooping and giggling, they blow their smokes above their heads and guzzle their drinks. André would have offered them some weed if he hadn't smoked it all before getting to the bar. Thirty minutes haven't passed and already there's a few empties on the table. In a moment of silence Eric plucks at his wispy beard. Hiking up his beer, he proclaims that they, the five guys at the table will vote, YES, for independence, YES, for Quebec sovereignty. He holds up his beer in a toast that includes the entire bar. "*Le Québec aux Québécois*," he shouts in a voice deepened by liquor.

The barman glares. A couple of stragglers applaud. The waitress picks up the empties and strides off.

"Eh Guimauve, she likes you," Benoit says.

"Nah, I already have a girlfriend. She likes Eric. He promised her a cupcake."

"How about another round," André says.

"*J'ai plus d'sous*," Benoit says.

"Steve has money."

"Yeah–"

"Eh, Steve, lend us a few bucks."

Steve clasps the stem of his partially drained glass and stares at the curlycue mustache on the men's door. Benoit is probably rich enough to own a bank in Switzerland and Steve has already overpaid for one lousy soft drink.

There's a clang of glassware at the bar and a moment later the waitress slides five beer steins onto their table. Who the hell could have ordered? The boys scramble for money. Shaking them off, she points her chin at a couple seated in one of the banquettes. The man raises his fingers in a salute and smiles.

Benoit lifts his glass to him. "Shouldn't we thank them?"

"It's a mistake." Eric's convinced of it. "They've got us confused with someone else. You think corporate affairs is going to send us beers? *Voyons donc.*"

The couple are discussing something over papers spread between them. Steve sips his beer, his mouth puckering at the bitterness. It's André who approaches the business persons with offers of cigarettes. The woman mouths something indiscernible. She has a way of cocking her head when she smiles. Looking at her, at that smile alone, the whiteness of her teeth, is enough to make you leak in your pants. André returns with business cards and pamphlets and a batch of blue and white flags, the *Fleur-de-Lys* of Québec, as if they didn't have enough of them at school. Almost all the boys have flags taped inside their lockers and binders. They're not allowed to display political symbols. Too disruptive a practice, according to Père Jean-Marie who doesn't want a clash between the small percentage of Canadianophiles and the Quebec nationalists.

The man in the suit grins at them. "*Merci les militants*," he calls.

Eric waves his little flag.

The two pack up their briefcases. On his way out the man brings his flushed cheeks to their table. He holds out his hand and begins a round of shaking that ends with his hand in Benoit's. He gives Benoit a final, sincere squeeze and introduces himself.

"*Je m'appelle Lucien Boucher.*" He laughs. "*J'suis pas le grand Lucien, mais quand même proche à ses rêves.*"

No kidding. He isn't vaguely like Lucien Bouchard, is about half his size and half his age, is in his thirties maybe. He looks more like a red-faced Irishman then a French Canadian even though the guy talks as if Lucien Bouchard is his best friend.

The real star is Lucien Bouchard. Now he is a statesman. Everything he says is true. He's coming to speak to the district. Would the young men like to join the rally?

The guys look at each other.

"Bring your friends. The more the better. Monsieur Bouchard needs to know that he's being supported."

*

There's a buzz at the table. Eric cups his hands over his jaw. His face contorts. Looks like he has a toothache. Or the beer's too cold.

"*On va faire tout ce qu'on peut,*" Benoit declares.

"*Mais oui.*" Eric jostles away Benoit. "You can definitely count on me. I'm a devoted militant. I've been handing out Parti Quebecois literature and Quebec flags everywhere." Eric holds his hand out to the Irishman. He's as stiff as a statue in a park and very loud even with the clenched jaw. "*Vous pouvez conmpter sur nos votes. Et les votes de toutes nos familles.*"

Another minute he'll offer the votes of every last person he's ever bumped into, better yet the entire province. Benoit wrinkles his nose through his smirk.

Eric writes his name and number on a sheet of paper and hands it to Boucher. Maybe the rest of them would have done the same if Guimauve didn't suddenly run off to the washroom dragging André along.

Boucher glances at his watch. "I must run. I'll be in touch." He rolls up Eric's paper and scoots out the door.

Steve doesn't know what they're talking about. Apparently, they're expected to cast their votes and do something for the party at the polls. That's a good one. The idea of driving and voting and drinking beer makes him hiccup with laughter. The one beer he had makes him thirsty for another. Guimauve swears that it's not his fault if he desperately had to pee and besides, they're not allowed to talk about politics in his family. His parents probably won't even vote. Or if they do, one will vote Yes, and the other No. And one minus one makes zero. So what's the point?

"Yeah, elementary school math, guys. So what is the point?" André taps his pen on the table to the tune of a song nobody else can identify.

Eric gets up. "Let's go. The movie's finished."

"Pumpkin time," Steve says.

Nobody laughs. They never get what he says.

Eric straps himself into the front passenger seat. The rest of them roll hooting into the car with their big tangled feet. The drive home could be much more fun than their time at the bar except that Eric keeps rapping at the window with the ring on his finger.

"Eh, Eric," Steve warns.

Benoit puts a hand on Eric's arm. The two muscles on either side of the guy's fuzzy jaws look like boners.

Chapter 35

Day after day Steve arrives home from school and there's Mariette at the kitchen table peeling potatoes, radio blaring the same theme: Better vote Yes, why not vote Yes, wise people vote Yes, vote Yes with confidence, vote Yes, Yes, Yes. Mouth pinched, Mariette nods in bleak agreement.

Before that butcher of an anglophone murdered her daughter, she'd have voted No. She'd never have risked their retirement funds or her children's ability to make a living or the future of the trees or the sun above their heads. Separation from Canada comes with the possibility of war. Or a financial depression they might never climb out of. And if in their new country the 1930's return, they'll have to go back to bread and lard. Or less perhaps. When she was a girl, men knocked on the door to bargain an hour's work for a bowl of soup. Sometimes her mother did not open the door. Beans stretched by water only go so far. Quebecers could be placed in that same position if North American anger holds its grudge. But to gain freedom for her Steve, she is going to take that chance. As to the barest possibility of war– she isn't going to think about it.

She places a muffin on the table for her grandson, presses him into his seat and wavers in her determination. Her tall boy needs to be fed. She tucks her fists under her chin. If she doesn't stop herself, she'll take every dish in the cupboard, every glass, everything, everything in her sight and slam them against the walls. No. The way to bring a fair change into the world is to vote in the right direction. Steve glances at her. Quickly, she curves up her mouth in the one sure movement that expresses her love for him.

The moment Lou-Lou met that man and wanted to take him for a husband, she should have known that things weren't right. Why take that Horvat'? God knows, he wasn't anything to look at. In his twenties he was already jowly, spider webs mapped red and blue on his face. Except for the lick of a black beard around his chin, there was no man in him. Louise couldn't even speak his language. And him, French? He didn't even try.

And there was no convincing Louise. All her life she was a stubborn girl.

"*Y'a peut-être quelque chose qui n'va pas avec lui.* There's a blood spot on his nose," Mariette once ventured to her daughter.

But that's all Mariette ever said. All the signs were there and she ignored them. All she saw were Louise's bright smiles. Worse, she wanted to share in her daughter's pleasure. The plans for the wedding reception were Mariette's. She showed off the fiancé to all her friends. That's what she did– show off– her daughter's immaculate white gown, the champagne reception they had to borrow for– the groom with the stained face.

If she could only go backwards, reconnect every shard of her broken plates. She holds herself by the elbows, her arms crossed like an amulet over her breast. No. She's being punished for her pride. There's no way to erase that Horvat'. Even dead, that Horvat' is too close. She'll have to separate herself and her little boy from him and all of his. She rinses her rag under hot water till her fingers burn. Then she turns and smiles at Steve, a real one this time. Lucien Bouchard will not let them down.

Chapter 36

Guimauve slides a sheet of twice-folded note paper onto Steve's desk.

'Militants,' it reads, 'tonight, my house, 17:30. Eric P.

On the other side of the room, Benoit lifts his chin and gradually lowers it.

Great. Another long-winded show starring that bossy big mouth, Eric Poulin. More time Steve can't afford to waste. His homework weighs as much as his car.

Like an affectionate granddad, the Premier of Quebec beams full-faced through a twenty-seven-inch screen into Eric's basement. Half the math class is standing in front of the tube, their blazers and shoes piled along the baseboards. A bag of Oreo cookies is going around. The camera beams on the Premier of the province. Eric shushes them.

As if waiting for the silence Eric ordered, the Premier cocks his chin deliberately before leaning into the microphone. To the sound of Eric's growl, the boys become more attentive to this news conference than they ever are to a lecture. Never glancing at a note, Jacques Parizeau informs the province that he has appointed Lucien Bouchard as chief negotiator for the province. Following their certain victory, it will be Monsieur Bouchard who will arrange an agreement with Canada in order to establish for once and for all, the sovereign nation of Quebec. The Premier goes on with the roll call of Monsieur

Bouchard's attributes: his experience in federal politics, his diplomacy, his strength, his courage in the light of a recent illness that cost him his leg. Jacques Parizeau smiles at the boys in the suburban basement. A grim pleat between his eyes, he raises his arms in a giant V and urges the party militants to forge on.

Eric shoots up his fist in a salute. "Don't worry, Monsieur Parizeau," he shouts to the future prime minister of their country. "I'll bring you plenty of votes."

The guys break into a cheer. Benoit crouches to the floor and in less than a minute, almost everybody's hands are stacked in solidarity. Steve licks Oreo cream off his fingers and leans against the safety of the wall as the boys disengage, push their feet into their shoes and break out of the house.

Steve runs home so fast, his dinner plate is still warm when he arrives.

Mariette sits on a kitchen chair smack in front of the ten o'clock news. To the Premier, she murmurs a litany of loving words– My dear, we stand behind you. You made the right decision with Lucien, *le pauvre,* so courageous without a leg, so morally strong, so sensitive.

Réal snorts into his camomile. All night Mariette stays crimped in her corner of the bed. She has no intention of allowing Réal to cancel her vote with his.

*

In the hours following the telecast, the English press talks about how desperation forced the premier to call in Lucien Bouchard. Snickering loudly enough to produce an echo, The No side claims that the premier's baggy morale has sunk past his navel.

The Yes side chugs on— one vote at a time. Militants grab their compatriots by their sleeves and urge them to vote with their hearts. Nationalistic pride surges. The official French-Canadian language glues people together. Songs and novels about snow tighten the bonds. Those who remember the taste of a good tourtière at Christmas feel for once, that politics will bring them home to their heritage. And if they look inside their pockets, the citizens of Quebec will understand that the feds are helping themselves to everything that rightfully belongs to them. Face it, the party militants inform their people, there's a fiscal imbalance. We're the only province to pay tax federally and provincially. The feds owe us.

A little girl who looks as if she's about twelve, smiles into the vestibule. The blue and white 'OUI' pin shines on her lapel.

"Yes," Mariette says to the girl at the door. "I am voting, Yes."

"I congratulate you for making a wise choice." The girl presses a bundle of leaflets on Mariette. "Pass these to your undecided friends. When they have the correct information, everybody on your personal list will vote, *Oui*."

"I will." One thing she trusts is her ability to talk. Many of her friends call her for advice, or did before her daughter was killed. She's something of an authority when it comes to making jams and pickles. She used to sew all her own clothes and the little outfits her children wore. She knows all about wild mushrooms, can differentiate the edible from the poisonous. Not too many people can call themselves experts.

The girl grasps Mariette's hand and presses it between hers. "*C'est moi qui vous remercie.*"

Such a familiar voice, sweet, so much like a daughter's.

A personal list– such a smart girl. Mariette sits at the kitchen table to write out a few names. Marc, maybe her friend Lyse. She knocks her pen against the paper and purses her lip. Her other friends are too polite to discuss politics. Well. Never mind them. Réal should top the list.

Mariette mashes potatoes and dips a few sole filets in milk and flour. Political activity is all about determination. The shield and the sword, that's what. She washes her hands, swipes them against her apron and picks up her pen to cross Réal's name off her list. The clear path to a stronger future is already forming itself in her head. Spiralling towards the clouds are the words with which to prove her point. She'll say: Réal, when we break away, nobody can tell us what to do. *Nous*, us– Quebecers will make their own decisions. Not somebody in some other part of this continent. They don't know who we are or what we need– or even how to say hello in the language of the people. Shouldn't take long to convince him.

She tucks one of the leaflets under the TV's remote control and another in the bathroom inside Réal's most recent carpentry magazine. A third she puts on his pillow and a fourth in the pocket of his bathrobe. She fluffs up her hair and waits on the edge of the sofa. From the back of the house, she hears Steve grunting into the phone. He has friends, thank the good lord.

The minute Réal enters the house, she leaps up and throws her arms around him.

"Is something wrong?" He smells like the wet concrete of a cellar. His skin too is damp.

"Take your shower. I have good news for you."

"First give me *les bonnes nouvelles*."

"Go shower."

He returns pink cheeked and warm. "Anybody have a baby? *Non?*"

She opens her mouth.

"I already know. You joined the parti Quebecois."

"Not yet. I–"

He grins, places his hands over his ears and turns his backside to her. Two pamphlets stick out of his pockets. "*Non non non.* Not for me."

Well too bad. A husband is obliged to vote with his wife.

*

Mariette will not stop. Each time she serves coffee she drops a couple of words about how they're paying absurdly high taxes to the Canadian government in Ottawa for no reason. And how they're supporting Canadian embassies in every single country of the world where their so- called representatives do not speak even a basic *bonjour*. And how a woman from Trois Rivières, robbed and beaten limp in a third world country, could not be understood by her own embassy. The poor thing had to wait forty-eight hours in a hospital crawling with vermin, without a cent for a bowl of soup, before a French speaking clerk could be found to aid her. So what's the point of belonging to Canada, she tells him. Might as well separate.

Réal doesn't mind. Mariette is livelier since she's taken up the cause. And some of her arguments would be almost sensible if they could be trusted. Nothing true comes out of the mouth of her adored radio personality. As for the quick words of the Parti Quebecois– he certainly won't chance his luck with them. So-called intellectuals support that party– like they ever worked a day in their lives. All they do inside the brick walls of their universities is write articles that make as if Quebec will become perfection itself the minute they're out of Canada's grasp. Green grass and riches for all. A republic– whatever they want to call to call it– where every citizen will charge around the countryside shaking hands in French only. *Ha.*

The truth is, you can't get too far without the English language. His friend Jean Bolduc, who can switch seamlessly from French to English is the one with the sailboat in Florida and the two apartment buildings in Côte-des-Neiges, both completely rented.

That's how Réal sees things on Mondays, Wednesdays and Fridays. The rest of the week he isn't sure. Even when not one newspaper enters the house, media opinions are being thrown at him from morning to night. His stomach hurts. Since his daughter died, a thumb is jammed between his ribs. He wants only to be left in peace. And he wants to feel that thumb on his ribs forever.

Mariette ignores her husband and pays five dollars to become an official member of the *parti Quebecois*. She'll devote herself to the cause. One thing she trusts is her ability to talk. Many of her friends call her for advice or did, before her daughter was killed. She's something of an authority when it comes to making jams and pickles. She used to sew all her own clothes and the little outfits her children wore. She knows all about wild mushrooms, can differentiate the edible from the poisonous. Not too many people can call themselves experts.

Chapter 37

Above a tie knotted so tightly it might have squeezed the tongue out of his mouth if he had one, is the ever-smiling effigy of Ecole Notre Dame's model schoolboy. He's often plucked from the principal's closet and brandished at the real boys of the school in order for them to know what a perfectly clad student should look like. For fifteen minutes Father Turgeon lectures his fidgeting audience on how young men of distinction comport themselves either in or out of the school gates and another fifteen on how if they ever intend to become men of precision and polish, they will need to wear the school uniform: grey slacks, white shirts, blue blazers, the regulation school tie correctly knotted at the throat, grey or black socks, oxford lace-ups, a watch with a simple black band and nothing else. That means Na-thing. Nothing. They are to rid themselves of their bracelets and their little earrings and all the political paraphernalia that hangs off their clothing *tout de suite*. That means right now.

"All of you, stand up and remove the junk from your persons."

There's a rustle amongst the students as they untack and unplug and even tear off the objects that are not associated with permission. For the form, they grumble. But they expect to be reined in. Steve looks at the guys. Benoit stretches back his lips in a skeleton's grimace as he knots his tie. Steve hitches up his pants and drops his Yes pin into his pocket. They all do. Except for Eric. He's the only one whose tie is always secured around his throat. He has the tailored look of a lawyer on the front page of a magazine. He folds his arms across his chest and sits absolutely still.

Eric goes about his classes with his chest puffed. The profs are too much in love with his perfection to notice the pin displayed on his lapel. The students on his side thump him as he passes. Steve always remembers to give him a thumbs-up. Sometimes Eric acknowledges Steve's good wishes with something resembling a smile. Sometimes Eric doesn't even see him.

A couple of days after the assembly, Eric actually stops him and says, "*Salut*, Steve."

Steve raises his thumb.

"How much do you charge?"

"Charge?"

"Eh, you forgot? You're tutoring English, aren't you?"

Maybe Eric can't manage an A plus for the robotic phrases he might produce.

"You come to my house. Be there tomorrow at sixteen hundred." Eric swivels around and stalks down the hall.

It appears that their relationship has moved up a rung. Later they'll become real friends and when that happens, Steve will charge him half price for the lessons.

*

Benoit takes the pose of a lone monk at the far corner of the cafeteria. The crusts of his sandwich are lined up like a retaining wall in front of his folded hands.

"So. You're giving English lessons now," he says before Steve has a chance to pull up a chair. "Everybody saw your little ad on the bulletin board. *Tuteur d'anglais*. Reasonable rates."

"Yeah. What's wrong with that?"

"What-is-wrong-with-that. You mean you don't know? You can't be that stupid."

Steve clenches the neck of his lunch sack.

"Go on. Eat your lunch. And I'll tell you what-is-wrong-with-that."

"I'm just trying to make a few bucks."

"In the new nation of Quebec, we will not need English. Quebec is a French nation."

"So?"

"Nobody wants to waste their time learning English."

"Yah?" Steve bites into his sandwich. Salami. His favourite. "Eric does."

In the crammed halls, you can't tell by the way the boys stand or jiggle or comb their hair, how they'd vote if they were allowed to. The only sure thing is that the No-sympathizers are definitely nerds with a capital N. Or they're in love with one of their dead English grandfathers. Or they're Asian. There are three of them in Steve's English class. For some reason, their English is so clean it practically squeaks. Even if at home they speak Chinese.

Lately the Asians huddle so closely, it looks like their socks are sewn together. Benoit and Steve pass them on one side. As Eric brushes past on the other, their circle tightens in self- protection. Steve turns away as they close ranks, acting as if he doesn't notice. They're different but not. Their accents are indecipherable from his. Without looking, you'd think they were *de souche*, as entrenched in the French-Canadian culture as anybody else. Unaccompanied by his buddies, Steve makes friendly overtures in their direction each time he passes them by, the barest of nods usually, but still a little something. He could have been part of their circle just as easily as his own. Or part of nothing at all, a bead rolling without direction. But now– he's part of another kind of people– the cool ones.

Guimauve runs to catch up with them, his book sack hanging off one shoulder.

"Eh, Tuan," he shouts as he passes the Asians.

Tuan Lo breaks away from his buddies and runs alongside, talking like a battery-operated toy. Just before they reach Benoit, he stops in his tracks and races back to his friends.

Steve isn't sure what made Tuan pull away, Eric's glower as he glanced at him or Father Turgeon's starched black coat bearing in on them like a speeding oath.

Chapter 38

One Jesus glows beneficently under a halo. The other drips with blood. The principal sits at his desk between the two photos and glares at Benoit. "Tie up those laces and get to your class."

Steve tugs surreptitiously at his drooping tie while Benoit bends over his laces. As he slithers out of the room Turgeon eyes Steve then turns his attention to the soldier-stiff Eric.

"*Monsieur* Poulin. I will look away while you remove that pin." He turns his chair to face an entire library behind the desk and pulls out a volume on butterflies.

Eric folds his arms across his chest.

Turgeon flips through the butterflies. Steve flexes his calf muscles. He keeps one eye on the principal and with the other, tries to appear interested in books.

Turgeon peruses the Monarch at some length, turns the page and glances up. "Ah, Steve, you may leave." Then he jerks his chin at Eric and points to the chair facing his desk.

"Sit," he orders. "Monsieur Dumont, please close the door behind you."

What happened? Tell us. The guys stand like grazing sheep outside the school gates. Steve's never been so popular. He pulls his tie up and down and tells them that Eric stuck out his tongue at the Jesus pictures when Turgeon was picking out his pretty book.

"Eh–"André interrupts. He blows a trail of smoke at the school. "One of his parentals took him home." He points his yellow fingertips at the study hall window. "I saw him get in the car."

"Alright. Let's go," Benoit says. He jerks his head at Steve and they go.

Like pencils strewn, André, Guimauve, Alex, Benoit and Steve lie hodgepodge on the beige Berber while Eric paces between them.

"He doesn't like your beard." Alex angles his smooth face at Eric. "I'm clean, that's why the religios love me."

"Has nothing to do with it."

"What did you do?" Benoit asks.

"What did I do? I did nothing more than stand up for my rights.

I'll bet you pasted your snot on Turgeon's door knob," Alex says.

"I should have."

Those who always talk, talk:

Benoit: Alright, stop running around. Give us the story.

Eric: Turgeon told me to remove my Yes pin. I said, No. Then he turns around and kicks me out. Three days suspension.

Alex: Freedom.

André: As long as we're imprisoned between the walls of the school there's no such thing as freedom.

Eric: Some guy complained that he doesn't feel comfortable in my presence.

Benoit: He told you that?

Alex: Fuck him.

Eric: Basically. He says the guy doesn't feel free in his own school.

Alex: Fuck freedom.

André: Freedom is in here (he taps his noodle). And here. (He jerks his thumb at his gullet). It's the right to think in any political language available and to spit out your beliefs anywhere and anytime you please. The guy who complained doesn't want another person's opinion staring at him. Well too bad. That's life in the free world.

Alex: Yeah. Like every time he looks up, somebody's telling him how to think.

Guimauve simply says, "Tu-an." He says it smooth and soft, butter in his mouth.

It shuts them up.

Eric stops pacing. The murmur of heat flows through the pipes.

"You have no proof," Benoit says to the ceiling.

"Tu-an," Guimauve repeats with a mixture of reverence and disgust.

"Tu-an," Alex grunts.

They know. The whole school knows that the Asians stand around like pillars for the No side. They're too chicken to say a word about politics out loud, but the word, No, fairly spews from their blank faces and their closed mouths.

Benoit thrusts his foot toward Guy's head. "Tu-an's too preoccupied with grades to bother complaining about anything. Even when the exam's ten years away all he ever does is review his notes."

"Yeah? Maybe it's Tu-an maybe not. I don't care."

"Yeah," Alex says. "What do you care. You get three days off.

And everybody thinks you're a hero," Benoit says.

"I am."

And Steve laughs louder than anybody else because he can't think of anything important to say and up until now, felt like a ton of hollow bricks.

"Eh–" Eric says, "give Tu-an a big kiss for me."

The guys snicker.

"*J'suis sérieux.* If he's the one who delivered me to the evil headman, then he's the one who made me come to my senses. *Les gars*, sometimes you have to have a revolution."

Alex grunts and races up the stairs to the toilet. André follows. Benoit starts a longwinded lesson on the quiet revolution, how Quebecers have already achieved an enormous amount with determination and solidarity alone and how, if Gandhi was leading them, they'd get all they wanted without doing anything more arduous than exerting their dignity.

"Gandhi, sure," Eric says. "And who else should lead us? Robespierre? Benjamin Franklin? How about Napoleon?"

"I wasn't trying to annoy anybody."

"You know what? The so-called quiet revolution wasn't so quiet. The FLQ woke people up. And if you ask me, a bomb here and there will make it very clear how serious we are."

"*Quoi, tu veut tuer le monde?*" Benoit snorts.

"Don't be stupid. We won't kill anybody. Not even that asshole with the hyphenated name."

Back from the toilet, Alex points his index at the gang and mouth-pops them with a theatrical jerk of his neck. Guimauve drops, raises his finger, and ra-tat-tatting away, shoots them all.

All night long Steve kicks and sweats. What kind of English Eric wants to learn isn't too clear.

"Not English class English," he told Steve. "Don't waste my time with that crap."

"*Eh– c'est toi. Quelle heure est-il?*" Eric waves him in.

"It's four already. You been sleeping all day?"

"Are you kidding?" He's still in his ironed pyjamas and socks looking like he didn't bother to sleep. Didn't need to.

"Uh– I came for your English lesson."

"I know why you came." He turns and strides down a hallway. "*Eh–* What are you waiting for?"

Steve takes off his shoes and scurries after him.

A huge pizza box lies on the centre of Eric's bed. Other than that, the room looks as if it belongs in a hotel. Two glasses stand on the desk beside a water pitcher. There's a notepad and pen on a corner of the desk. Nothing more than a photograph of a hill flecked with skiers decorates the pale blue wall. There's no shoes or clothing, no homework, no clutter of daily living.

"You know what's good about being kicked out of school for no reason?"

"A holiday?"

"*Ben non.* It's the awakening of the parentals. The curtain has risen." Eric raises his arms. "What's your problem? You have to pee?"

"No– just wondering if we should uh– maybe speak English?"

Eric flips open the pizza box. Patches of brown bacon are scattered over a greasy slick of cheese. "Want some?"

Steve shakes his head then remembers to speak. "*Non merci,* no thank you." He doesn't actually know what they should talk about. Sports, maybe hockey. Except that the words in both languages are pretty much identical.

"I love bacon pizza. Could you imagine? My mother ordered it for me." Eric chews reflectively. "They'd pull me out of the school if I let them. You know what I told them?"

Steve shakes his head.

"I told them that the only thing I really want is for them to vote Yes. And you know what?"

Steve glances at his watch wondering if he should start to charge for the lesson right this minute or wait for Eric to utter at least one English word.

"I'll bet you they'll vote exactly as I ordered."

Once they figure out what to talk about, Steve could teach conversational English. But if Eric is expecting grammar, forget it. Steve speaks and writes more or less grammatically but doesn't know how it happens, wouldn't be able to explain it. In Steve's mouth, the word pizza could sound either French or English. To start off the lesson, he says pizza in English.

"Yeah." Eric saunters to the pizza and gazes into the box. "It feels really great to tell your parents what to do." He reaches for the ball of dough at the centre of the extra-large and stops midway. "*Eh.* Have a look at this. The future of Quebec is laid out right here, right on this pizza. Each one of these is a cabinet minister." He presses his finger on one of the cheesy wedges. "Get what I'm saying?"

"Pizza," Steve corrects.

"This, for example, can be Benoit, Minister of Justice, since he's planning to be a lawyer. André can be Minister of Health." Eric lifts out a slice and takes a bite. "We'll all have some role in the cabinet. Even you."

Eric tears off another slice and proffers it to Steve. "You must be hungry."

Steve takes the pizza with the edge of his fingers, not wanting to make a mess.

"Go on. Eat. *C'est ben bon.*"

The thing is stone cold. Steve chews and swallows.

Eric pulls out a Kleenex from the box beside the bed and hands it to Steve. "I'll bet you're wondering why in the world I want to study English. Well you're right. In a French country, it's a useless waste of time."

When there's money in raking leaves the real waste of time is right here.

"Anybody who doesn't serve us in French should be jailed. That's what I'll do. I'll put them all in jail. I'll crush them." He crumples a piece of paper and smacks it into the garbage pail. "You didn't ask me why I want the extra English."

"Why?"

"Sit down. You can't teach me anything while you're jiggling."

Steve flushes, relieved by the mention of the lesson.

"*Quoi?* There's something wrong with your voice?"

Steve scrambles for an English word that won't get him thrown in jail and comes up with, "Okay."

"Okay." Eric nods at the chair. *"Assis-toi.* The way I see it is, if Jacques Parizeau speaks English, so should I. You can't negotiate with Canada unless you understand their language."

Big surprise. The future Prime Minister of the country of Quebec is Eric the dough ball, smack in the centre of the pizza, higher, crustier, more dignified than everybody else.

"The thing is, if we get every word they say, the Canadians won't be able to feed us shit. We need to join the party and move on in the ranks quickly. So– I'm making a plan."

"Uh– *Veux tu parler* in English?"

"Yes sir." Eric's accent is startlingly precise, his anglophone R rolled back in the throat. "We speak English right to-day." But as if his mind is programmed in only one direction, he proceeds in French.

"I'll find the recipe for a bomb from some FLQ manual. All we have to do is buy a few chemicals, stir them up with baking soda and vinegar and there you go. Boom."

It sounded like Eric said the word bomb, but no, he must be talking about some kind of recipe.

Steve turns his tongue in his mouth and in clearly enunciated English says, "Bomb."

Eric gazes at him, pours himself a glass of water and proceeds in his usual language. "I don't think a bomb will necessarily bring on new voters. Takes a big explosion to do that. But people will come to their senses. Get what I'm saying?"

Steve only knows that it feels weird in this hotel room. "We didn't do much English and I have to go home soon. How about if you repeat after me?"

"*Pas d'problème.*"

"I - like - popcorn - too."

Eric removes twenty bucks from his pocket and holds it out. "We'll have another session next week. Same time."

Steve snatches it, dashes down the hall, jams his feet into his boots, and runs home.

On Monday morning Eric shows his wispy beard at the school without the Yes emblem on his blazer. None. He murmurs to Benoit after which Benoit meanders past the guys, stopping at each ear till he reaches Steve's. "*Après les classes. Devant les portes.*" The time and place of the meeting, nothing more.

Steve slips into the washroom and locks himself into a stall. He might as well have a stomach ache and not go. And if Beardie takes a fit over it, who needs him anyway? There's plenty of other ways to get twenty bucks.

Somebody runs into the washroom. Steve cups his face in his hands and listens to him pee. The faucet starts and stops. Within the ripping paper comes the sound of the bell.

"Eh– *t'est la*?" The guy bangs at Steve's door. "*La cloche a sonné.*"

Benoit. Always on his leash.

"Steve?"

"*J'ai mal au ventre.*"

"Wipe your ass and flush. I'll give you a Tums."

"I really don't feel well."

Benoit rattles the door. "Get out. If you need to go to the infirmary, I'll take you."

Steve flushes and throws open the door.

"You look fine to me."

"Yeah. I'm fine." He passes his hands under cold water and wipes them on his pants.

*

Six obedient cabinet ministers stand on the front steps of the school. Eric eyes them till they're quiet, then points at Alexandre with his chin. "*T'as quel âge, toi?*"

"*Seize?*"

"*T'est idiot*, Alexo."

The boys snicker.

"*Eh–*"

Eric rubs the boy's smooth cheeks. "*Eh nono– t'as dix-huit ans.*"

Alex opens his mouth.

"*Ferme-la. On va croire que t'as un bébé.*"

The boys burst. That's a good one and true. When Alex's round mouth forms his special little O, he looks like a two-year-old.

"Guess what guys– you're all eighteen except for André. He's nineteen."

André raises his arms in a pirouette.

"Yeah, strip off that uniform," one of the boys shouts.

"And, because I'm the only one with the chin hair to prove it, I am twenty. The board of directors will be issuing new ID cards. Even you, Alexo *le bo-bo*, can look like an eighteen-year-old as long as you have an ID card to prove it and wear a turtleneck up to your nose."

"Yeah?" Benoit stands with his arms crossed, his legs apart. "What's wrong with the IDs I got?"

"Nothing. They're great if all you want to do is get a beer." Eric smiles so widely his little beard fairly quivers. "*Mais*– if you want to vote in a provincial referendum, you'd better have some identification that's a little more sophisticated. Let's just say– a passport.

"You're *fucké* man. We're not Canadian. We're Quebecois."

"*Eh* Benoit, relax. Every vote counts. We can make a difference." Eric keeps talking, the smile broadening till his cheeks reach the bridge of his nose. He repeats stuff about statistics and regions and opinion polls and maybe even an opera on TV. The guy probably sleeps with a dictionary under his pillow. As the group disperses, he follows Benoit and Steve down the street yakking the whole way.

When Eric finally turns in the direction of his house, Benoit grasps Steve by the shoulder and shakes him.

"*T'as pas peur?*"

"Afraid of what? He didn't say anything about a bomb."

"Don't you get it? He wants us to vote in the referendum. *C'est pas légal. On peut aller en prison pour ça.*"

"They don't put you in prison for a little tick mark on a piece of paper."

"If you believe that, you're an idiot." Benoit stops to light a cigarette while Steve measures out his steps, two per paving stone. Two times three to the corner.

"He thinks he's some kind of hero.

The Premier," Steve mutters.

"Hey, are you even listening?"

Steve waits for his friend at the curb, his toes on the very edge, about to tip.

Benoit arrives panting. "You can't argue with Eric." He begins to laugh sluggishly, his narrow shoulders rounding like an umbrella under his blazer. "*J'adore les rayures.* Man, won't we look sna-zzy behind bars."

"Doesn't work like that."

"What?"

Steve shrugs. Benoit might be the crown prince of grammar and history but he knows nothing about crime. When Steve commits crimes and not the kind Benoit thinks is a crime, it's because he has to. The second one, taking the money, is less criminal than the first because he really only borrowed it. It isn't his fault that he hasn't paid it back yet. He will as soon as he gets himself a real job. It was his aunt's fault anyway, how she practically pointed arrows to her purse and left money floating around in there as if it was garbage. She knew perfectly well that being pure and good wasn't in his genes.

"Yeah you're right. You can't go through an honourable life without being a political activist."

"I'll vote even if it's not legal," Steve says. It won't matter. He's already on the verge of going to jail. Once you start being a criminal there's no going back. Drinking at the bar was illegal and didn't even feel illegal. You could get arrested for pretending to sleep under the bed while your mother gets killed. He got away with that one because the police were too busy feeling sorry for him to figure things out. They asked about a million of the wrong questions and not once did they wonder why the hell he was under the bed, his big fat stupid fingers in his ears. His grandmother says that he was under the protection of Jesus Christ and Mary and the Holy Ghost and who knows what else. But it's not that. It's just the way things go for invisible people.

Chapter 39

In about three minutes Benoit emerges from Père Turgeon's office with the gold key to room 4. Eric unlocks the door. Except for a few delaminated wood benches and a warped table, room 4 is barren. Six ministers file into their so-called study hall bearing armloads of books. Without a word between them, they fall into line on the one shaft of daylight permitted by the frayed edges of the flannel blankets that cover the windows. As soon as Eric closes the door, they burst into unanimous giggles.

"*De l'ordre*," Eric commands.

Still tipsy, they settle around the table in the centre of the room leaving Alexandre to hiccup against the wall.

"Alex, sit your ass in here," Eric drums the table till his acolyte joins the group on one of the two warped benches around the table.

"Gentlemen, I made an important contact and have arranged for us to receive–" Eric pauses like Jacques Parizeau would - "official, and I mean official, drivers licenses."

"Who's your contact?"

"Your brother."

"Yeah Eric," Benoit sneers, "that's real official. Besides, you already have a license."

Eric lengthens his neck and smiles. "You forgot, *mon cher* fellow voter, you need to be eighteen to vote. That is what our official paperwork will prove. Now, *messieurs*, as I call your names, please stand up."

As the boys stand in turn, he hands each a card.

Steve stares at his plastic identification. His own eyes glare back at him. "Where'd you get the pictures?"

"My brother still had them, I'll bet," Benoit says.

"I got them for free given the nobility of the cause."

André examines his. "I don't know–"

"*Ça veut dire quoi ça?*"

"*Ben–* It isn't that simple. We have to register for the vote."

"Yeah. Don't worry about it, we'll register."

His fingers rigid on the steering wheel, he hears himself sigh. Whatever it is they want him to do, he's not afraid.

Each time Steve goes to Eric's with nothing more than a backpack loaded with lists of English words, he makes twenty bucks. The minute Eric's parents realize that he isn't learning much, Steve will certainly be fired and even be obliged to return the money. He could open the garage and slide in behind the wheel of his barely used car and back out. He unfolds his wallet and pulls out his permits. They appear equally fake, as fake as the English lessons. The crooked line of his mouth in both photos dares him to be a real person. To ram the car into the world right this minute.

Yeah, but nobody will know. He'll make two or three more twenties and take off forever.

André and Eric are at the kitchen table facing the same pizza as the week before, regenerated just for the English party.

"I'd offer you a piece, but there's only enough for two." Eric contemplates André, eyes shiny with obvious admiration while the guy chomps with his yellow teeth.

André tips back his chair, wipes his lips with the back of his hand and nods at Steve. "Is he taking part in the plans?"

"Benoit swears on him."

They gaze at Steve as if, chosen from a row of suspects, he's not too trustworthy.

"You planning to stand all day?" Eric says.

"What about the English lesson?"

"You just sit and listen. We're making important plans."

"*Restes debout si tu veux.*" André smells of cigarettes, his blazer smudged with sticky crap and loose hairs. According to Benoit, the guy's a brainiac even though he hasn't figured out a way to get rid of his dandruff. He stuffs the last wad into his mouth and turns to Eric. "*Alors*, we're all set to vote?"

"They won't let us register."

"*Non.* They won't."

"*Tu-l'savais.* Why didn't you tell me?"

"You never know till you try."

"*Sacré Jesus.* You wouldn't believe the questions they asked. I thought they were going to ask for my toenail clippings next. Sit down Steve, you're making me nervous."

"Sit here." André taps the bed. "The dead don't talk you know." He glances at Steve. "And, the funny thing about information in governments is that it's passed around really slowly, *len-te-ment*. Did you notice how long that word is? It's long so you can say it sl-ow-ly. You know what I'm getting at?"

"Of course I know," Eric answers. "But go ahead, lead on *maître*. I love the discourse."

André's chair claps to the floor. "Eh– first I need a smoke. You guys coming?" He dashes out before they have a chance to stand.

"Maybe you could practice your English while we smoke."

"You don't get it, Steve."

"You don't want to learn English?"

"Not right this minute. I have more important things to do."

"Leave him alone." André's voice floats in through the open door. "He doesn't want a career in politics. He wants to be a barber for the English community in NDG."

Eric runs out of the house. "Nah. He wants to be a cab driver." The two of them laugh. Steve turns back into the house.

"He's too damned serious to be a cab driver. Eh Steve," André shouts, "that was a joke."

"Steve, relax. You can be Minister of Transport."

The hyenas laugh like he's in another country never mind ten steps away from them, invisible behind the open door, his ears wide open. Rigid, he peers at them between the hinges. They inhale loudly, letting a haze of stinking smoke rise above their heads.

"Now listen," André leans back against the building bricks. "When a person dies, the government finds out in about a day or a week at the most. Some doctor fills out the paperwork and zap– somebody in death department number one gets all the details. But the voting department, either because it's in another building or it's one-hundred-and-thirty-fourth on the list of departments to be advised, or the employees are half dead themselves, doesn't find out that person XXX moved underground until far later– weeks, even months."

"*Oui mais*, when we have our own country, the system will be much more efficient," Eric says.

André smiles. "*Ecoutes ben*. We can get a list– let's say for a school project– of people between the ages of eighteen and twenty-two who died in the last month or so. Next, we correlate it with the voter's list. All we'd need after that is a photo ID that gives their name."

"We have IDs," Eric says.

"Right face, wrong name. Let me explain further. Dead people can't show up at the referendum polls even if they're on the voter's list and they really want to vote. But if some dead guy's name is on your ID card, you can vote in their place. That would be a very nice memorial to them, don't you think?"

"*Y'a pas beaucoup d'mort jeunes*," Eric says.

"Ah— there's tons of them. Car accidents, drug overdoses, cancer, a murder here and there. Suicide."

"And when the bomb explodes, we'll have a few more."

André laughs.

Some big joke. Steve unzips his backpack and pulls out the sheets of English vocabulary. He feels the nausea in his empty stomach. Yeah, like Eric thinks he won't have to pay him for the lessons.

Eric fist-punches the sky. "They'd feel happy to have died for a good cause."

"*Ben oui*," André answers. "But don't bother killing Tu-an. He's too young to vote."

Chapter 40

All night, Marnie's authority blusters wisdom inside Paula's brain— Go on, what are you waiting for? Didn't I tell you to be a doer? Do something. Get those voters on board. Win that race. Bring the boy home. Celebrate his birthday. Gather up those voters. Go on, quit sitting around. Get off your butt. Do something.

The floating turban refuses to shut up. As Paula presses a palm to her ear praying the speech will rattle itself into the floor, the country's falling apart. What seemed like a big joke isn't funny anymore. And Steve is miles away, in a country of his own.

A warehouse nowhere near the bus stop houses the Liberal party. People cluster about looking as if they know exactly where they should stand and why this one act of standing is of great national importance. With more experience in politics, Paula too will learn where to stand. Meanwhile, she leans against a wall and waits.

A patter of applause starts up as a speaker calls for silence. Everybody gathers forward. A couple of boys set a few folding chairs haphazardly throughout the room as the speaker thanks his audience for coming. He says a few words about success generated by people like them and again, thanks them. If Paula could catch just a glimpse of the speaker, she'd hear him more clearly. She weaves her way closer to the front. He tells them that in this, their last stage of the fight, they'll have to roll up their sleeves. Paula cocks her head. She can roll up her sleeves like the best of them. And then what? Attack the problem the way she does her cleaning, one blast of disinfectant after another. That's not too hard. The minute she gets her instructions, she'd tell the right things to the right people. With a specific action plan, things will start shaking.

For a long time, the speaker explains things in a French that is indecipherable to Paula, then switches to English. "All we want you to do is ask questions," he declares. "Approach your friends and acquaintances, and very gently," he raises his fingers as if to conduct a symphony. "Ask them if they are *sure* they have made the right decision. A gentle nudge is all it will take. The Liberal party believes in the psychological method. Gently, gently, we will bring the voters on board."

After a smattering of applause, the young man shouts. "If each one of us does just a little, we will accomplish much."

Paula lines up for a work detail.

"Six blocks of door to door? Do I look like I can't walk?"

"You need to speak French."

"Of course I speak French."

Her purse waded with leaflets, she's psyched, ready to go. Her address list is in the mail.

Three days later she unfolds the page. Somewhere on the other end of the city are people who need to be told how to vote. She balls up her fists and calls Shelly.

Shelly begins his litany of complaints. "You didn't tell me we'd be driving all the way to Timbuktu." He pulls up to a block of two-story duplexes. "Look at those buildings, Paula. That's fifteen winding staircases times two. We've got six F-ing blocks of this."

"Wonderful. We save the nation and become physically fit at the same time. And you know what else? For once, we're on the same team. Now go." She pushes Shelly ahead of her and starts trudging up the stairs.

Up and down three times. Nobody answers. They don't answer even when the sound of the TV pipes on. Paula stuffs pamphlets into mailboxes. At the fourth address, Quebec's blue *fleur-de-Lys* flag is draped over the door.

Shelly turns back. "No way. We're not stopping at this place."

"Then what's the point?"

"You think they'll change their minds when they hear your accent?"

"Your accent, Shelly. That's why you're here."

"It's enough, we've done enough."

Paula turns away from the blue door and pushes Shelly up the next flight. At her third ring, a woman eating an apple cracks the door. "*Oui?*"

Paula gives Shelly a couple of pokes as if to kick-start her moody television.

"*Bonjour*, hi, *Je suis* Shelly Shapiro and I'm with the Liberal Party."

It's up to Paula to continue except that her mouth is frozen over the French words she's practiced for hours in front of the mirror. She's supposed to ask something friendly and unthreatening, something like, I see that you're crunching into an apple. Well you know what? That apple was probably grown in Quebec. Great! But did you know that apples grow all over Canada? She wants to form her thoughts into sentences but Shelly's already done his bit. No time. It's her turn.

She bites her lip. "*Il fait froid?*"

The woman wraps her arms around herself, the apple pinched between index and thumb. "*Ben oui.*"

Wow, converted already. Paula offers the woman a pamphlet and to the closing door, a Welcome to Canada smile.

Shelly thumps down the stairs, climbs into his car and slams the door. "Get in, Paula."

She peers into the open window. "Why? She was nice."

"You tell her it's cold? That's the political message?"

"That was a subtle way of saying we're all Canadians. We're not supposed to annoy anybody."

"Yeah right. Now get in."

"We have to finish the list."

He turns on the motor. "We're wasting our time."

Paula looks at the impenetrable row of facades, every household curtained against her opinions and advice. She gets into the car and refuses to say another word.

Too early for bed, Paula sits at the kitchen table and gazes through the window. Across the alley, in her neighbour's illuminated kitchen, a grey silhouette stir-fries vegetables, or tosses a salad. As from the perfection of television, Paula sees him comb his hair. She wants to tell him, if he in fact is a he, to be smart and vote No. Forget the shy questions. She should act like a person with a heart, should fling open the window and shout, Just vote No! But the polite politics of her party disagrees with such tactics. Politeness itself drives her to close her curtains when he lifts a fork to his mouth. Or white-faced, waves at her.

Apart from this ghostly neighbour, Paula knows absolutely nobody to whom she could pose the courteous question mark. Everybody in Paula's Anglophone circle and beyond will certainly vote No. And immigrants? Guided by pure fear and the desire to keep their imported languages on their tongues, new citizens of Canada-Quebec have no other choice but to vote No. None has signed up for a country in turmoil. They could have stayed home for that. Which leaves the Francophones. No way to know by looking at them where their sympathies lie or even what language they speak in their own homes.

So, who must she convince? She ponders her options till the mailman hammers at her door.

"Hey," she says to him, "What do you think? Shouldn't we just let things be?"

He thrusts plastic boxes of books on tape into her hands and rushes off to the next mailbox.

Chapter 41

Sharon seats her mother in the corner of the room and allows her to watch as she places dishes in boxes. Two young men take away the sofa and the bed that was Sharon's since she was sixteen. Paula waves at one of the boys, tempted to ask the Is This Really What You Want, question except that he looks too young to vote. As he bends and lifts the sofa, the blue and white pin on his T-shirt winks at them.

After they leave, Paula says, "He was laughing at us."

"No Mom. He's a lawyer in family court. The guy never smiles."

"Even lawyers vote the wrong way?"

"Two sides to every argument."

Sharon unhooks the living room curtains. Toronto is grabbing the best Quebec has to offer: its people, its industry, its banks and insurance companies. Its chrome kitchen tables and worn-out cotton. Even its language is finding homes elsewhere.

The sun prints a tattoo against the walls. Paula shades her closed eyes with a pair of dark glasses. This sun, so craved by other people makes her crazy.

She says, "Let me help," but doesn't mean it. Earlier Paula broke a glass and immediately after, a hand-crafted bowl.

Sharon cloaks her mother's head with a squashed straw hat. "There. Better?"

While Sharon fills the last of her boxes, Paula dozes. She's awakened late in the afternoon with a paper cup of tea. The apartment is chilly in its bareness. Sharon leans over and kisses her. Paula holds onto her hand. Toronto isn't too far. But if Paula were to drive, it would take a month or more, maybe a year to get there. What Sharon looks like now will alter as she ages. Already Paula can't recognize her in a crowd. She takes a deep breath of her daughter, her smell of soap and newsprint and presses her face to Sharon's moisturized cheek.

"Maybe you should leave some of your things with your father."

"Mom—" Sharon shakes herself away.

Paula takes hold of the table. She has to clutch something. "That way you won't have to tow them back and forth."

"Mom. There's nothing for me here."

"But you speak French."

"What don't you get, Mom? They don't want us here."

In the familiarity of her home and in the dusk that calms her, Paula remembers the way Sharon held the lawyer's eyes. From eye to eye, a passage of understanding connects Sharon to everybody she meets. Eye to eye for people who are not Paula. Amidst the street chatter of multiple languages, nobody makes eye contact with Paula. It makes sense for her to feel unwanted. But not Sharon, surely not her. Yet she said it herself. Handicapped by politics, Paula's child is not wanted here.

Paula rubs the back of her head till her hair stands. No. She won't let it happen to Sharon. If she has to convince people to vote No, she will. Even if she has to dig total strangers from the phone book. Even if she has to hocus-pocus them out of thin air. She'll twist their ears till common sense pours into their brains.

Paula grips the receiver. She knows that phone number by heart because in her heart she's dialled it hundreds of times. The conversation, warm in her blood, burns through the phone line. Without the faintest idea of what to say, she dials.

"*Allo–*"

It's always her.

"*Allo?*"

Through the hammering in her ears, Paula says, "Hello. *Bonjour.*" There's a long silence, that woman's usual schtick. Just as she had at her door-to-door campaign Paula says, "Hello, *je m'appelle* Paula–"

"*Vous n'avez pas le droit de parler à Steve.*"

"I know. I'm not calling him. I'm calling you."

"*Qu'est-ce-que vous voulez?*"

She wants nothing that isn't hers.

"*Ma-dame. Qu'est-ce-que vous voulez?*"

All she wants is to ask a simple question. Is Mariette Dumont sure? Has she thought about the consequences? Would she please tell Sharon that Quebec is her home, that she's more than welcome here?

And if it isn't such a big deal, please damn it, put Steve on the line. Paula only wants to hear his voice. She hears instead the strident click of the receiver so brief, it's almost polite.

Between the walls of her apartment, there's nobody to speak to in either language. The last of Sharon's breezy conversation sits hard on her. On Sharon's last day of work, she was taken out for lunch by the gang of translators.

"Everybody's sad. It's like, they all want to go with me but they're too chicken."

"Me too. I want to go." The words escaped their guarded cell.

"Now people are saying that Montreal should separate from the province. I mean, if a province can separate, why can't a city? If there weren't so many separatist lawyers, they'd be jumping to defend that one."

"If you want, I'll move to Toronto too. Better for the cause, isn't it?"

"Better for the cause is to stay here and fight. It's just that I have no choice. Don't be worried about me. Are you worried, Mom?"

"No sweetheart. You do whatever you have to."

Paula takes out a dish and a knife and fork and sets them on the table. She'll have to put food on the plate. She opens and closes every one of the cupboards then passes her hands over the length of the counter. Her fingers bump into the plastic case of the fossilized Happy Birthday Steve cake. Cake or sandwich, it's all the same in the end, a brain silencer down her throat. Paula arranges the cake in the centre of the table and cuts out a massive wedge. Mouth wide, she bites off the Happy. Before ants dare take possession of the cake, she chomps down piece after piece. If it wasn't so damned hard and so damned stale, she might have enjoyed it.

She awakes with the slime of frosting in her mouth. How the cack disappeared in its entirety is too embarrassing to recall. She'd have eaten through the very walls of the apartment if sleep hadn't demanded its share of her body. In one abrupt movement, Paula clamps her hands over her ears. Stop thinking about it. Stop. She pulls her hair till her scalp feels as though it's about to separate from her skull. Quivering, she throws on a jacket. Get out of this place. Go.

There are fifty, maybe sixty steps that lead from the mall entrance to Marnie's paisley curtains. A line of little girls wait their turns. Paula swallows her saliva and careens past them through the drawn paisley into the booth.

The teenager perched on the chair gapes.

Marnie slams the table. "Hey. Ever heard of privacy? When the curtain is closed, that means, Keep Out."

"It's an emergency.

Wait your turn."

The girl closes her mouth over her braces and gets up. "That's okay. I'll come back another time."

Paula shrugs off her jacket. "Take my advice child. Hang on to your hormones. If he really loves you, he'll wait."

"Mind your own beeswax," Marnie says as the girl's red face disappears past the curtains.

"So— are she and her boyfriend getting back together?"

"That'll be twenty please."

Paula places a coin on the table. "I only want a loonie's worth."

Sighing, Marnie takes the dollar. "Talk fast. Your time is running out."

"I just want to know if I should move to Toronto."

"Why? What's in Toronto?"

"My daughter's going."

Marnie grunts. "I told you already. Be a Doer. Not a Mover."

"It sounds like the same thing."

"If you move, you'd be a Follower. Doer, means doing."

"I did. I joined the Liberal party."

"And?"

"All they want us to do is ask stupid questions."

"Going to the unity rally tomorrow?"

"What rally?"

"Don't you read the papers?"

"You know perfectly well I can't read."

"I mean, listen to the radio, watch— I mean listen to the TV." She's like a live wire buzzing. "Every politician in the country's showing up.

The entire country's in arms." She lowers her voice. "Go Canada," and begins to sing. "Ca-na-da. One little two little three little provinces. Weeee love you, now we are twenty milli-on." The '67 Olympics song. "Remember that?

Remember the national anthem? Might as well sing it while we still can." She leans closer, singing on in a whisper, "*O Ca-na-daaa terre-eu de nos-aieux*," like the song's telling a secret. "*–ton front est ceint, de fleurons glorieux! Car ton bras sait porter l'épéé –eu, il sait porter la croix! Ton histoire est une épopée-eu des plus brill-iants exploits*," Stretching the last syllable, Marnie drums her chest with her knuckles and without pause continues in English. "God keep our land, glorious and free! O Canada we stand on guard for thee, O Ca-nada we stand on guard– for thee-ee." She applauds either for herself or for the land, for its snow or its hockey players. From coast to coast to coast, she applauds. She stops and bows her head. "Thank you for coming. Please go now."

"You didn't tell me anything."

"That will be twenty dollars."

"You owe me."

"Twenty please."

Paula fishes out ten.

"Alright alright." Marnie snatches the bill. She stares at the woman's cap of uncombed hair. Hard like a rock, that one. Such an impenetrable coconut core. "Look at me."

Paula takes off her sunglasses. Her eyelids hang over her eyes. She blinks and looks away to the far side of the curtains.

"Look-at-me."

"I am."

"Go on, open up those eyes."

Paula opens her mouth, widening her eyes.

Marnie grips Paula's chin and gives it a wobble. This woman's thoughts are not in the right place. Some clients you have to shake up so their thoughts can settle into clean, readable lines. Oh, but there he is, in Paula's eyes, bleary in the centre of her pupils, rumbling around in a small green car. He's driving too fast, a smear of red in his windshield– anger, blood, lust, one of those. "It's your boy. He's on the wrong road."

"What do you mean?"

"I mean, if you're any kind of mother you'll get in there and stop him."

"Steve? I'm not his mother."

"Some things don't end well."

"But, what's the problem?"

"Either you care or you don't. And if you put ten bucks on this table, I can tell you more."

"I already gave you eleven and last time I gave you twenty and you were supposed to make me some kind of special. You think I'm a millionaire?"

Paula's ribbon of information coils itself into an illegible spool, tightening with each of her complaints. Too much constriction. Too many clients to worry about. There's a lineup out there, willing to pay.

"Thank you. Come again." Marnie pulls Paula up by the elbow and leads her out of the booth. "See you at the rally."

Chapter 42

There's this thing called a political rally where you shout, *le Québec au Québécois* till your throat gets raw. Usually, it's in some kind of auditorium. In those rallies, politicians give speeches about the new country. Or the country that will be new after the referendum. A huge *fleur de lys* is always pinned across the stage. When everybody in the auditorium stamps their feet and claps their hands and shouts and sings, it feels like being at a rock concert. Doesn't matter if you don't understand the words. And once, it was Lucien Bouchard on stage– the real star of the show– Wow, they almost couldn't breathe. The moment the gigantic screens flared and Bouchard's bushy eyebrows appeared, a roar of pure love and loyalty erupted from the crowd. It couldn't get any more sincere, made your skin itch. And when the guys went for sundaes at MacDonald after the rally, it was really fun.

Five days before the referendum Mariette watches her two boys unfold their napkins. Politics, with its all-encompassing girth, has become a voracious guest at their table. And in spite of winter's approaching growl, the state of the weather is ignored altogether.

In a week of suppers, she's dropped tidbits of information about their future country, making each remark as incidental as a crumb on the table. Réal drinks an entire glass of water before taking the first bite of his favourite Boeuf Bourguignon. Mariette has much more to say but will not utter a word before his hunger is soothed. She cuts food that does not need to be cut and forces herself to eat. The moment Réal dips his bread in the sauce one final time and wipes his mouth, she lays out her accounting of how everybody plans to vote.

Marc, they already knew, is a vehement No. Céline isn't about to say a word about it either way. She's become thinner, her elbows more bony than drawer knobs.

Réal laughs. The concept of a sovereign state is risky and foolish, so vaguely defined, it would be like voting for an ice sculpture.

Now Luc, Mariette putts on, is planning to vote Yes. Definitely, Yes. He's entirely confident with his choice and he's the one most educated in this regard. Who else to trust but a lawyer?

Réal swipes another piece of bread in his sauce and has an out-loud thought: "What about our son? He's not a lawyer but he's as intelligent as that Luc. I'll bet he reads more than Luc. He reads those books and manuals. He has his university. He deals with his clients in the two languages. And tell me what will happen to him and to the children if you," he sweeps his arm over the table, "wipe away his future with a mark on paper?" He smiles. "My dear, what a treat you made us. I'll just have another little spoonful. How about you, Steve?"

Steve concentrates on his plate counting down till the end of the dinner. In this house, you can't eat too fast. Even when your plate is empty you have to wait for everybody else to finish before clearing the dishes. And the meal still goes on. They always want you to have something sweet– apple sauce or pudding out of a little glass bowl.

He hates the hidden stew vegetables but eats everything on his plate because if he didn't, one of his grandparents would follow him to his room and talk about the immense fortune God blessed them with and how the poor don't even get a morsel of bread and here he is tossing out what other people are desperate for.

He and Réal clear the table. When the chairs are in place and the cactus centred on its doily, Steve motions the door.

"*Où vas tu?*"

"School project," Steve mumbles.

"You're going to work with one of the boys we met??"

"With Eric."

"Oh yes, the one who drives. You have good friends." Réal pats him on the shoulder. "And your books?"

"Oh yeah." They pad back to Steve's room.

Réal settles on the bed, his toes trailing the floor. "Your grandmother and I are married almost fifty years. You need only one book?"

Steve packs a few notebooks, hesitates, and tosses in a bunch of pens.

"Together we have since I was fifteen and she was just a little girl, thirteen years old but in those days thirteen is already the mind made up. I knew she would be my bride and four years later she stood beside me."

Steve glances at his watch.

"When you get old, you're not in a hurry anymore even though time is short. *Eh ben*. For me, time is too valuable to rush. Maybe you're too young to think about that, *hein* Steve?"

Steve casts a look around the room. As far as he's concerned, it's in order.

"Maybe for you, time goes too slow?" Réal bobs his head at his knees. "Because you're young. But— time for your mother finished too fast. Because you know, she was your mother and she was to you, maybe very patient. But that came later. When she was sixteen, she worked in a restaurant— do you know this story? My fault. I wanted her to work. I wanted her to grow up. It doesn't matter now. She wasn't the girl for the school. She couldn't read too too much. She couldn't—" He patted the bed beside him. "*Assis-toi. J'ai besoin de te parler.*"

"*Oui mais—*"

"Sit beside me. Five minutes only."

Steve has about five minutes to get to Eric's. He sits.

"You know, she was romantic, your mother. Maybe in her housedress, she seemed old to you but no—" He lifts his shoulders and with a loud breath, drops them. "So romantic girls, how do you think it is with them? The first man who winks at them well— he must be the one. Oh *Papa*, he's the one. He's wonderful. He's this, he's that. She wouldn't let go one minute. Not one." He takes Steve's hand in his. "Well. Maybe there were things she couldn't do. Who's perfect in this world? He chose her also. He married her. In sickness or in health, for better or worse, rich or poor, that's the way it is. He made his choice. And she– made hers." His clasp tightens. "She was a lot like your grandmother. My Mariette has her own ideas. I don't know where she gets them. Sometimes I think, what can she be saying, this nonsense, these things without logic. But– even if I don't agree, even if I think she's crazy, I married her. You see what is the difference between her and your mother?" He leans toward Steve. "Your grandmother– chose the right man."

He lets go of the boy's hand and watches Steve roll off the bed like an automatic toy, pick up his school bag and take off. Run off.

Réal sits on the bed a while longer. The child is in almost every way a Dumont. His nature, his sweetness, his very appearance comes from his mother– even the way he runs, a skinny whirlwind. But something in the boy doesn't add up. He looks away when you speak to him no matter what the subject is. His father– that Oscar Horvath– was the same way. The same slide to his eyes. Men like that never accept a helping hand. Nor will they listen to reason. Just that, is enough to make Réal pray.

Chapter 43

To make the announcement, Eric crams the guys into the furnace room and lines them up against a shelving unit piled with canned and packaged goods. A six-foot exercise machine shaped like a humanoid stands on the right side of the shelves and on the other, a rowing machine rusted orange. Legs apart, Eric unscrews a two-litre bottle of decaffeinated cola, takes a long swig and passes it to André who chugs it back and passes it along. After the bottle has gone around twice, Eric caps it with a pop. Guimauve starts to giggle.

"*Ça suffit!*" Eric points a rolled-up sheet of loose leaf at him. "Quit it, I said." Then, as if to anoint them with his blessing, he points his wand at each of the guys. "*Messieurs,*" Eric intones, "your new identities are– he unfurls the magic wand: Christian Laforet, Gary Junis, Yves Rimmel, Patrick Jodoin, Sebastien Wong, Mathew Andrews, *et* Hovig Azounikian."

They look at each other. The furnace rumbles.

"That was seven guys. There's five of us here."

"Benoit, I thought you couldn't add," André says.

"We would have been six if Alex the baby was allowed to go out on weeknights." Eric grins and they burst into jittery laughter.

"Bet he won't even vote."

"He'd better."

"Eh, *c'est quoi ça*, Hovig Azounikia?" Guimauve interrupts.

"*C'est toi idiot.* And Hovig, guess what? You can drive even if you don't know how."

"Why do I have to be him? I can't even pronounce my own name."

"If you weren't him you'd have to be Marshmallow the idiot. So shut up." Eric flaps his paper at Guy, just to show how much the guys really love him.

The assignations go on with Mathew Andrews going to Steve because Mathew Andrews sounds like an English name and Steve speaks the best English. The last of them, Sebastien Wong, goes to Benoit.

"I can't be him."

"Why the hell not?"

"Wong is a *caliss* Chinese name. Do I look Chinese to you? Guimauve looks more Chinese than me."

"I don't look Chinese."

"Do you think, when I go into the voting station they won't notice? Oh. Mr. Wong, go ahead and vote. We're blind."

"Relax. You'll wear sunglasses."

"Eric, what's wrong with you? Why did you have to go and pick a Chinese name?"

"I didn't pick."

"That's all there was in the proper age group and appropriate voting district. I didn't want to do anything stupid," André says.

"What are you talking about?"

André rolls his eyes and gallops up the stairs for a smoke, Guimauve at his heels.

Steve wants one too but until Benoit goes out, he'll wait.

"We only need six names," Benoit says. "Get rid of Wong."

Eric shakes his head. "He's the only one who died with dignity. Cancer. He deserves the right to vote."

"Died?"

"There's no dignity in drug addiction. You can't count on drug addicts for anything, never mind taking care of their country."

Benoit's glasses are smeared with sweat. "Why are they dead?"

"Ask André. He's the one who deals with philosophy." Eric jerks his head at André, just returning from his smoke. "One of them, Christian what's his name, was strangled."

Guimauve pulls the collar of his T-shirt noose-like around his neck and squawks. "Who strangled him?"

"How would I know?"

"Maybe you." André leers at each one of them. "Or me."

"One thing about dead people is they can't get to the polls."

"Unless they're ghosts," says Guimauve.

"So who's going to give them their God-given right to vote? Us. That's who."

"It's only fair," André says. "Except that poor old Christian's name was all over the papers. We don't need anybody wondering how some dead guy got out of the grave with his voting card. His picture was in the Journal too. A blond guy wearing a gold earring. Remember?"

Nobody does.

"Steve should be him," Guimauve says.

"Does Steve look blond to you?"

Guimauve snickers.

"*Caliss de merde de–*" Benoit would go on swearing if it weren't for Steve, colourless against the wall, stiff as a pole. "Eh– are you okay?"

Staring at his feet, Steve nods.

"Have a drink." Guimauve passes him the coke.

Steve swallows. "What about Mathew Andrews?"

"What about him?" Eric glances at his notes. "Nineteen years old, food poisoning. That's not noble. Only stupid people die of food poisoning."

Staggering across the room, Guimauve clutches at his throat. "Awk, some people can't be trusted. Awwwk, they aren't real *Quebecois*." He squawks out a series of strangulated names that all sound like Wong and Wing.

Even Benoit snickers.

"Don't worry, Steve," Eric says. "Mathew Andrews is allowed to vote even if he's stupid."

Steve doesn't laugh. They'll let him vote. And drink from the same bottle. But whether he's Steve Dumont or Mathew Andrews, he still amounts to the same stupid, un-noble guy.

Somehow he slipped in. As long as he's Steve Dumont, he's in. But if he's Mathew Andrews, the whole jigsaw could fall apart. And if he's Steve Horvath, it would for sure.

Guimauve rolls to the floor, dead, supposedly.

Benoit lays his hand on Steve's shoulder. "*Viens, on va prendre une cigarette.*"

Okay yes, a smoke– to calm him. Benoit drags him upstairs. At least it feels that way, as if the hand on his back is pushing him up. By the time Benoit pokes a cigarette between his lips and he inhales, Steve's hands are shaking.

"It's cold."

"You must be getting sick. Here–" Benoit rustles through his pockets, comes up with a peppermint. "If you have a sore throat, this will help."

He doesn't have a sore throat. He has a headache– that smell of turpentine in the furnace room. And he's nauseous. He breathes in tobacco and coughs into the bushes. With another cough, coke and saliva steam out.

"Eh– you'd better go home. Maybe I can call my brother to drive you."

Steve shakes his head. "*Non ça va. J'ai avalé de travers, c'est tout.*"

"Yeah. Maybe you swallowed the smoke. Better stop. Anyway, all that smoking– it'll only make us sick." Benoit snuffs out his cigarette. He watches while Steve taps out the lit end of his and returns it to its carton. "That Wong with the cancer– maybe he was a smoker. Even if he didn't actually die from smoking, it probably made things worse."

Steve is still queasy. "You have to die sometime."

"Yeah but not so soon. My mother feeds us whole wheat everything. Even spaghetti. It's disgusting but if it's good for you, I guess it's alright." He taps Steve on the shoulder. "Don't worry. I'll get my brother to change my ID to another dead guy. I'm not stupid enough to vote as Wong. And you? *Ça va*?"

Yes, he's okay. But now he really wants to get out of here fast. Steve careens down the street, away from the whole weird gang of them, his three identities lurching in his stomach.

Chapter 44

People who rarely speak to Paula– a cousin in Oshawa, an old friend in Fredericton– make long-distance phone calls to bridge the vast expanse of the country. A bunch of us are thinking of coming to the rally, Oshawa says. –We love you, we love Quebec, Fredericton says. Please don't let our beautiful country break up.

Such great responsibility thrown into her lap. Paula has every intention of doing whatever she can. But what? Along with the entire country, she counts down. As the sovereignists take over the hearts and minds of the Franco majority, gathering enough votes to start their new country, she twiddles her thumbs.

Three days till the referendum. A tick-tock heart beats out the minutes.

A roar more immense than the one rising from Niagara Falls emerges from Phillips Square. Paula's never seen such a swaying carpet of humanity. They left their jobs and their schools and filled Metro cars to arrive. They've come in cars and buses. They've come in planes from every part of the country. Federalists, all of them. The flags of Canada and Quebec rustle red and blue in the breeze. Declarations of affection for Canada and its errant province can be seen everywhere– Quebec, we love you– scrawled on placards, painted on faces, worn as crowns. So much optimism. So much hope. If this lawn of people wearing the No insignia on their lapels could be hugged, Paula would crush the entire mass against her heart. She'd kiss Marnie if she could only find her.

Paula wanderers among the throng, waving her paper flags in one hand, the red maple smooching with the blue fleur-de-lys. A cheer rolls in from the far reaches of the square, billowing louder and louder amongst the horde. One single word is repeated– Canada Canada Canada—CanadaCanadaCanadaCanadaCanadaCanadaCanada... Paula screams out her loyalty till her voice disappears in her throat and the chorus is washed away in the wind.

At the far end of the square, a long podium faces the crowd at which politicians are likely delivering speeches. A barely amplified buzz is followed by the spattering of applause. Holding hands, the couple on her right munch granola bars. To the left, a group hams up the latest sitcom, retelling jokes with no humour. They could be at a campground or on a beach. A boy begins to pluck out the national anthem on his guitar, the red stripe of a folded maple leaf bandanna gleaming damply across his forehead. Around him, people pick up the melody. By the time Paula joins the discordant voices on the last verse, the crowd has begun to dissipate.

The big question is what exactly they achieved in one afternoon of flags. The politicians on the pulpit surely offered solutions to the unity problem. But proclamations lost in the flaky clouds can't possibly be effective. Paula checks out the grounds, waits to be given an instruction manual for sewing up a nation.

Her mother could have done a better job. She taught them exactly what to do in their daily lives– brush your teeth, comb your hair, say thank you, open the door for that lady, pick up your toys. That's how you maintain order in a household. If you know what to do, life is simple. In countries too, some kind of order, some kind of mutual understanding exists among citizens. There are laws and taxes that kind of make sense. As long as the rules make sense, everything can roll smoothly. But as soon as politics creep in– there's a mess. Paula closes her eyes, obliterating the misguided hope in the faces of the people around her. It's all a sham. The fact of the matter is, rally or no rally, if all the federalists do is make speeches to the converted, they could well lose.

Instead of waiting to hear platitudes from the blank mouths at the podium, she should scream the only words that could shake them into action: Be a Doer! Follow the turban that foretells the future!

Paula turns to a cluster of gossipers. "You might as well throw away the red drapes. It won't work. Your best bet is the fortune teller. She knew about the unity rally before it came on the news."

They close ranks taking cover under the bonnet of their flag.

"Trust her," Paula shouts. "For twenty bucks, she'll tell you what to do."

Calling out her name, Paula roves the grounds searching for Marnie. The assembly of people blinks and wavers, pinheads in motion. But this, Paula is not aware of. That her grey version of the world is not everybody's, she's long forgotten. Eyes bleary in the glare of the sun, she peers at faces through her two pairs of sunglasses. They all step back from her stare as they drag away their flags and high spirits.

In the morning– oh yes– she remembers. *Your boy is in a bad place.* She pressed the snooze button and now the alarm's smoking. Or did Marnie, looking for her too, transmit the warning to Paula in the form of an anxiety attack? Sweat coats her underarms.

Be a Doer. Call him.

The number's imprinted in her memory. Often, she dials and hangs up or almost dials, her one-finger connection to Steve faltering with each loss of confidence. This time she dials straight through, no pause no hesitation. In her mind's eye, she pictures him cupping his hand around the receiver, a secret pipeline between them.

It's the old woman who answers. Always her, the same careful *allo?* Paula launches in. "*C'est* for Steve. He's in some kind of trouble. I don't know–" The phone slams. Paula punches at the keys again. This time the phone on the other end slams before she can say *please.* Burning to the roots of her hair, Paula's in a complete sweat. She dials again and slams the phone against the receiver. Bang, bang, bang.

There. Three times– that bitch. The heat around her ears may be caused by her descent into menopause but the way her heart resounds is pure triumph.

As the referendum countdown approaches zero a number of people on both sides feel ill enough to vomit. Critics of the unity rally say that it backfired. Previously undecided voters, insulted by the declarations of love made by total strangers to Quebec, now choose sovereignty. And who, pray tell, paid for all that insincere hoopla? Corporations? Governments? No. Their own tax dollars of course. Quebec is for Quebecers. Nobody can tell a citizen of Quebec what to do.

Paula burps up her lunch, swallows antacids, and gulps down tea. One and a half days to go.

The lawyer comes bearing down on her burning stomach in his suit and tie. Like an idiot, she lets him in.

He says, "*Madame*, I come to you because I believe your telephone is not on the hook."

Paula points to her neatly cradled receiver without telling him that after the old hag slammed down the phone, Paula wanted to pluck out that woman's hair and instead, yanked out the cord.

"May I speak one word with you?" He lowers his head, acting polite.

"Why? What do you want?"

"It's for your nephew."

"Ha–" There it is. Whatever he's about to tell her– whatever they did to him– can only be–. The ball of lemon in her chest leaks. If that old biddy bothered to listen, that lawyer wouldn't be standing in front of her now with his head hanging.

She needs to ease the acidity. "Want some tea?"

"*Merveilleux*, yes."

Why she offered tea, she doesn't know. She doesn't want him in her house nor does she want him to open his mouth shooting off bad news. But she needs to know. She dips her used tea bag in two mugs of boiling water and plops them on the kitchen table not about to put out anything fancy for him. No sugar, no milk, no napkin. He can very well wipe his mouth on his sleeve for all she cares.

"*Merci. Un bon thé.*" He takes a sip. Hopefully, the boiling mouthful will burn off his tongue. But no. "*Alors*, madame. You are well? Yes? When you did not answer your telephone I was worried for you."

"What for?" She tastes his reedy cologne in her tea.

"Madame Horvath, you are Steve's aunt. We want you to be very much healthy."

"You want me to be dead."

"No no, Madame Horvath," He laughs. "I have come to you because we must understand each other."

"Yeah, yeah."

He smiles using all his teeth. "You know Madame, I know that you want so much good for Steve. *N'est-ce-pas*?"

"Get to the point."

He nods, folding his hands on the table. "Madame. You are not to be in contact with Steve until he has passed his seventeenth birthday. This is in the custody agreement."

"No way. Why would I agree to that?"

"Madame. You signed."

"I signed to give them custody. I didn't sign to never talk to him. What idiot would do that?"

"The agreement was clear. Every word in English for you. This is for Steve to have time to get used to his new home. It is a transition time. Very important for him."

"Well it didn't work. He's in trouble, isn't he? And now you're trying to blame it on me." He watches her, doesn't get it.

Be a Doer.

"If Steve is in some kind of jam, I can get him out of it. I can watch him." She flings out her arm, her index pointed. "And lead him in the right direction."

"But Madame, *Steve est très très bien*. He is good in his school. He has friends. He is happy."

"Happy?"

"Ha–py. Yes, Madame."

In her relief and her sadness, she pulls in her arms and hugs herself. "So what are you here for?"

"I came for the *thé*." He laughs and takes a sip. "And I must tell you to please do not call the Dumonts."

"I'm going to call whoever I please whenever I please. So please and thank you to you too."

"You signed."

"I didn't. I signed only to give custody."

"Madame Horvath. You must always read carefully before you sign."

"Do I look like I can friggin read?" She lifts her eyelid with her index and glares at him. "I don't even know if you're the real lawyer or a fake. For all I know, you're just some guy off the street."

He stands and pirouettes. "I am Luc Richard. I am the lawyer for the Dumonts. I am not your enemy. I am here to work with you for the benefit of your nephew. For Steve, we will work together." He bows and sits down.

She sees it then, a little blue emblem on his lapel. He's a separatist clear and through. What absolute nerve he has to show up with that. Paula sweeps away his cup. Too bad. Tough luck. No more tea for him.

"I have the documents with me here. I would like to go over them with you," he says.

"I want to see my nephew."

"In less than one year he will be–"

"I mean– now."

The lawyer smiles at the ceiling. He looks as if he's enjoying the view That guy will say Yes for the federation of Quebec, Yes to break up Canada and No to anything she asks for. There are millions of shimmering dots in front of her eyes and millions of things the lawyer will say just to make her miserable. Well too bad. It's her turn for good luck. Marnie said.

"I want you to know that I am voting No with a capital N. No. No. No,"

He chortles. "I will vote *Oui*. With a capital O. Or Y, if you wish. Yes, Yes, Yes."

"Of course you will. Why am I not surprised? I want to know what you people are so pissed off at. We live in a perfectly good democracy. Some people would give their eye teeth to live in Canada. This is the best country in the world." She's saying far more than she means to and is about to clam up. But then she remembers. Be a Doer. "I mean, if you don't agree with everything the government does, so what? Nobody does. If Quebec separates, really bad things could happen. We might be forced to use American currency."

Another laugh. You'd think she put laughing gas in his tea. "Yes. Canada is a beautiful country."

There. It isn't so hard to convince people. She'll offer him another tea. Keep him at the table. Those lawyers bill by the second. A nice tall bill for the Dumonts. They'll be charged for every sipping minute.

"I travel everywhere. I have been to Eastern and Western Europe, Africa, Australia, many places in *Asie*. I love to visit new locations. And I love to return home. But do you know what happen when I visit, for example, Vancouver?"

"They don't speak to you in French."

"They don't. But that would be no problem if they would make here and there, the gesture. A sign in French, a simple *bonjour*, some welcome."

She opens her mouth and closes it. He won't stop talking.

"You know, the worst for me is in the hotel. The menus everywhere is in English of course. But then they are also in Chinese, Japanese, maybe Spanish. Not one word in French. It is as if where I live is even more far than China. And more strange."

"But everybody came to tell you how much they love Quebec." She feels herself sputtering. That smiling wall of his. Nothing's going to move him.

"*Eh bien*. It is too late for that. Now. For Steve. Maybe I can arrange a little meeting between you and your nephew. I will have to discuss this with the Dumonts but I will work hard to convince them. I will let you know." He stands and holds out his hand. And in spite of everything, they shake on it.

Chapter 45

The voters form a silent lineup all the way up the stone stairway that leads into the school building. They exchange barely a nod as they shuffle in. Marching down the path, Steve's grandparents pass stiffly into the building, unaware that on the far-left side of the wide stairs, a group of boys watches them. Had Eric been there to offer Mariette his arm, they'd have seen their boy crouched on the bottom step, three feet away.

While Eric exercises his civic duty at Christian Laforet's polling station, the rest of the gang waits for his report before exercising theirs. For what feels like centuries, the boys loll on the stairs crunching vinegar chips. A very pleasant sun keeps them warm. A series of clerics join the line. One of them waves to them and approaches.

Le Père Jean-Marie nods at the boys and holds out his hand to Steve. Steve scrambles to his feet.

"We always pray to God for help," the priest warbles. "And now we must help God. We must vote." He smiles at the sky. "*Le petit Jesus nous a donné* a perfect day to be out of school."

Steve gets the feeling that every word is being addressed directly to him– a reassuring message from God that tells him that he must vote. And that he'll be safe. And that Eric, proud of the extra votes he created, will not blow anything up even if he says he will. Steve nods, going at it with too much vigour. Le Père Jean-Marie squeezes Steve's hand and lets go– a sort of blessing.

"What's wrong with his voice?" Alex mutters as soon as the priest goes in to vote.

"How come you're such big buddies?" André says to Steve.

"Throat cancer," Benoit says. "He used to teach History when my brother was here. Now just hangs around."

"Too many cigs," André says.

They pass around the chips.

Steve slouches against the stair. The salt in his mouth stings. Maybe the priest meant for them to vote the other way. If Eric never shows up, he could cross off one more item from his To-do list. So simple, as long as Eric is happy.

At around lunchtime, a couple of minutes before they give it all up, there's Eric looking like a bank manager in a grey blazer and striped tie. Grinning, he strides across the lawn giving them and the entire voting public a generalized thumbs up. He high-fives each of his buddies in turn and tucking himself on the stair between Benoit and Steve, gathers the gang into a huddle.

"Nothing to it, men," he whispers. He tells them how the worst part of it was having to wait for a full hour in a lineup of old ladies before getting his turn. "You guys are lucky you're going after lunch. Eh, I had to walk a zillion miles to the polling station." He fist-pings André on the side of the arm. "You're a genius man. The guy at the desk took Christian Laforet's name without even bothering to look up. I could have been Wing or Wong or Patricia with a blond wig, anybody on earth and it wouldn't have mattered. The guy was too busy crossing off names to notice anything."

"Thank you for your confidence, *Monsieur* Poulin. And by the way, your father wears very elegant ties."

"Of course. It was a little Christmas gift from his favourite son." Eric unwraps a squashed and half-eaten peanut butter and bacon sandwich and gulps it down.

"So there's no problem? We just go and vote?" Benoit asks.

"No problem. Except for one minor little thing."

"There's no sandwich at the polling station?"

"Eh, Guimauve– not only is there no sandwich, you have to walk two days to get there. In other words, unless Hovig has a car, you won't make it."

"Eh, don't tell me I can't vote."

"You'll vote. You can be Mathew Andrews. He's not too handsome but you look like him, so no problem. Steve can be Hovig."

"What about the ID?" Benoit says.

"Stop screaming. Want the enemy to hear you? Now listen. Every old lady in the Nation just waved her ID like a tennis racket and still got to vote. They don't actually look at your ID."

"No way," Benoit says.

"Listen, I was there. You go in, you get to the desk, you tell your name to some kid younger than me, and all he does is glance at your license and cross your name off a list."

"They're supposed to look at your picture," Benoit says.

"They don't. They're too busy folding bits of paper into fans. That's the ballot– a mini fan. Then they give you the fan like they're giving you a joint and you go to a baby desk that's panelled off for privacy. You open your ballot, tick off Yes, and fold it back exactly as you got it. After that you give them back the fan, they cut some part of it off and give it back to you like there's something wrong with their brains, and you put it in a box. The ID part is purely symbolic."

What exactly Eric's mumbling about was lost way back when Steve suddenly became Hovig. Because he isn't Hovig. He owns neither the guy's squashed-up face nor his squashed-up accent. If he has to uncurl his tongue and let go of the vaguest word, they'll know.

"Democracy with dignity," André says.

"Where's the dignity of voting in a cardboard box? Cardboard. When Quebec becomes a real country, we'll have wood boxes. "

"Maple," Benoit says. "From our own forests."

"*Eh, les gars,* time to get going. *Faut voter*. Steve, switch IDs with Guy."

"What do you mean? It's not my face on that ID."

"Don't you ever listen man? You guys are twins. You both have big feet. And it won't matter. Guimauve, put on a tuque. You'll be fine."

Standing up, he places his hand over his heart and begins to croon, his voice close to their rubber soles, *"Mes chers amis, c'est à votre tour..."* He raises his head and with his voice blaring as high as the sun above, he repeats the line till André stuffs a cigarette in the round little hole framed by his mouth, and lights it.

Eric hooks Steve by the elbow and won't let go.

Mariette's cheeks are taut. The smell of acidity escapes her pale mouth as she offers them soup and milk and celery sticks from a water-filled glass. Eric declines for both of them. He flashes his real driver's license while Steve explains about practicing his driving and how Eric has offered and how Eric drives as neatly as his clothes and how–. Eric yanks at his sweater before Mariette understands a word.

Hovig Azounikian's voting station is on some street called Balfour or Ballard or Beaufort. Eric can't remember. "It doesn't matter what it's called. Just go straight. It's at a blue church. We can't miss it." He unwraps a granola bar.

They drive forever. Steve pronounces Hovig Azounikian in his head and visualizes it in huge round lettering. "You think we passed it?"

He'll be asked to sign in he assumes, fill in some kind of certificate. He can't remember Eric's– what you're supposed to do explanation and won't ask. There's something about a folded paper and cardboard boxes and dignity. Voting is about choosing something, but really it's about the law. And maybe it's like sitting in the judge's office with carpets and white curtains and big wide halls that lead you there. Or was she a lawyer? She brought her chair around to his. Her hair swung over her face as she leaned over him and explained that he would live with his aunt. It didn't matter what he wanted. It never does. You tell people. You write the stuff you want to do in a letter. Nobody cares.

"There's the steeple. Turn, it's right here."

Steve swerves toward a blue church.

It's weird to go into this building not to pray. Not that he's ever prayed but when he was small, his mother brought him to church where she lit candles and sometimes, murmured to *le petit Jesus*. In this church, he follows a silent line of voters down a flight of stairs to the basement. He's tempted to beg the little Jesus for something. There's no Jesus in the hall and nowhere for him to go but forward. Otherwise, he'd bolt. Let this be easy, he mutters inside his brain. His mother used to hug him so close he could neither see nor breathe.

At the front of the line is a table. A pair of glasses asks for his name. Whether the person behind the specs is male or female, he can't tell. For some reason, his eyes are misted.

The glasses regard him. "*Votre nom*, please."

He's supposed to be some undignified guy who died in a car accident, an asshole, a moral irresponsible. He feels inside his pocket for his new identity card. Oh, but that one's not him right now. The one who looks like him on the card is the person he used to be. His name for voting or maybe forever, Hov– something, is gone from his head. Instead, he remembers the other H name, the name his mother also used. The unshakable Horvath name is clamped to his tongue. If he opens his mouth, it might pop out. He glances over his shoulder. At the back of the room Eric is biting his bottom lip, his little beard pointed like a finger.

"Horvath," Steve says, "Azounikian."

"I'm sorry?"

"Azounikian."

"Your identification, please."

Eric has disappeared. Nobody can help him. In Steve's pocket is the card with the right name and the wrong face. He's supposed to wave it like the old ladies with the rackets. His arm is too stiff, too attached to his rigid armpit. The card falls on the table.

"Ho-vig A-zou-ni-kian?" The man with the glasses looks at Steve, at the face on the card, then at Steve. "Do you have another identification? Medicare card?" He looks up and waits for Steve to produce the proof. "You're very nervous, this must be the first time you vote?"

You're supposed to answer, but he can't. The man waves down somebody from the back of the room and a moment later Steve has to stand at another table, this one with three people who all look hard at the Hovig card. They examine his face, then the face on the card. They huddle up over a discussion that sounds like Maybe the eyes aren't quite, but then again, they are sort of like– and the mouth definitely seems to be– but who could tell with the shaven-off beard, young people all look– he doesn't seem genuine– he's only shy but there's no way to decipher a chin under a beard– and those who talk too much– shy– too nervous– my own son is– One of them says, Yes he is definitely the person in the picture. Louder and quite firmly, another of them says, I doubt it, no, not a chance and the third, pursing her lips, continues to glance from him to the guy in the picture.

His armpits are soaked. He won't look at them. Nothing matters now. He's going to jail. And when he goes, he'll unfold his hands and show them every crime he took part in.

Then one of them tells him, "You'll have to bring another piece of identification."

"I can't," he hears Hovig say. "I don't have time. I have to go to work. I need to vote in this referendum." And he does need to. Eric is somewhere out back, watching. They are all watching. Watching and listening to him breathe, listening to somebody's squashed accent.

"Look," the woman says. She holds up the driver's license. "They're both very thin and very pale. Even through the beard you can see that. And the nose, well, it looks a little different in the picture because of the beard. We really have no choice but to accept the identification."

They all talk at once– yes, no– have another look– fair– so skinny. Somehow they all agree. Maybe they're too tired to care. Somebody brings him back to the man with the glasses. The guy scans his list and points to table four.

Three more people sit at the next station about to test him all over again– who he is, what he looks like, if his hair is parted correctly. The woman in the middle rolls out her anglophone R's and L's through regulation French making it obvious how she voted. Steve wants to speak to her in English and would if it didn't appear forbidden to utter that language. He can't remember what he looks like when he speaks English. He's ugly no matter what language he uses. But maybe when he speaks English, he's uglier still.

He remembers to pronounce Hovig Azounikian like it might sound, like he's the real guy and right this minute, maybe he is. He used to speak English to his father and French to his mother never noticing who he sounded like. It was pure instinct. Like turning on a radio. You push a button and automatically a language emerges. Except there's not even a button. The man on the right passes a ruler down a paper and draws a line across Hovig's name. Another woman pleats the ballot into a tiny accordion and passes it to the English one who hands it to him. She nods to the cubicle behind the table.

In the privacy of the cardboard barrier, he closes his eyes. The ballot, or whatever it is, is pinched between his thumb and index exactly as it was given to him. Sweat trickles along his neck but this, he can't wipe off. Eric told them what to do. You get in there. You put a giant X on your ballot. *Et tu fous l' camp.* Steve wants to follow the part of Eric's instructions that say to get the hell out. But first, he has to vote. He finally wipes his forehead with the back of his sleeve and sits at the desk. He peers at his paper but can't see where on these folds to place the X. If he opens the paper it will become invalid. That much he understands. He steadies his shaking hands. What the method is for voting isn't clear to him. He feels the time tick. He has to make a move. He has to be fast, do something that makes sense and get out of this cardboard box. He scribbles Yes on one of the creases of the ballot and writes over it as neatly as he can in darker print. He takes a deep breath and leaves the booth. At the back of the hall, he sees Eric lick his lips. The blue sleeve of his blazer touches his face. One of the examiners at table four waves Steve over, takes the ballot, and tears off a piece of it. He returns the rest of the fan to Steve and helps him glide it into the piggy bank slot of another cardboard box.

Chapter 46

The entire province– no, the entire country, sits in front of a television on the night of October 30, 1995. Those who decide not to watch the outcome of the referendum on sovereignty do so for deliberate reasons– maybe a headache or high blood pressure, often the threat of family discord. Some people refuse to let politics control their lives. Others are so infuriated by the whole debate, they want no part of it. And for some, there's plain, blind, fear.

Eric is forced to go out for chicken with his family. He watches his poky sisters masticate, his teeth clenched over his one mouthful. His parents drag out their meals over coffee and refills and bread pudding and after paying the bill as slowly as possible, offer to take them to a movie. On a weeknight. When history is about to be made.

He taps at his watch. "You know perfectly well I'm busy." The Poulins grin at one another. Big joke.

"We'll drop you off," his father says. "Maybe your comedy will be better than ours." Eric gets home barely ten minutes before André, smelling of sardines, arrives.

"*Merde*. Don't you ever shower?"

"I can't do everything."

The rest of them trickle in, all except for Benoit who calls to say he has a fever. Eric sends André to the washroom with a towel and a bar of his sister's mandarin soap. The others flop onto the divan in front of the television. Guimauve demands beer.

"Shut up, *asti* and wait for the results. How the fuck do you think we're going to celebrate if you finish the beer before the announcement?"

"Can't we have a little sip?"

"I said no. Am I the only one with a brain around here? All you care about is drinking yourself drunk."

Steve puts up his hand.

"What is it? You have to make *un pee-pee*?"

"What if we don't win?"

"Are you weird or something? Of course we'll win. Don't you listen to the polls?"

"Yeah Steve, don't you listen to the polls?"

Steve turns away. His car is parked in front of Eric's house, his grandparents too far on their own moon to have noticed that after waving them goodbye, he let the car glide out of the driveway backwards on gravity and with a quiet little swish, eased onto the street to Eric's. And now, all he has to do is drive off. Way off. Before Eric blows up the neighbourhood.

"How about some chips?"

"Shut up."

Guy won't shut up. He and Alex honk like geese while Eric fusses with the television. Steve doesn't open his mouth. Alex and Guimauve are so damned loud, he'd like to cut off his ears. André comes downstairs, his hair dripping over his shirt.

"Eh Eric, get us some chips," Alex says.

He probably didn't even try to vote and still has the nerve to make demands and laugh like a buffoon.

"Go get them yourself dammit."

The light is sober on the broadcaster's narrow face. Bernard Derome begins with, "Welcome, *mesdames et messieurs*." His grave pucker leans right into the basement. "The polls have closed. The countdown has begun."

From the centre of the divan, Guimauve wraps his arms around Alex and André and cheers. Steve sits on the floor to one side of the couch while the guys drill through their chips. On the edge of a folding chair, Eric glares at the television five inches from the screen.

The first region is tallied. Les Iles de la Madeleine comes in with a resounding Yes! Arms raised, Eric jumps off his perch. It's looking good. No, great, really great. Region by region, the votes are posted. The Saguenay too has voted hugely Yes. The guys roar with delight, high-fiving each other every other second.

"Eh Eric, we're winning. You're a fucking genius."

"You should be *le premier ministre*."

Steve watches Eric. The guy's hands are clasped in front of his midriff. He's already accepted the nomination.

"I'm becoming a journalist."

"Eh, you could be like René Levesque."

Yeah yeah. Just like his precious hero, journalist first, then premier of the province. Oh. Wrong. Premier of Quebec, the country. The Nation.

"Benoit's more like René Levesque," Steve mutters. They're too busy rattling the chips to hear him.

André goes out for a smoke and charges back two minutes later with the case of beer. "It was under the balcony," he shouts.

They get down to their celebrations. Steve gulps down one then another. If he's Hovig, he might as well *be* him, too drunk to know when he's driving drunk. Too drunk to become morally responsible. Too drunk and dead to vote the way he wants to.

Soon enough Steve laughs and shouts with the rest of them. He squeezes in on the divan and they laugh through much of the telecast. Eric tells them to shut up each time some important bit of news is announced but they won't let up. He stares morosely at the TV, his eyes as expressionless as Bernard Derome's. The rest of the boys swig back beers and beat tattoos on their empty cans. André keeps flipping channels for better coverage till Eric orders the asshole to stop.

There's a point at which only Eric listens while Bernard Derome calmly recites the tallies as if he's calling out bingo.

"Wow," Eric murmurs. "It's looking great. We're heading straight to victory. History in the making, the real thing. And my baboon parents are watching cartoons."

Then– the Quebec City results come in. Eric slumps to the floor. He slams his fist on the TV stand. "Shut up, shut up, *gang de mardeux*," he shrieks at the clowns on the divan. "There's something wrong. It isn't supposed to be like that. Quebec City's supposed to be on our side. That's what the polls predicted."

They're quiet at last. The votes from Montreal are showing up largely as No's, no surprise given the amount of Anglos who control the city. Still, the count is awfully close. They appear to be leading. Yes, leading. Inching on. But not the turtle and the hare. They're ahead. They must be. Eric's fists are clenched. His face is red. Behind his looming back the guys can barely catch a glimpse of the report. Nobody dares say a word. Steve needs a little snooze. He closes his eyes.

Across the country, Canadian arterial tension rises as its citizens hear about the choices made by Quebecers. The desire to stay or not to stay within Canada is divided by a hair. A couple of thousand votes this way or that or maybe one hundred either way, or maybe only one– will seal it.

*

*

The phone at the wrong time. Rings and keeps ringing till Eric seizes the thing only to make it shut up.

"We won," Benoit shouts. "Why the fuck didn't you answer? They just announced it."

There's a roar in the basement. But Steve is not part of it. Shaken awake, he hears Bernard Derome speaking deliberately: *A vingt-deux-heures-vingt, heure de l'est, Radio Canada prévoit que si la tendance du vote se maintien, c'est l'option du Non qui remportera ce référendum.* –therefore, for the second time in fifteen years, a majority of Quebecers have rejected that Quebec should become a sovereign country and choose that Quebec remain in Canada–

Possessed by illegitimate joy, the Anglophones on the tube are cheering. On the other side of the split screen, the Parti Quebecois militants are completely silent, some of them crying just as Eric is crying. Across the dangling phone line, Benoit too is crying. Because some stupid idiot on the other station predicted too soon, predicted wrong, the margins so impossibly thin. And he's the one who called it, blaring out the false news with his fool's trumpet.

Steve stares at his shoes. Win or lose, he doesn't care either way. He realizes it now. A country, a home in that country, is not his, so what difference does it make? His grandmother will be tearing out her hair but his grandfather will be pleased, at least in secret. There's balance in that. And then on the other side, his aunt Paula will be tooting it up, running through the apartment with her New Year's horn. Those who lost will very very soon forget their sadness. People do. He knows that for a fact because nobody on earth could have been sadder than he when his father took lives that didn't belong to him, not even his own. Not too long after they were buried– a week, a month– a couple of hours maybe, Steve had already started to laugh.

The stricken faces of the losers appear close up on the television. Jacques Parizeau, the leader of the party, stands at the podium. His eyes are narrow and pouchy. "*Mes amis, mes amis–*"

His supporters begin to sing and he too joins in the chorus ... *c'est à ton tour de te laisser parler d'amour...* It is your turn, they croon, to talk about love. Then the Premier claps his hands along with his audience while they cheer him up. See. Nobody's ever sad for too long.

Jacques Parizeau begins again. "It's a failure, but not by much."

Eric buries his face in the crook of his arm.

"And it's a success in part–" The Premier waits for the cheers to subside. "We– eh, let's just stop talking about the francophones of Quebec. Let's talk about us. At sixty percent, we voted for-r–" Oh, the cheers. With both hands, he taps his chest. "Hey, we fought well–"

Well, they had. Eric certainly, and André and maybe Guy. And Steve did too. But not in his heart. He followed them like *un petit toutou* without an opinion either way.

"We fought hard. We fought and we– clearly indicated what we wanted. We lost, but not by much. A small margin. A few tens of thousand votes." He pinches his fingers to show them all how ridiculous it is. "So, in a case like that, what do we do? We spit in our palms. And start again!"

The people on TV cheer. While Steve rubs his eyes, Eric, the entire gang in the basement shout out their support.

"We were so close to our country. Well. We were put back a bit, but not for long. Not– for long. And, it was beautiful to see, in the assemblies, the young people who came in larger and larger numbers, and who said, *le pays, on l'veut, le pays*. And as long as the young think that way, we will have– we will have our country."

Eric stands at attention. André joins him in front of the TV. Like soldiers in a row, Alex and Guy follow. They want their country. They whistle and holler and wave their blue flags. From the couch behind them, Steve feels obliged to waggle his.

"It's true," the Premier leans into the microphone. "It's true that we were beaten. But by what?" He frowns at them all. "By money and the ethnic vote."

The guys shout. Steve places his hand over his pocket. There's a wad of bills in there. It always comes down to money.

"Which means that next time, instead of voting sixty percent Yes, we will be sixty-three or sixty-four percent, and it will be over." The premier waits for the surge of applause to subside. "My friends– in the proceeding months– listen, some people were so frightened that the temptation for vengeance against us will be *something*. So now, nothing will be more important than to have a government in Quebec that will protect us till the next time."

The screen switches to the winners' camp and Eric slams off the television. The sound of his thumb shuffling in and out of his fist is louder than what he says. "*Qu'est-ce-que tu fous sur le divan, toi?*"

Alex begins to gather up the bottles. "Eh, let's get those out of here before the parentals get home." Guimauve races around the room in search of empties. Steve starts to get up. Eric pushes him back.

"Eh, *às-tu même voté?*"

"Of course I voted. You were there. You saw me get into the little cubby. I wrote it right on that paper."

"You mean," André points at him with a beer bottle. "you ticked off Yes, you X'd it off, you darkened it."

They all stare at Steve. The shuffling of Eric's thumb sounds like something being packed in a tube, like how he'd pack the ammunition in his bomb. Steve looks at the floor. He feels a soft tremor in his chin. In his knees and his hands.

"Well? Did you X it or tick it? Do you even know what it said?"

To still his hands Steve tucks them between his knees.

"I said, what was the question?"

"I don't know what you're talking about."

As if reciting his chaplet, Eric begins to call out the words of the referendum question, "*Le Gouvernement du Québec* has made public its proposal to negotiate a new agreement with the rest of Canada, based on the equality of nations; this agreement would enable Quebec to acquire the exclusive power to make its laws, levy its taxes and establish relations abroad– in other words, sovereignty– and at the same time to maintain with Canada an economic association including a common currency; any change in political status resulting from these negotiations will only be implemented with popular approval through another referendum; on these terms, do you give *le Gouvernement du Québec le mandat* to negotiate the proposed agreement between Quebec and Canada?"

Every last word the guy knows by heart. But really he's talking about the Horvath Steve who never belonged. And about the money. Always the money.

"You didn't vote, did you–"

"Of course I did. I wrote it out. *O-U-I.* Yes."

André begins to laugh.

"Shut up," Eric raises his fist to the level of his ear.

"I put the paper in the box. You saw me."

"So, you're the *trou d'cul* who made us lose the vote." His fist against Steve's jaw– not a punch, just a little something to lock him in.

Steve picks up a corner of his lip to show that he gets it, a joke, right? But Eric shoves him back against the couch. And back again when he tries to get up.

"Eh–"

"Shut up."

Eric's breath is as loud as the blowing furnace, his fist locked against Steve's jaw.

"*Qu'est-ce-que tu fait?*" André steps in front of his friend.

The clinking of bottles has ceased.

Steve tries to explain– the picture on the ID–

André tugs at Steve's shirt. "*Va t'en,*"

"But–"

"Just go."

An inch away from Eric's next lunge, he slides off the couch, up the stairs, and out.

Chapter 47

Who knew it could be so cold in October. Steve has only his jean jacket for warmth. He ignites his car and wheels away, cranking up the heat till it blasts his face. Warm now. He swerves onto the boulevard that leads to his grandparents' house, sees the outline of the bricks. The light in the living room window glimmers in his pupils. No. Like a wind, he passes the driveway and led by fathomless streetlights, crosses an intersection. Further and further from his grandparents, the car veers left and right and left again beyond residential streets of ornamental trees and cement stairways. Lampposts fall away leaving the narrow road ahead pitch dark.

A roar in the silence lets his ears pick out purple flashes in the thickets. It's up to the white line on his left to show him the way. If the road has no end, it's no big deal. The trusted line is clear and straight. Wherever it goes, he'll go. His eyes close and snap open. He isn't tired. He's just thinking too hard. He tries to spit out the thoughts that jerk around in his brain but can't decipher words from thought except for one. The money word opens its monstrous mouth and eats everything around it.

Harvested and vacant, fields whizz by. His car leaps above the black asphalt. Just a matter of taking it higher into the flossy clouds and there, resting his burning eyes while the wind ferries them on. Now it's a different road. Whoosh, he and his car are riding on a surge of wind. He loosens his right leg, feels the car swerve. The car drops from the sky, hits gravel and skids to a halt on a slick of grass. A yellow sheen lights up the ground. They must be in some other part of their endless country– their giant country. Steve opens the door and falls onto rigid tufts– the cuttings of a harvest, maybe corn, maybe hay.

It's cold on the ground. He rolls under the Malibu. No, the other one– the green car– and feels his pocket for money. Safe. Close to the muffler, he takes a deep sniff of rust and oil. Mufflers he knows about but not much more. His father made a list of car parts for him– the axle, the drive train, the transmission, on and on, meaningless names. He squints at the pipes that feed off the underbelly of his car and presses his finger on the gritty muffler. He hears his father say– Muffler even though he almost never talked. Minutes before the world fell apart he said– Come, Steve. Steve, I'll take care of you. Help me, I'm cold. You and me, we're together, boy.

Steve grits his teeth. He lies here– lay, under the gleaming coils of his sagging bed, in a cave protected by the bed skirt. No. It's a metal cave. He's under the car. In a field of nothing.

His father would not shut up. –Steve, come sleep with me, boy. Come, come to bed. Oscar rolled onto Steve's mattress, sobbing and muttering. –Stevie boy. Stevie, I need you.

Steve brings his fingers to his chest and tucks them under his shirt. It is icy. He feels the mattress on his ribs. Oscar began to kick and scream. Steve kept dagger stiff. Later, when the old man quit crying like a two-year-old, he'd go. He'd bring him something hot to drink.

For a few minutes or hours, Steve could not say how long, Oscar screamed. But Steve did not understand the whole phrase, only heard the higher pitched, *bear it. Bear it!* Then Oscar was very quiet. Something fell. Steve saw the blue cuff of his father's shirt on the floor beside the bed skirt. His dad must have gone to sleep. For a while, Steve closes his eyes.

Oscar was quiet. He watched the end of the day's sunlight glint on the blade. With the residue of blood on the steel, it was pretty. Such a fine wedding gift Marc had given them. Oscar straightened his wrist and turned the point to his chest. No. That would not do. His shirt was not too worn. He unbuttoned it and slipped it off, letting it slide to the floor. Ah, the blade flat on his chest was cool. Shivering, he slid it over and around his nipples. It tickled as if Louise was with him, her teeth nipping at his skin. She was as soft as the blanket he lay on. Then he remembered that he could not bear it. I can't bear it. And rolling onto the pointed knife, he screamed, I can't–

Steve lies under the car warming his fingers. He unclasps his belt and slides his hand into his pants. His penis shrinks. From warmth to warmth, it begins to harden. He tightens his fingers around it. Oh. Never is he completely alone. Always surrounded by people and by people who aren't. So often his father– his mother– but they're somewhere else now. Back and forth his fingers make their pass. Back and forth, free from thought, free. He gasps and yanks till puss squirts from his penis. Sticky on his hands it smells of the putrefaction he was born with. He cries out loud enough for the moon to gaze at him with its impassive face. He sobs and sobs to the quiet moon, his hand clutched to his stickiness.

Around him, the fields shine gold. He had to drive a very long way to find this yellow island to cry on. But there's his dad, at it again– *Bear it.* Steve spreads his arms till they touch the limits of his cave. And bears it.

Steve creeps into the car. He buckles his seat belt and stares out the windshield into the barren dark. In a minute he'll drive away from the field and when he gets home, he'll count it again though he knows the number to the last penny. Two-hundred-and-ninety-four dollars and eleven cents are in his pocket and another three-hundred stashed in *Les Malheurs de Sophie.* Five- hundred-and-eighty-seven for Aunt Paula. Four dollars and eleven cents for him.

Chapter 48

The money and the ethnics. The money and the ethnics
The money and the ethnics The money and the ethnics
The money and the ethnics The money and the ethnics The
money and the ethnics The money and the ethnics The
money and the ethnics The money and the ethnics The money
and the ethnics The money and the ethnics The money and the
ethnics The money and the ethnics The money and the ethnics The
money and the ethnics The money and the ethnicsThe money and the
ethnics The money and the ethnicsThe money and the ethnicsThe moneyand
the ethnicsThe money and the ethnicThe money and the ethnicsThe money
and the ethnicThe money and the ethnicsThemoney and the ethnicThe money and
the ethnicsthe money and the ethnicThe money and the ethnicThe money and the
ethnicThe money and the ethnicThemoney ethnicsThe money and the

The residents of Quebec become aware of the colour of their skins, the
shape of their faces, the odours that cling to their bodies. Every one of
us does. In whatever language they dare think, they compare the bed
they sleep in to the one they were born in– the spices in their stews to
the ones of their neighbours. And the French Canadians too, as *Pure
Laine* as they can be, are no longer pure. Somewhere in their pedigree
remains a vestige of Native or Irish blood. They are the Métis of
Europe, of the Ancient Norse, of the Inuit perhaps, the Mohawks and
the Cree. Darkened by Africa, stained by one small Jew– they are
embarrassed to the depths of their souls. Ashamed to have heard from
the mouth of our leader, that one phrase– the money and the
ethnics–.

*

Paula too will never forget, now that the Premier has put it to them, that she's English or Jewish or perhaps Hungarian. The only sure thing is that she was one person before the telecast and another afterwards. She clicks off and wrings her hands at the faceless television. Apart from the crackling radiator and the whispering pipes, she's surrounded by utter silence. The respectful fridge observes a brief moment of bereavement. Paula strokes the inside of her white forearms feeling for the blue veins that confirm her very life. She swallows a rising sob and rushes to the phone for comfort. To commiserate with somebody, to listen to Sharon Say– It's a good thing I'm leaving, didn't I tell you they don't want us– is better than listening to her own numbness. Even hearing Shelly's postulations of doom doom doom, would be agreeable. She grabs the receiver and when the dial tone refuses to resonate, remembers how she wrenched the wire from the wall. Standing slack in the middle of her living room, she lets tears course down her cheeks. The government has slithered into her living room, glared right into her eyes to measure her strangeness and with one deft motion, chucked her aside.

Paula presses her hand to the cold wall and lets it guide her around the circumference of the room to her small garden of photographs. One picture at a time, she peers at her daughter in all her ages. Wise in a mortar board, Sharon smiles back. And in her aqua bathing suit, the authority of her scowl tells her mother to be a Doer. In Paula's mind's eye, Marnie scrutinizes her crystal ball. Be a Doer. Vote that party right out of office. Why wait for spring? Do it now.

Through the window, Paula looks at the street. One little woman will not do this to her. It is Paula, Paula who will Do. There are buses that go all the way to the South Shore. She'll take the first one out and get off that bus with her hands stretched in the direction of the path that leads to the house of a little lady whose blue eyes, huge with anger and grief, surely gaze at the photos of her own pale daughter in all her ages never to get older. And in that house across the river, past the tremulous mouth of a sad old lady, is a sixteen-year-old boy whose smiling picture has not yet been taken.

Somewhere in her apartment, Paula has a camera. She has a pair of sturdy legs that will take her to the metro that will take her over the bridge and to the bus, and to the road that will lead her right up to the Dumont's door.

She knows how to smile. She knows the one word that will open that door. All she has is say is, Bonjour. Bonjour, bonjour, bonjour.

end

About the Author

Terry Ades was born in Egypt and brought up in the bilingual city of Montreal. While her first language is French, she was obliged to attend English school.

After receiving a degree in creative writing, her intention to author stories was derailed when as a young mother, she lost her eyesight. No longer able to read her narratives, she gave up on writing. Multiple surgeries and the aid of 31-point font later, she completed several short stories and two novels.

She was awarded first prize in McGill Street Magazine's "Writes of Passage" competition for *Part of a Small Left Eye,* a short story based on her experience. A still-to-be-published novel was a semi-finalist in the Chapters/Robertson Davies First Novel contest.